"This is a trap."

"Obviously," said Brigid dryly. "But what's the point of it?"

"Do we really care to find out?" Lakesh inquired.

Kane smiled crookedly, glancing over at the three snarling heads of Cerberus on the wall. "I think we should. Lilitu as much as claimed she'd launch an attack against us if we didn't go along."

Lakesh's dark face creased into a frown. "If we help her to achieve her goal, the fate of Cerberus will be intertwined with hers forever."

"Not necessarily," Brigid interjected. "If we can end the threat of Tiamat, the scope of our operations will be expanded considerably."

"And if Lilitu isn't successful," argued Lakesh, "and our complicity in her attempted coup is discovered by Enlil, we can expect no mercy."

Other titles in this series:

James Axler
Outlanders®

DARK
GODDESS

A GOLD EAGLE BOOK FROM
WORLDWIDE®

TORONTO • NEW YORK • LONDON
AMSTERDAM • PARIS • SYDNEY • HAMBURG
STOCKHOLM • ATHENS • TOKYO • MILAN
MADRID • WARSAW • BUDAPEST • AUCKLAND

First edition November 2007

ISBN-13: 978-0-373-63856-7
ISBN-10:   0-373-63856-6

DARK GODDESS

Special thanks to Mark Ellis for his contribution to
the Outlanders concept, developed for Gold Eagle.

"And I, the Instructor, proclaim His glorious splendor so as to frighten and to terrify all the spirits of the destroying angels, spirits of the bastards, demons and Lilitu, who falls upon men without warning, to lead them astray from a spirit of understanding and to make their hearts desolate."

—From *Song for a Sage,*
The Dead Sea Scrolls

The Road to Outlands—
From Secret Government Files to the Future

Almost two hundred years after the global holocaust, Kane, a former Magistrate of Cobaltville, often thought the world had been lucky to survive at all after a nuclear device detonated in the Russian embassy in Washington, D.C. The aftermath—forever known as skydark—reshaped continents and turned civilization into ashes.

Nearly depopulated, America became the Deathlands—poisoned by radiation, home to chaos and mutated life forms. Feudal rule reappeared in the form of baronies, while remote outposts clung to a brutish existence.

What eventually helped shape this wasteland were the redoubts, the secret preholocaust military installations with stores of weapons, and the home of gateways, the locational matter-transfer facilities. Some of the redoubts hid clues that had once fed wild theories of government cover-ups and alien visitations.

Rearmed from redoubt stockpiles, the barons consolidated their power and reclaimed technology for the villes. Their power, supported by some invisible authority, extended beyond their fortified walls to what was now called the Outlands. It was here that the rootstock of humanity survived, living with hellzones and chemical storms, hounded by Magistrates.

In the villes, rigid laws were enforced—to atone for the sins of the past and prepare the way for a better future. That was the barons' public credo and their right-to-rule.

Kane, along with friend and fellow Magistrate Grant, had upheld that claim until a fateful Outlands expedition. A displaced piece of technology…a question to a keeper of the archives…a vague clue about alien masters—and their world shifted radically. Suddenly, Brigid Baptiste, the archivist, faced summary execution, and Grant a quick termination. For

Kane there was forgiveness if he pledged his unquestioning allegiance to Baron Cobalt and his unknown masters and abandoned his friends.

But that allegiance would make him support a mysterious and alien power and deny loyalty and friends. Then what else was there?

Kane had been brought up solely to serve the ville. Brigid's only link with her family was her mother's red-gold hair, green eyes and supple form. Grant's clues to his lineage were his ebony skin and powerful physique. But Domi, she of the white hair, was an Outlander pressed into sexual servitude in Cobaltville. She at least knew her roots and was a reminder to the exiles that the outcasts belonged in the human family.

Parents, friends, community—the very rootedness of humanity was denied. With no continuity, there was no forward momentum to the future. And that was the crux— when Kane began to wonder if there *was* a future.

For Kane, it wouldn't do. So the only way was out— way, way out.

After their escape, they found shelter at the forgotten Cerberus redoubt headed by Lakesh, a scientist, Cobaltville's head archivist, and secret opponent of the barons.

With their past turned into a lie, their future threatened, only one thing was left to give meaning to the outcasts. The hunger for freedom, the will to resist the hostile influences. And perhaps, by opposing, end them.

Prologue

The former barony of Beausoleil, the Tennessee River Valley

Sean Reichert moved in quickly, knocking the cudgel aside and striking the slagjacker hard in the belly with his right fist.

Air exploded from the small man's lungs with a sound like a protracted, phlegm-saturated cough. The wooden club clattered to the floor and the man clutched at his midriff, doubling over. Reichert drove a knee into the slagjacker's face, enjoying the sensation of the man's nose collapsing under the impact.

Blood spewing from both nostrils like an opened faucet, the man collapsed to the floor of the tavern and lay there, twitching. Reichert swept the people watching from the tables with a bright-eyed stare and boyish grin. "Want to see me his kick his head loose of his shoulders?"

The patrons of the Tosspot Tumor didn't answer. The few who hadn't averted their gaze glared at the young man with angry, resentful eyes. Larry Robison, sharing a corner table with a nude woman with hair the color and texture of a hayrick, called out, "Yeah, we *so* fuckin' want to see it."

He chucked the blonde beneath her chin with a finger. "Don't you, baby?"

The woman blinked her glassy, unfocused eyes and reached for the bottle on the table. "Uh-huh."

"That's what I thought," Reichert said. "So, here goes—"

Grin widening, he drew back his combat-booted right foot, then kicked it forward. The thickly treaded sole skimmed over the prone man's face as Joe Weaver caught Reichert by the collar and pulled him off balance.

"That's enough, you bloodthirsty moron," Weaver snapped, dragging the younger man across the room. He slammed him hard against the slab of rough-hewed pine that served as the bar.

Reichert struggled, but Weaver applied a wrist lock to the youth's right arm and kept him in place. Reichert strained to get free for only a few seconds. "I showed the son of a bitch," he shouted jubilantly. "I put him in his place, by God. Nobody disses us—Team Phoenix for America, fuck *yeah!*"

Despite his Germanic surname, Sean Reichert was Latino, with straight black hair, a dark complexion and a carefully maintained mustache. Although only of medium height, his athletic body carried tightly packed muscle.

Joe Weaver was considerably taller, heavier and older, his square-chinned face framed by a bronze-hued beard. A pair of round-lensed spectacles covered his slightly slanted eyes. Wearily, he said, "The poor bastard didn't dis you. I think he's hard of hearing."

Reichert paused, glanced at Weaver, then at the unconscious man whose blood filled the cracks between the floorboards. "Well, he's fuckin' hard of *breathing* now, too."

He laughed uproariously at his own joke and with a disgusted head shake, Joe Weaver released him. Larry Robison joined in with the younger man's laughter. Tall, with a deep chest and wide shoulders, Robison had a big head covered by a mop of dark brown hair. Like Weaver, he affected a beard, but trimmed closer to the jawline. The nude woman caressed his beard with trembling fingers, then she slid sideways, draping herself over his lap.

The Tosspot Tumor tavern was fairly typical of most such establishments in the Tartarus Pits of any barony—one big common room redolent with the reek of home-brewed liquor and unwashed bodies. A makeshift bar coursed along the rear wall, a row of wooden barrels with rough planks nailed atop them to serve as a buffet. A scattering of tables and chairs completed the furnishings.

The tavern did double duty as a brothel, so a single doorway behind the bar led to a small, dark bedroom. From the room came a hoarse cough and then a gravelly male voice snarled, "For fuck's sake, can't a man get a decent night's sleep anywhere in this shithole world?"

Reichert and Weaver glanced toward the shadows shifting beyond the open door, hearing the squeak of bedsprings and the thump of booted feet on the floor. "Sorry, boss," Reichert called. "We didn't know you were supposed to be sleeping."

"Besides," Robison said, "it's near the middle of the afternoon."

A teenage girl stepped through the door, brushing a strand of brown hair away from her eyes. She clutched a frayed sheet around her thin frame, leaving one knobby shoulder bare. Robison was reminded of a sorority girl returning from a particularly boisterous toga party, but he doubted she was old enough to attend even the most liberal-arts college. He never was quite sure what a liberal-arts college was supposed to be, but he presumed it was a place that liberals sent their kids to learn how to be artists, so he hated them as a matter of course.

Mike Hays lumbered out of the room, absently smoothing his shaggy silver mustache with a scarred thumb. His burly body was clad only in olive-green boxer shorts with the words Hays, Maj. stenciled onto the elastic waistband. A pair of unlaced combat boots flipped and flopped on his feet. From his right hand dangled his Belgian Fabrique Nationale Mag-58 subgun. He didn't even visit the outhouse, much less sleep, without it.

"Fighting with the locals again?" the gray-haired commander of Team Phoenix demanded.

Reichert leaned against the bar, propping his elbows

up on the edge. "What the fuck else is there to do here, Major? This is the only ville we've found that ain't controlled by Magistrates, so there's nobody to fight *but* the locals."

Hays hawked up from deep in his throat and spit on the litter-strewed floor. Pushing between Reichert and Weaver, he asked, "What've you been taught about winning hearts and minds, Sergeant?"

Robison brayed out a short, scornful laugh. His female companion laughed, too, but very querulously. "Whoever came up with that shit never tried to make a life for themselves in fuckin' twenty-third-century Tennessee…in the fuckin' Tartarus Pits, no less."

Hays rapped his knuckles autocratically on the bar top, and the man behind it sullenly placed a bottle half-filled with amber fluid in front of the ex-Marine. He also put down a glass tumbler, which Hays contemptuously slapped aside.

Picking up the bottle by the neck, he said flatly, "Maybe we can all go back into the fuckin' deep freeze. Sleep long enough, we'll wake up where we started."

"That's assuming the nature of time is circular, instead of linear," Weaver said. "So far, it seems pretty much like a straight line. And speaking of circular…do all of you guys have to use 'fuck' every other word?"

"It's part of our mission statement," Reichert replied. "'Team Phoenix for America, fuck *yeah!*' I thought you knew that."

"I knew it," Weaver said. "I guess I've been trying to forget it."

"Me, too," Hays agreed gloomily. "So we're stuck here, in this place, in this century, with nobody to fight."

"The eternal lament of mercenaries during peacetime," Weaver commented.

"Fuck, there are definitely wars out there," Robison snapped, pushing back his chair and rising from the table. His female companion fell onto the floor and appeared to go instantly to sleep. "There's a big-ass fuckin' war going on."

"Yeah, but those Cerberus pricks won't let us fight it," Reichert said.

"Won't let us fight it with *them*," Joe Weaver corrected. "Guess we shouldn't have killed all those friends of theirs, huh?"

Hays shrugged, not responding to Weaver's sarcasm. "Bunch a' ersatz injuns with feathers in their hair and paint on their faces. Good old collateral damage. No loss."

"Not to us, mebbe," Robison agreed. "But Kane sure seemed to set big store by them."

At the mention of the man's name, an image of Kane's pale, cold eyes flashed into the mind of Major Mike Hays and he repressed a shiver. He involuntarily glanced over his shoulder, made uneasy by mere utterance of the name.

Although he and his subordinates had promised to never speak of what actually happened when they had been lured into the trap laid by the Cerberus warriors, Hays still shuddered at the most oblique reminder of the encounter.

Mike Hays gusted out a sigh, then tilted the bottle to his lips and drained it in several noisy swallows. Reichert watched him with slitted eyes. "Fuck, this is worse than that Rwanda mission…didn't do nothing there but drink and fuck."

Hays dropped the bottle to the floor and made swooping and rising gestures with his hands, intoning a prolonged, "Smoo-o-oth."

Weaver pinched the bridge of his nose and whispered, "Jesus Christ."

"Oy," the bartender said angrily, "don't drop your shit on my floor."

Hays speared him with a challenging stare. "I drop my shit where I please."

"Yes, I can see that," the man shot back. "That's why I mentioned it."

Hays locked eyes with the bartender, hoping he would notch up his objections from the verbal to the physical. He wished he could vent a fraction of his frustration by shooting several holes in the man's head with his Mag-58.

His frustration sprang less from boredom than the knowledge he had once again failed to achieve an erection, even under the ministrations of the girl he had bribed with several MRE packs.

When the bartender dropped his gaze, Hays announced loudly, "I think it's time we leave this fuckin' burg and take the fight back to where it fuckin' belongs."

Reichert groaned wearily. "Not more fuckin' Indians."

Hays scowled at him. "It don't have to be Indians, but—"

He broke off when a high-pitched whine touched his hearing. Hays, Weaver, Reichert and Robison stared around in puzzlement. Little sprinkles of dust sifted down from the ceiling as the drone grew in volume.

"A chopper?" Robison asked. "One of those old Apache 64s the Magistrates call Deathbirds?"

Reichert shook his head. "We'd hear the fuckin' rotors."

Hays spun toward the door, hefting his subgun. "Let's recon."

The four men rushed out into the humid afternoon air and stood in a muddy street that twisted between ramshackle buildings, past hovels, shacks and tents. There was no main avenue, only lanes that zigged in one direction and zagged in the other.

They looked toward the latticework of residential Enclave towers connected to the Administrative Monolith, a massive round column of white rockcrete that jutted hundreds of feet into the sky.

A featureless disk of shimmering silver twenty feet in diameter hovered above the flat top of the tower. The configuration and smooth hull reminded Joe Weaver of the throwing discus he had used in his college days. Perfectly centered on the disk's underside bulged a half dome, like the boss of a shield.

As the four men gaped in silent astonishment, the craft settled down on top the monolith and from the rim sprouted three tentacles of alloy. They curved out and down, plunging through the slit windows.

"What the fuck is that?" Robison half gasped, voice quavering. "It's like a fuckin' flying saucer—!"

"No fuckin' way!" Reichert blurted, but he didn't sound completely certain. "Maybe we'd better get Bob warmed up—just in case."

"Just in case what?" Weaver asked, a slight mocking edge to his voice. "Just in case it *is* a flying saucer?"

Sean Reichert glared at him through narrowed eyes, then he nodded. "Yeah. Just in case."

The four men sprinted down a narrow alley running alongside the Tosspot Tumor. The alley opened up into a wide courtyard where Bobzilla was quartered. The huge, armor-plated LAV-25 had been modified by the Phoenix Project designers to serve as the team's rolling base of operations.

As they reached the rear hatch, a shadow momentarily blotted out the sunlight and in unison they heeled around, necks craning, heads tilting back. Reichert's face paled despite his dark complexion, and he muttered, "*Fuck.*"

Another silver disk hovered barely five yards overhead. As it slowly sank toward the courtyard, Robison fumbled with the hatch latches and swung the heavy metal panel open on squeaking spring hinges. "Let's get our asses heeled!" he bellowed.

Swiftly, he took an AK-108 and then passed one of the lightweight carbines to Weaver. Hays reached around Robison and snagged an FIM-921 Stinger shoulder-fired antiaircraft rocket launcher. Reichert grabbed an M-203 grenade launcher combined with an M-16 rifle. With expert fingers, he loaded the weapon with three blunt-nosed 40 mm explosive rounds.

The disk slowly descended, but it didn't come to rest. From the half dome on its undercarriage snaked out three gleaming legs. They in turn sprouted three claws that sank deeply into the muddy soil and lent the machine a resemblance to an old-fashioned milking stool coated with a shifting sheath of quicksilver.

A chill fist of dread squeezed Weaver's heart and he said to his companions, "Let's not jump the gun, boys. We don't know what we're dealing with here."

Hays snorted in derision, placing the tube of the launcher on his right shoulder. "I'd say it's those fuckers that don't know what they're dealing with."

Weaver fearfully eyed the tripodal machine. "Heard that before, Major. But this time we're not facing a bunch of childish savages with bows and arrows. We need to discuss tactics before we—"

The disk emitted a harsh, electronic hoot, which to Weaver sounded like a warning to get out of its way. Three legs moving in unison, the machine took a weirdly graceful step forward.

"Here's your tactics, Joe!" Hays bellowed. "Turn out the dogs!"

The weapons in the hands of the four men spit flame, thunder and multiple kinds of projectiles. The courtyard became a crashing, exploding, blazing inferno. Steel-jacketed bullets sparked a dozen miniature constellations on the rim of the disk ship's hull.

Mike Hays squeezed the trigger of the FIM-921 and the Stinger rocket leaped from the hollow bore, propelled by a wavery ribbon of smoke. It struck the disk ship broadside, the warhead detonating amid a billowing mushroom of black smoke and a blinding gush of flame that rolled over the hull.

The flurry of grenades fired by the howling Sean Reichert burst all around the tripod, eardrum-compressing detonations blooming against and below it. Dirt and mud erupted, raining down in all directions.

Smoke billowed, a shroud of gray enveloping the courtyard, completely obscuring the disk from view. As the roiling canopy of haze and smoke spread, Team Phoenix ceased fire.

Coughing, fanning the air in front of his face, Robison declared hoarsely, "Overwhelming firepower trumps tactics every fuckin' time."

Hays dropped the rocket launcher and gusted out a satisfied sigh. "Smoo-o-oth."

He and Reichert bumped knuckles. The young Latino crowed triumphantly, "Team Phoenix for America, fuck *yeah!*"

Weaver squinted through the thinning vapor, his leaking eyes picking out the orange smears of flame. He realized that the entire rear of the Tosspot Tumor tavern had been pounded into a litter of broken, fire-laced kindling. The roof had collapsed, but he saw no sign of the silver tripod.

Weaver lifted his spectacles and cleared his blurred vision with swipes of his fingers. When he was able to see more or less normally again, he realized why he couldn't find the disk. The craft had simply retracted its three legs and floated soundlessly above the barrage. It hovered thirty yards above them, not so much as a smudge mark visible on its iridescent hull.

But where the tripodal legs had been planted now stood three motionless figures. The drifting scraps of smoke imbued them with an eerie, ghostly quality. Although all three of them wore formfitting silver-blue armor, two of them were almost identical in physique and features. Set deep beneath jutting brow ridges, their white eyes did not blink, nor did their craggy, scale-pebbled faces register emotion.

Ovoid shells of alloy rose from the rear of their body armor, sweeping up to enclose the back and upper portion of their hairless skulls. From the undersides of the shells, hair-thin filaments extended down to pierce both sides of their heads. Conduits stretched down from inch-thick reinforcing epaulets on their shoulders, connecting to the alloyed gauntlets that sheathed their extended right forearms and hands.

From raised pods on the gauntlets rose three small flanges, curved like the letter *S* cut in halves. The ends of the flanges flared out like cobras' hoods, and red energy pulsed in the gaping mouths of the stylized serpent heads.

The third figure was leaner, slighter in stature, but still obscured by floating planes of smoke and settling dust. "How dare you threaten a member of the Supreme Council? Lay down your weapons and beg me not to have you killed where you stand!"

The tone, pitch and timbre of the voice was sharp, imperious, and although holding a sibilant echo, it sounded undeniably female.

Major Mike Hays stiffened in surprise and his expression molded itself into one of contempt. He glanced toward Robison and Reichert. "That's just some mouthy bitch out there!"

Sighting down his Mag-58 subgun, Hays snarled, "Beg *this*, bitch!"

Although he had no idea of what kind of council the sharp-voiced woman referred to, sudden terror galvanized Joe Weaver to slap down the barrel of the Mag-58. "Mike—no!"

Reichert uttered a sneering laugh, bracing the stock of the grenade launcher against his hip, aiming it at the three armored figures. He roared, "Team Phoenix for America—"

A series of crack-sizzles cut off the rest of his mantra. Bolts of energy, glowing like globules of molten lava flung from catapults, struck Sean Reichert directly in the head, blowing away his trim mustache and face in a pinwheel burst of flame.

Frozen in place, Joe Weaver watched two more balls of seething energy explode against the heads of Mike Hays and Larry Robison. He caught only a fragmented glimpse of the one blazing toward him before his world turned to a dazzling orange flare, instantly followed by impenetrable darkness.

LILITU WRINKLED her delicate nose at the concatenation of odors wafting throughout the Tartarus Pits. During her ninety years as Baroness Beausoleil, she had never ventured within a thousand yards of Tartarus, fearing that she would contract loathsome diseases. Now she realized she had not suffered from an infection phobia so much as the place simply stank.

Narrowing her vertical-slit-pupiled eyes, Lilitu glanced up at the Administrative Monolith. The sunlight winked on the surface of the disk of smart metal still attached to the roof. The uppermost floor of the high, round tower had served as her sanctuary and home for many years—no, not a home, she corrected herself, but a cocoon, one that had sheltered the chrysalis form of the baroness until she shed it and emerged as Overlord Lilitu.

Gesturing diffidently with the metal-shod fingers of her right hand, she waved toward the four smoldering corpses of the humans who had threatened her.

"Make sure those dung beetles can crawl no more," she commanded her armored Nephilim. "Then begin razing this entire cesspit."

Quarlo, her personal bodyguard, glanced toward her, no emotion in his dead white eyes. "The complete barony, Goddess?" His whispering voice held a hollow quality, as if only the echoes of his words passed his lips.

Lilitu's beautiful, scale-patterned face creased in a smile. "And everyone who still lives in it. They no

longer serve my purpose, and the mandate of the
Supreme Council of the Annunaki has ever been that
all humans must serve a purpose for their gods."

Chapter 1

Coral Cove, the Gulf Coast of Florida.

Kane raced through the night, cursing the heat and cloying humidity that sapped most of his stamina. His legs felt as if lead weights were tied to his knees. The sweat that stained his camo-striped T-shirt and flowed down from his hairline stung his eyes.

He wanted nothing so much as to fling himself facedown in the palmetto scrub and drink from his canteen. He also wanted to forget why he had agreed to lend Cerberus's support to a rebellion against the coastal pirates led by the ridiculously named Billy-boy Porpoise.

Over the rhythmic boom of the surf, the faint baying of hounds and shouting of men reached his ears. Kane swore beneath his breath, but he continued to run. Twice bullets had skimmed very close to him, and once he had nearly been caught beside the waters of the drainage canal that cut in from the Gulf of Mexico and served as a moat around the Porpoise estate. Only the fact that he could dive and swim like an otter saved him.

The pillared trunks of cypress, pine and palm trees surrounded him. Palmetto plants, their fan-shape fronds gleaming with patterns of ebony and silver in the moonlight, rose up on either side of the narrow trail. Insects chirped and buzzed from the shadows. His chest feeling as if it were pressed between the jaws of a tightening vise, Kane halted in the murky lee of a log overhang, where lumber had been piled to use as palisade walls in the settlement.

He breathed deeply, regaining his breath. He ran a hand through his longish dark hair. It was soggy with sweat, stiffening with salt. His clothes reeked of sewage and brine, but he took a little solace in the fact he knew he had smelled worse.

A hoarse male voice bellowed beyond the far edge of the canal. The words were unintelligible, but the tone was angry. Kane's palm itched where his Sin Eater would have fitted if it were not packed away with the rest of his equipment in the settlement. He stepped deeper into the shadows, his movements fluid but cautious, like a man in a jungle wary of poisonous snakes. He often thought of the world in which he lived as nothing but a snake-infested jungle.

Kane struggled to tamp down a surge of homicidal fury at his pursuers, but he was honest enough to admit that distaste at playing the role of prey fueled his rage, not that his attempt to breach the Porpoise estate had been stymied.

Fleeing didn't come naturally to a former Magistrate like himself. He was a tall man, as lean and sinewy as a timber wolf, and his pale eyes were the color of dawn light touching a blue-steel knife blade. A three-inch hairline scar cut whitely across his clean-shaved left cheek.

Kane had considered growing a beard for the op, so he could infiltrate Porpoise's crew, but he couldn't stand to go without shaving for more than a few days. His years as a Cobaltville Magistrate had instilled in him a loathing of whiskers longer than an eighth of an inch.

He heard a dog bark and he clenched his fists. It was bad enough he had been discovered while trying to climb the wall around Porpoise's compound, but now he felt the hot breath of death on the back of his neck.

When Kane heard the men's voices again, their words drowned out by the baying of the hounds, his lips peeled back from his teeth in a silent snarl. They were much closer, and he knew he had to start running again.

The brief rest had done him little good, but his anger added renewed vigor to his muscles. The men and the dogs probably viewed him as little more than a weary fox, fleeing before the hounds, but he felt more like the timber wolf. A wolf was a wise animal that had learned all the tricks of staying alive, spinning out the odds with a gambler's skill to continually outwit death.

Kane sprinted full-out, achieving a long-legged, ground-eating stride, running on the balls of his feet. He swatted at the mosquitoes that made strafing dives at his eyes. Straight ahead, past a row of gnarled cypress roots, lay a stretch of mudflats that led directly into the ville of Coral Cove. There he would find alleys and doorways in which to hide until he could make his rendezvous.

The soles of his high-laced jump boots sank into the muck, releasing the sulfurous stench of marsh gas. Behind him rose the frenzied yelping of the dogs. Kane lurched into a shadowed area just inside the half-completed log wall surrounding Coral Cove and risked a glance backward.

Three bearded men held a trio of long leather leashes in their right hands, and rifles were slung over their shoulders. At the ends of the leashes strained and slavered six of the biggest mastiffs Kane had ever seen. The black-and-tan dogs yipped and bayed, eyes rolling, tongues lolling, froth dripping from their fang-filled jaws.

Kane wasn't sure if the men had seen him, but they released the leashes. The mastiffs bounded forward, a line of red maws and yellow teeth pounding right through the mudflats at blinding speed.

Blinking back the sweat from his eyes, Kane whirled and sprinted into the ville, the snarls and yelps of the dogs loud in his ears. Coral Cove's buildings were old, many of them close together, arranged around a makeshift town square, the centerpiece of which was an old, immense and deep-rooted live oak. He glimpsed a slatternly woman dumping a pail of slops out of an upstairs window of a big frame house. When she caught sight of him running across the square, she retreated quickly, snatching a curtain closed.

The settlement wasn't very large, but according to the Cerberus database, Coral Cove had been a small fishing village turned vacation resort. Of course, that been a very long time ago, before the skydark.

Kane's eyes darted back and forth, looking for cover. He didn't care for the idea of digging in and standing fast, since the dogs could surround him and tear him to pieces. He had not gone armed on the recon mission, taking the precaution that if he were apprehended, he wouldn't provide more weapons to the enemy's arsenal.

But Kane was never completely helpless. He dug his hand beneath his shirt to the waterproof utility pouch at his waistband and carefully pulled out a metal-walled sphere about the size of a plover's egg. The pressure-fused CS powder grenade, usually employed as a diversion in a limited area, would cause extreme discomfort in a small room. To have flung the grenade back at the dog pack would have been useless—there was not enough concentrated spread in the vapor.

Kane sprinted to the trunk of the oak tree and leaped high. He caught hold of a thick, leafy branch and managed to swing up and balance himself precariously upon it. The limb swayed like a hammock under his weight.

Looking across the town square, he saw the first of the mastiffs bounding into view, tongue lolling, savage eyes glinting. The other dogs raced behind it, their smooth dark coats clotted with mud. Their teeth gleamed like ivory daggers.

The dogs milled around uncertainly, sniffing the ground and whining quizzically. Far back across the mudflats there were shouts, the thump of running feet. Kane held the grenade tightly in his left hand as he watched the mastiffs casting about in confusion.

The first dog to have entered the ville growled and slowly advanced on the tree with a twitching muzzle, nose still to the ground.

"That's it, sweetheart," Kane breathed. "Nose to the dirt. Don't look up."

The limb upon which he crouched suddenly creaked. Kane grabbed a branch overhead as the limb sagged half a foot. Wishing he were fifty pounds lighter, Kane kept absolutely motionless. The dogs would know he was nearby through scent alone, but if their attention wasn't drawn upward—

The limb suddenly bent and the splintering crack of wood filled Kane's ears for an instant.

With a startled growl, the mastiff circling below looked up, caught sight of him and barked ferociously. The other dogs clustered around the base of the tree, yipping and yelping. They slammed into one another as they all tried to squeeze around the trunk.

Kane wasted no time. He dropped the grenade straight down into the mass of milling dogs. One of the mastiffs snapped at it and the casing burst open, the small explosive charge within it detonating with a low, smacking explosion. A heavy cloud of white CS powder erupted, spraying in all directions, like a miniature blizzard.

Instantly, the baying of the dogs turned to high-pitched whines, whimpers and squeals. Pawing frantically at their eyes, the mastiffs reeled away, staggering, snorting and sneezing. Kane jumped down from the limb, landed on the far side of the tree and ran toward the nearest house, a rambling two-story structure built in the old antebellum style. The windows were boarded up, so he decided the door was mostly likely secured and began to angle away.

A black mass shifted in the shadows cast by a balcony overhang. *"Kane!"*

The urgent whisper cut through the cacophony of the distressed dogs, and Kane darted into the murk. The black shape was a small figure huddled within a mass of rags and tatters, decorated with gray streamers of Spanish moss. Under green stripes of camouflage paint he saw streaks of milk-white flesh.

"Inside! Be quick!" The figure scurried sideways and a door opened and closed.

Panting, Kane groped over the door, searching for a knob. His fingers touched nothing but damp, slightly warped wood. He pressed a shoulder against it, then the door swung inward and he stumbled into an unlit foyer. A small hand clutched at his right wrist with surprising strength and hauled him forward.

"In here, idiot!"

Kane caught a whiff of mildew and urine. The door

closed, and he heard the faint snick of a locking bolt being drawn. Fingering his nose, Kane whispered, "And I thought I was the only stinkard here, Domi."

"Shut up."

Kane stiffened at the angry intensity of the girl's voice, but he fell silent, listening to the yowling of the hounds. He heard men's voice raised in breathless curses, the cracking of whips and the piteous yelps of the dogs.

"Where'd the son of a bitch go?"

"Guess for your own self, Lucas! Got my own problems with this goddamn hound—"

"Billy-boy ain't gonna like it if we lose 'im."

"Shit, tell me something new…but he's gonna have to live with it."

Ear pressed against the door panel, Kane listened to more whining, whimpering and cursing as the men got the dogs released. They didn't intend to continue the pursuit. Although the citizenry of Coral Cove put up with a great deal from Billy-boy Porpoise and his gang, they wouldn't tolerate a midnight door-to-door search. After a few minutes, the sound of the dogs and their masters faded away.

A flashlight suddenly glowed, startling Kane so much that he jumped and cursed.

"Relax," Domi said softly. "Windows boarded over—nobody can see."

Kane squinted toward her as she flung back the hood that shrouded her close-cropped, bone-white hair. An albino by birth, Domi was a small white wraith of a girl, every inch of five feet tall. Eyes like red rubies stared up at him through the mask of combat cosmetics she had daubed over her cream-white complexion.

"Had you goin' there, huh?" Laughter was in her high-planed face, and the faint mockery added piquancy to her features.

"Yeah," Kane said dryly. "You're a gifted comedian. What would you have done if the dogs had caught me?"

Domi's small right hand eased out from beneath the ragged cloak. Nestled within it lay her Detonics Combat Master .45. The stainless-steel autopistol weighed only a pound and a half and was perfectly suited for a girl of her size.

"Shoot 'em," she replied frankly. "Then kill the men who made them killers."

Kane nodded. "Figures. Where's Grant?"

Domi shrugged out of the tattered cloak, letting it drop to the floor. "Upstairs. He was keepin' an eye on you, too."

Stepping around the heap of rancid rags, Kane pinched his nostrils shut. "Why does it stink so bad?"

Domi shrugged. "Cover up my own scent, in case the dogs got after me. Old Outland trick."

Kane regarded her gravely. "You peed on it, didn't you?"

"Among other things." Domi turned toward a stairwell, casting the beam of the flashlight ahead of her. She wore a black tank top and tight-fitting denim shorts that only accentuated her compact body, with its pert breasts and flaring hips.

Kane followed her up the stairs, reflecting that after five-plus years of working with her, he shouldn't be surprised by anything Domi did, even wearing a cloak soaked in her own urine.

The stairs opened onto a small room that led out onto a balcony. Grant stood there, peering through a screen of oleander leaves. The buttsock of the heavy Barrett sniper rifle was settled firmly in the hollow of his right shoulder. He pushed it forward on its built-in bipod as he leaned down to squint through the twenty-power top-mounted telescopic sight.

Without turning toward Kane, he said in his lionlike rumble of a voice, "I thought you were going to be in and out of here like the wind."

A big man standing several inches over six feet, Grant had exceptionally broad shoulders and a heavy musculature, but with a middle starting to go a little soft. Beads of perspiration sparkled against his coffee-brown skin like stars in the night sky. Gray dusted his short-cropped hair at the temples, but it didn't show in the sweeping black mustache that curved fiercely out from either side of his grim, tight-lipped mouth. Like Kane, he wore camo pants and T-shirt.

In response to Grant's sarcastic question, Kane replied, "That was the plan. I guess they smelled my wind."

Carefully, he moved to the balcony's rail and looked down into the ville. He could still detect the chemical tang of the CS powder.

Grant stepped away from the Barrett and tapped the scope. "They caught more than that. Take a peek."

Obligingly, Kane stooped and peered through the eyepiece. He glimpsed a tall figure standing just outside the log wall, trying to hide himself in the shadows. The rifle he cradled in his arms looked like a lever-action 30.06.

"They left one behind," he commented. "A spotter."

Grant nodded. "They want to see which house you come out of. And to find out if anybody in town is helping you, so they can be made an example of."

Kane shrugged. "I don't think they got a good look at me. And since you two didn't arrive until after dark, they most likely don't know you're here."

"Porpoise is probably sure it was you creepin' around his place," Domi stated matter-of-factly.

Kane cast her a quizzical glance. "Why do you say that?"

The girl shrugged. "He only saw you and Brigid together—stands to reason he'd figure you'd be the one to try and sneak in and steal her back from him."

Chapter 2

The morning sky melted, pouring down heat. Kane stood on the shoreline, listening to the noise of the surf and gazing through the smoky spume rising from the breakers.

Although sunglasses masked his eyes, he squinted against the glare glimmering on the blue surface of the gulf. There was nothing to be seen except the blaze of white sand, sparse stalks of beach grass and the long line of combers lapping at the shoreline. He perspired heavily, as if the rising sun were a sponge sucking liquid from every pore of his body and soaking through his black T-shirt. Although he felt the sting of sunburn on his arms and face, the heat failed to thaw a hard knot of ice inside him.

Acceding to the demands of Billy-boy Porpoise, he was completely unarmed, not even carrying a jack-knife. The only concession to his standard complement of equipment was the Commtact, a flat curve of metal fastened to his right mastoid bone and hidden beneath a lock of hair.

Despite heat that turned the beach into an oven, Kane stood motionless, hands loose at his sides. He knew he was being watched, and he figured Billy-boy would wait until he had virtually sweated out all of his strength before sending someone to fetch him.

But Kane had learned stamina in a hard school, a killing school. He retained vividly grim memories of former colleagues whose stamina failed them at the last critical second. Stamina in this case consisted of standing steadfast, husbanding all of his resources until they were needed.

A burst of static filled his head and Grant's voice said, "Testing, one, two, testing."

Resisting the urge to turn and look in the direction of Coral Cove, Kane reached up behind his ear and made an adjustment on the Commtact's volume control. The little comm was attached to implanted steel pintels; its sensor circuitry incorporated an analog-to-digital voice encoder embedded in the bone.

Once the device made full cranial contact, the auditory canal picked up the transmissions. The dermal sensors transmitted the electronic signals directly through the skull casing. Even if someone went deaf, as long as he wore a Commtact, he would still have a form of hearing, but if the volume was not properly adjusted, the radio signals caused vibrations in the skull bones that resulted in vicious headaches.

"Receiving you," Kane subvocalized in a faint whisper. "Do you read me?"

"Reading you. Status?"

"Lots of sea and sand. I think I spotted a crab a few minutes ago."

The Commtact accurately conveyed Grant's grunt of disgust. "The bastard believes in making people wait for him."

"I guess Billy-boy thinks it increases the anticipation."

"No sign of the spotter he left behind?"

"No. He probably hung around until just before daybreak and then moved on."

Grant didn't respond for a long tick of time. Then he asked dourly, "How did such a simple op go so goddamn complicated?"

Kane almost lifted a shoulder in a shrug but stopped himself. "Happens sometimes," he retorted with a nonchalance he did not feel. "You know that as well as I do."

"I do," Grant said. "I also know Brigid hasn't answered any of our thousand and one hails, so we may want to—"

"Her Commtact is probably malfunctioning," Kane broke in harshly. "She was knocked into the pool when Billy-boy's crew put the arm on us. That's all there is to it."

"Right," Grant drawled, his tone studiedly neutral. "So let's cut to the chase here. Billy-boy wants to parley with you for Brigid's return. Why?"

"Why what?"

"He's already got her, so why does he want to bargain with you for her? What does he need you for? It's the Cerberus armory he wants, not her...unless he thinks having two bargaining chips is better than one."

"That possibility occurred to me," Kane admitted. "He was pretty disappointed when we came to him yesterday bearing no gifts, particularly of the lethal kind."

"I got that. But I don't think you can trust this son of a bitch to do a simple exchange, Brigid for blasters. You may have to—"

"I hope you're not trying to prepare me for the possibility that she's already dead," Kane interrupted.

"Now that you've brought it up," Grant said, "what if she is? This guy reps out as a stone-cold murderer, not a businessman."

"If she is," Kane intoned flatly, "then all the more reason for me to be in Billy-boy's company. If she has so much as bruise on a leg, he is most definitely a dead man."

"And what about you?" Grant argued. "You're waltzing in there unarmed and even if you manage to get close enough to kill the bastard, there's no way we can extract you before you're killed, too."

Before Kane could formulate a response, he heard the grinding of an engine.

He turned toward the south and saw a red Jeep emerge from a copse of royal palm trees. The chassis was painted a bright cherry red with the illustration of a shocking pink porpoise emblazoned on the hood. The vehicle rolled smoothly on oversize beach tires across the expanse of searing sand where it met with the surf line.

The driver was a tall man who looked half Viking

and half pirate. His long white blond hair was tied back in a foxtail, a sharp contrast to the deep bronzed tan of his naked torso. A black eye patch embroidered with the outline of a pink dolphin covered his right eye. Sunlight winked from the three-inch gold ring piercing the lobe of his left ear.

The man's single eye glinted with cobalt brightness, and his hands on the steering wheel were very big and powerful. As the Jeep drew closer to Kane, he flashed a taunting grin. His teeth gleamed startlingly white in his bronzed face.

A young woman sat beside him, her eyes the deep amber of a Siamese cat's, slanted, cold and dangerous. They looked at Kane with contempt. Her hair was a thick glossy black, cascading in loose waves over her bare shoulders. Little-girl bangs hung in feathery arcs, inky against the white of her forehead. Her eyelids and sullen mouth were heavily rouged, and the bright red blossom of a flower made a splash of color in her raven's-wing hair.

The woman's full breasts strained against the tight confines of her slate-gray bikini top. The cloth was almost the same color as the S&W Airweight .38-caliber revolver she aimed at him around the frame of the windshield. Kane had been introduced to the man and girl the previous day. Their names were Shaster and Orchid.

"Here's my ride," Kane murmured.

"Acknowledged," Grant replied. "Standing by."

Shaster braked the Jeep a few yards away and sat

with the engine idling. He stared at Kane and Kane stared back.

After a few seconds, the tanned man challenged, "Well?"

"Well what?"

"Are you trying to see how long it will take to pass out from heatstroke? Don't you have a breakfast sit-down scheduled with B.B.?"

"You tell me," Kane retorted.

"You do," Orchid snapped petulantly, gesturing with the short barrel of the revolver. "Get your ass over here."

Kane's mouth quirked in a smile. "Don't you want to frisk me, sweetheart?"

Shaster glanced toward the girl. "Don't you, Orchid?"

She shook her head impatiently. "Maybe later. Right now it's too goddamn hot. Besides, you were told to come unarmed, just like yesterday, right?"

The half smile disappeared from Kane's mouth. "Right."

"Good enough for me," Shaster said. "Climb aboard, muchacho, so we can get back to the pool and the piña coladas."

Swallowing a sigh, Kane crossed the stretch of scalding-hot sand, feeling the heat even through the soles of his boots. Orchid slid into the backseat, affording him a glimpse of her well-molded backside and the pink porpoise tattooed at the center of her back.

"Billy-boy really believes in this brand-recognition

thing," Kane commented as he climbed in on the passenger side. "Even on his hired help."

He felt the cold tip of the pistol press against the back of his neck. "Shut the fuck up, sec man," Orchid said, voice sibilant with spite.

Kane felt his shoulders stiffening at the epithet, then he forced himself to relax. "Sec man" was an obsolete term dating back to preunification days when self-styled barons formed their own private armies to safeguard their territories. It was still applied to Magistrates in hinterlands beyond the villes, so Kane figured Orchid was either a former Roamer or a Farer. Roamers were basically marauders, undisciplined bandit gangs who paid lip service to defying the ville governments as a justification for their depredations.

Farers, on the other hand, were nomads, a loosely knit conglomeration of wanderers, scavengers and self-styled salvage experts and traders. Their territory was the Midwest, so Farer presence in and around Florida was a little unusual. Regardless, Magistrates were feared and despised all over the Outlands by Roamer and Farer alike.

Shaster turned the Jeep and drove up the beach, the coarse sand flying from beneath the knobby tire treads in a double cresting of rooster tails. After a quarter of a mile, he turned off onto a bumpy asphalt road that led directly to a glass-walled toll booth. Within it sat a man wearing swim trunks and a gold chain about his neck, but little else.

He saluted Shaster with the barrel of a shotgun as

the Jeep rolled past. The vehicle followed a narrow lane stretching over a moat filled with brackish water and flowering hyacinths. The canal Kane had been forced to swim less than eight hours before fed the moat.

The lane curved into a community of pale pink stucco houses with red-tiled roofs. Palm trees sprouted from the small lawns. The houses faced a beach that sloped gently toward the waters of the gulf. White-winged gulls wheeled over the shoreline. A number of boats floated on the brilliant blue sea, and although most of them looked like fishing vessels, Kane knew a number of them were disguised fast-attack craft. The bows of several boats bore the outline of leaping pink porpoises.

The beachfront marina was one great open market, just like the intel had indicated. Shops and stalls were brightly painted, the vendors selling the wares looted from other coastal communities by Billy-boy's fleet. People from all over the region mingled with the tanned locals who came to trade, exchanging valuable items like drugs for guns or artifacts dredged up from the Gulf coast's plentiful supply of submerged ruins.

Shaster steered the Jeep through an open gate in a five-foot-high whitewashed wall. Bracketing both sides of the gate, painted in pink on the surface on the wall, was a pair of sporting dolphins. A deeply bronzed blond man, stripped to the waist and cradling a lever-action 30.06 rifle in his arms, pursed his lips at Kane, blowing him a kiss as the vehicle drove into the compound.

Shaster cast Kane a sly grin. "Lucas is checking you out."

"I noticed," Kane grunted.

"He didn't get the chance to formally meet you last night."

"That's a shame," Kane replied blandly.

Brigid Baptiste had described the Porpoise compound as the model of an exclusive beachfront estate—it had been built as such more than two centuries earlier, when land development was the chief economic force on the Gulf Coast of Florida.

Kane had been less interested in the history of Billyboy Porpoise's little seaside fiefdom than the man who had put it together over the past few years. The only reason he and Brigid had traveled from Montana to Florida was to learn what kind of man he was and if he could be recruited into joining their struggle, as other former and potential adversaries had done.

Diplomacy, turning potential enemies into allies against the spreading reign of the overlords, had become the paramount tactic of Cerberus over the past two years. Lessons in how to deal with foreign cultures and religions took the place of weapons instruction and other training.

Over the past five years, Brigid Baptiste and former Cobaltville Magistrates Kane and Grant had tramped through jungles, ruined cities, over mountains, across deserts and they had found strange cultures everywhere, often bizarre re-creations of societies that had vanished long before the nukecaust.

Due in part to her eidetic memory, Brigid spoke a dozen languages and could get along in a score of dialects, but knowing the native tongues of many different cultures and lands was only a small part of her work. Aside from her command of languages, Brigid had made history and geopolitics abiding interests in a world that was changing rapidly.

She and all the personnel of Cerberus, over half a world away atop a mountain peak in Montana, had devoted themselves to changing the nuke-scarred planet into something better. At least that was her earnest hope. To turn hope into reality meant respecting the often alien behavior patterns of a vast number of ancient religions, legends, myths and taboos.

However, Billy-boy Porpoise had exhibited behavior patterns that were all too familiar to Kane. After inviting the two emissaries from Cerberus to a council with the promise of giving their proposal serious consideration, he had chosen treachery over diplomacy. Although not particularly surprised by Billy-boy's choice, Kane had been enraged when Brigid was held hostage so as to force a new session of talks.

Shaster wheeled the Jeep down a crushed-shell driveway and braked to a stop at the foot of a flight of stone steps. Orchid stepped behind Kane and pressed the bore of the revolver against his back. "Let's move it on up, sec man."

Kane climbed the steps with the girl and Shaster walking behind him. At the top of the steps a gently sloping path curved through an area lush with shrubs and tropical plants—huge ferns, enormous, glossy elephant ears, green philodendrons and orange birds-of-paradise.

Kane heard the murmur of voices and the clanging rhythm of steel drums, as well as the bleat of trumpets and the wail of an electric slide guitar. He sidled between two date palm trees and came to a halt, looking down into a slightly sunken area dominated by a huge, blue-tiled in-ground swimming pool.

A score of people, most of them nearly naked and some of them completely so, milled around on the concrete deck of the pool. A four-piece reggae band played a vigorous piece that sounded like a tuneless racket to Kane's ears.

He saw only two people in the pool. One was an enormously fat man sitting in an inflatable purple rubber chair, floating motionless in the deep end. A pink foam dolphin bobbed in the water beside his right hand. It was almost the same color as Billy-boy Porpoise's bare skin.

On Porpoise's left hand, reclining in an identical chair, was a tall woman of five-nine or so with flowing curves, long, lovely and unbruised legs—and an abundant bosom almost completely exposed by the two narrow triangles of yellow cloth that were scarcely more than token acknowledgments of clothing.

The woman's thick hair shone with the fiery hue of

molten lava, and although Kane couldn't see her eyes behind the lenses of the sunglasses she wore, he received the distinct impression Brigid Baptiste was completely at ease as she lounged beside Billy-boy Porpoise.

Chapter 3

Kane strode down to the poolside, very conscious of how he was being ignored by the revelers. He wasted no time looking for hidden guns—it was enough to know they were around.

He saw a big moon-faced man, tall and wedge shaped, with a thick chest and wide shoulders that led to a size-eighteen neck. He had a flat face, with a bulging forehead and about two pounds too much jawbone. His hair looked like the sprout of black hog bristles. His skin was unhealthy, blotched, mottled by the scars of old radiation burns that came of digging around hellzones. The garish colors of the tropical-print shirt complemented his complexion.

The man's gristle-buried eyes followed Kane's every step, and the expression on his face was one of concentrated hatred. It took him a few seconds to put a name to the ugly face—Blister McQuade, the former pit boss of Mandeville who bore no one from Cerberus a feeling that even approximated goodwill.

A small girl, stark naked except for fluorescent pink body paint laid on in loops and a fall of blond, silken hair that covered her upper body like a cloak, glided up to him. Silently she handed him a fluted glass filled with a bright orange fluid.

Kane waved her off. "Too early for me, sweetheart."

He spoke loudly in order to be heard over the band. Billy-boy Porpoise's eyelids fluttered. His sagging pectorals with shocking pink nipples rose and fell. He inhaled, and then exhaled a deep breath, causing small wavelets to break at the pool's edge.

He peered up at Kane with dark eyes surrounded by pouches of fat. They were round eyes with no discernible lashes and bore no resemblance to those found on a dolphin. Kane figured they had originally been intended for a barracuda but due to a production error, ended up in Billy-boy's hairless head.

"Kane," he said in a soft voice.

"Billy-boy," Kane replied. "Sorry to wake you."

"Nonsense. We were just conserving our strength." He glanced toward Brigid Baptiste. "Weren't we, doll-baby?"

Brigid did not reply, her face expressionless. With the sunglasses concealing her eyes, she might as well have been wearing a mask.

Kane nodded toward her. "Good morning, doll-baby. You're looking rested."

Slowly, she lifted the sunglasses and regarded him with dispassionate, emerald-green, jade-hard eyes. "I don't know what would give you that idea."

A slender woman with a fair complexion, Brigid Baptiste's high forehead gave the impression of a probing intellect, whereas her full underlip hinted at an appreciation of the sensual. Her mane of thick hair hung in a long sunset-colored braid, tossed over her left shoulder.

As he sat up straighter in his floating chair, Billy-boy Porpoise's pudgy fingers pulled a lever that activated a small prop positioned at the rear of the seat. With a faint whir, the chair moved toward the concrete steps at the shallow end of the pool.

Grasping the handrail, Porpoise heaved himself out of the pool, rolls of fat jiggling as he mounted the steps in a slow, careful motion. Water streamed from his balloonlike belly, dripping down his tree-trunk-thick thighs. Although at first glance he appeared naked, he wore tiny Speedo briefs, almost absorbed by the multiple bulges of flabby, wet flesh. His dripping body was totally hairless, heavy pendants of fat creasing his torso and limbs. Barely visible within the folds of the man's triple chins wealed the trace of an old scar, the memento of a long-ago throat cutting. Sunlight glinted from the multitude of rings on his pudgy fingers.

Brigid rolled out of her chair and swam with languorous strokes to the edge of the pool, effortlessly heaving herself out of the water. She casually padded barefoot toward a buffet table. It required a great deal of effort on Kane's part to fix his attention elsewhere.

The girl who had offered Kane the drink picked up a multicolored beach towel only slightly smaller than a sail and carefully began patting every part of Porpoise's skin dry. He smiled at her fondly. "Thank you, Dixie."

He lifted his arms so Dixie could wipe down the undersides. Each touch of the towel sent little ripples jiggling over the expanse of pink flesh. Trying not to allow his revulsion show on his face, Kane guessed the man stood a little less than six feet tall, but probably tipped the scales at four-hundred-plus pounds.

Reacting to a gesture from Porpoise, the reggae band instantly stopped playing, as if a volume control knob had been turned all the way down. As the girl blotted the swag belly that rolled out and nearly hid his pelvis, the pink man said genially, "I'm a little surprised you came back, Kane…especially after last night's failure."

"What failure was that again?" Kane asked in a bored tone, as if he inquired only to be polite.

Porpoise shook his head in good-natured frustration. "It doesn't matter. It's enough you kept your word and returned here."

"It's not like I had a choice." Kane nodded toward Brigid, who was examining the items on the dessert cart with great interest. "You baited the hook pretty damn effectively."

Porpoise smiled. "Thank you."

"Is that what this party is about? Celebrating that I came back?"

"Hardly. I'm holding it in honor of a former acquaintance of yours who may become a business associate."

Kane glanced toward Blister McQuade, snapped off a salute with a finger to the brow and called, "Yo, Blister. How you been?"

To Kane's surprise and great unease, McQuade's lips writhed back from his broken, discolored teeth in a grin. "Gotcha, Kane. Finally gotcha."

"*You* got me?"

McQuade chuckled, a sound like old bones being crushed underfoot. "Well, you're sure as shit *got*, ain't cha?"

"You have a point."

Turning back to Porpoise, Kane demanded, "Is this whole routine just a trap to turn me over to some small-time trash like Blister?"

Dixie held up a pink terry-cloth robe and Porpoise thrust his arms into the voluminous sleeves. "Come now," the fat man said patronizingly. "You and Brigid are bright people. You're too valuable to me to waste you like that."

"I don't get you."

"You must've known when I permitted you to walk in here yesterday that there was a chance I'd take one or the both of you hostage."

"To force Cerberus to deal with you," Kane stated. "To trade our freedom for weapons. Like I said to you yesterday, it's not going to happen."

If Porpoise had possessed eyebrows, they would have arched upward over his scalp. "I think you're very much mistaken. It's not so much your freedom I'm bartering with, but your reputations."

Brigid dropped the pretense of being uninterested in the exchange. She turned around, demanding sharply, "What do you mean?"

"The so-called Cerberus warriors are more than just legends in the Outlands," Porpoise said, his eyes glinting shrewdly. "You're symbols, valuable propaganda tools, far beyond your reputations as baron blasters."

Like "sec man," the term "baron blaster" was old, deriving from the rebels who had staged a violent resistance against the institution of the unification program a century earlier. Neither Kane nor Grant enjoyed having the appellation applied to them. Their ville upbringing still lurked close to the surface, and they had been taught that the so-called baron blasters were worse than outlaws, but were instead terrorists incarnate.

Regardless, the reputations of the core Cerberus warriors had grown too awesome, too great over the past five years for even the most isolated outlander to be ignorant of their accomplishments, even if it was an open question of just how many of the stories were based in truth and how many were overblown fable.

Kane folded his arms over his chest. "How can our reps be of any use to you?"

Porpoise accepted a glass from the girl and sipped at it appreciatively. "In the three years I've run my operation from here, rarely a month has gone by without word of the notorious Cerberus marauders. Even before I settled here, reports were circulating about your group."

Brigid smiled coldly. "And you thought we were fairy tales?"

Porpoise shook his head. "No, I figured you were real enough. I wasn't sure how much of what I heard was true or just folklore…like how you assassinated Baron Ragnar, blew up a major baronial outpost in New Mexico, took out a couple of Magistrate Divisions, destroyed Ambika's pirate empire and royally screwed a big Millennial Consortium operation."

He raised his glass in Brigid's direction. "I really must thank you for that, doll-baby. Saved me the trouble of dealing with the competition."

"All true," Kane declared flatly. "And that's just the stuff we let our PR department circulate."

Porpoise's eyes flicked back and forth between Kane and Brigid. "I personally don't care about the other stuff or even it's true or not. What's important is if the outlanders believe it."

Brigid frowned. "Why?"

"Their belief in the tales makes you extremely valuable assets. Once word spreads that you're working for Billy-boy, whatever agenda Cerberus is putting together will fall apart. They'll be flocking to me as their new hope."

Kane opened his mouth to retort, then shut it. Porpoise was far more perceptive than his initial assessment. The Cerberus agenda called not just for the continued physical survival of humanity, but for the human spirit, the soul of an entire race.

Over the past five years, the Cerberus warriors had scored many victories, defeated many enemies and solved mysteries of the past that molded the present and affected the future. More importantly, they began to rekindle of the spark of hope within the breasts of the disenfranchised fighting to survive in the Outlands.

Victory, if not within their grasp, at least had no longer seemed an unattainable dream. But with the transformation of the barons into the overlords, all of them wondered if the war was now over—or if it had ever actually been waged at all. Kane often feared that everything he and his friends had experienced and endured so far had only been minor skirmishes, a mere prologue to the true conflict, the Armageddon yet to come.

The Cerberus warriors had hoped the overweening ambition and ego of the reborn overlords would spark bloody internecine struggles, but in the two years since their advent, no intelligence indicating such actions had reached them.

Of course, the overlords were engaged in reclaiming their ancient ancestral kingdoms in Mesopotamia. They had yet to cast their covetous gaze back to the North American continent, but it was only a matter of time.

Before that occurred, Cerberus was determined to build some sort of unified resistance against them, but the undertaking proved far more difficult and frustrating than even the cynical Kane or the impatient Grant had imagined. Even two years after the disappearance of the barons, the villes were still in states of anarchy, of utter chaos, with various factions warring for control on a day-by-day basis.

"For the sake of argument," Brigid said, "let's assume you're right, that our colleagues view us the way the Outlanders do. Wouldn't it make more strategic sense to be known as our ally?"

Porpoise sipped the piña colada. "Not really. From both a personal and business perspective, becoming a Cerberus satellite would be detrimental to my business model. I've got a lot of overhead."

"You're a goddamn pirate," Kane rasped impatiently. "Whatever you need, you steal. Overhead, my ass."

"I'm an entrepreneur," Porpoise countered defensively. "A visionary. I'm building a colony and when I'm done, I'll be the major trading port on the gulf. I've got big plans—a rut farm, casinos, a major marketplace. But I need personnel."

"Personnel?" Brigid echoed, a contemptuous undercurrent in her tone. "Slaves, more like it."

Porpoise snorted disdainfully, blowing orange froth over the rim of the glass he lifted to his lips. He gestured expansively to the people assembled at poolside. "Do they look like slaves to you?"

Eyeing the naked, docile Dixie, Kane remarked, "Now that you mention it—"

"Enough." Anger entered Porpoise's voice. "The colony I'm building will be self-sufficient and will not owe its existence to the fucking barons or to Cerberus. So here's the deal, Kane—I know you've got people hidden in Coral Cove. From the reports I've received, there's usually four of you out in the field…doll-baby here, an ex-Mag named Grant, you and a little albino piece. You're going to write out a list of what Cerberus will give me to expand my operations and I'll arrange to have it delivered to them."

"And what I am supposed to tell these contacts of ours?" Kane asked impatiently. "That me and doll-baby have decided to stay here and par-*tay* with you and Blister? You don't think they'll buy that, do you?"

Porpoise shook his head. "No, and that's why I'm not going to sell it. I'm keeping you here as hostages, plain and simple. That's the deal. If they don't accept it, then they can take parts of you back home, Kane. I'll keep doll-baby around until she bores me…which, after hearing her talk, probably won't be that far in the future."

Kane sighed, presenting the image of seriously pondering Porpoise's words. At length he said, "I have a counterproposal."

The fat man cocked his head at a quizzical angle. "Which is?"

Matter-of-factly, Kane said, "If you let us go in the next hour, those contacts of mine you mentioned won't raze this trading port of yours to the ground. It's an either-or situation, Billy-boy. The safety of your giant plushy-pink ass depends on you making the right choice."

Porpoise's expression did not change, but his gaze shifted, eyes looking beyond Kane. Glancing over his shoulder, Kane saw that Blister McQuade had moved closer. He was not alone. Shaster and Orchid stood slightly behind him and both of them were armed with pistols.

Billy-boy snapped his fingers and turned away. He said, "Hurt him."

Chapter 4

Kane's battle-trained muscles, tested and refined in a hundred situations where a fraction of a second gave him all the edge he needed, exploded in a perfect co-ordination of mind, reflexes and skill.

Kane jumped for Billy-boy Porpoise. The obese man yelled and tried to fend Kane off with one hand. Kane caught the flailing arm, hooked it at the elbow and wrenched it around ruthlessly in a hammerlock. He muscled Porpoise around in front of him. It was like trying to wrestle with a beached whale.

At the same time, Brigid Baptiste snatched up a short-bladed knife from the buffet table and laid the edge against the side of Porpoise's throat, right above the scar. Orchid, Shaster and McQuade rocked to halts as Porpoise squawked hoarsely, gesturing with his free hand for them to stop.

Orchid raised her revolver, sighting down its length, training the bore on Brigid. "Want me to kill your know-it-all bitch, Kane?"

Brigid pressed the knife harder against Porpoise's neck. "Want me to kill Billy-boy? No? Then stand aside or I'll finish what a throat slitter started a long time ago."

The woman's tone was hard, grim and confident. Even Kane knew she wasn't bluffing, so that meant her loathing of Billy-boy Porpoise was profound.

McQuade's eyes narrowed. "You kill him, then you'll die sure as shit."

"We know that, Blister," Kane said with a genial smile, bearing down on the hammerlock. "But if we do it our way, nobody has to die and this happenin' party place will stay standing. If we do it anybody else's way, then just about everybody here will be dead."

McQuade scowled, fists clenching. "You're so full of shit, Kane."

"Are you one-hundred-percent certain about that?" Brigid asked, a taunting note in her voice. "I don't think Billy-boy is…are you?"

Porpoise sighed heavily, sounding like a dolphin expelling air from a blowhole. "All right, all right. You two can leave. Neither one of you is worth all of this bullshit—"

To Kane, it felt as if Billy-boy Porpoise suddenly exploded within his grip. He twisted wildly to the left, then hurled himself to the right, kicking backward with both heels. The knife blade in Brigid's hand dragged along the side of his neck, drawing a thread of blood.

Kane tried to bear down on the hammerlock, to force Porpoise to his knees, but the man exhibited enormous strength. He kicked out with a huge splayed foot, catching Brigid in the stomach and driving her backward.

With his free hand, Porpoise jabbed up and behind him at Kane's eyes, fingers hooked like claws. Kane lowered his head and saved his vision, but Porpoise secured an agonizingly tight grip on his hair. He heaved with his shoulders, as if performing an expansive shrug, then tore free of his terry-cloth robe, leaving it in Kane's hands.

Releasing his grip on Kane's hair, Porpoise heeled around, snatched the hem of the robe and hurled it up and over the taller man's head. A fist pounded into his stomach, jarring him several feet to the left. As he tried to struggle free of the enveloping robe, a hard object struck the side of his head through it, and what felt like Billy-boy's forearm pile-drived against his chest, knocking him down.

A rain of blows and kicks fell on him, his ears filled with breathless curses and furious female shrieks. Pain flared all over his body. He heard Brigid's voice raised in anger.

Two more kicks, landing just below his rib cage, drew a grunt of pain from him. Rolling onto his back, Kane tensed every muscle in his body and performed what gymnasts refer to as a "kip-up," the easiest and quickest way to go from lying prone to an upright posture. He kicked his legs straight out at a thirty-degree angle, bent his knees swiftly, planted his feet and used the momentum of the kick to spring erect.

The draping folds of the robe fell away and Kane glimpsed a glitter above his head, descending in an eye-blurring arc. Half turning he caught a slender wrist in his right hand and twisted viciously, hearing bones snap like brittle wood. A female voice screamed in pain. Kane caught a fragmented glimpse of Dixie falling to her knees, cradling her broken arm. The knife Brigid had wielded lay at her feet.

Kane snaked his upper body to the right and spun backward with his right fist. The ram's-head punch impacted solidly with Blister McQuade's chin. Pivoting on his toes, he shot his elbow into the man's throat.

McQuade staggered backward, holding his throat in both hands, his tongue protruding from his mouth. He toppled into the pool, raising a great splash that sloshed water on everyone in the vicinity. Kane whirled toward Porpoise.

For all of his bulk, Porpoise launched himself forward nimbly, cannonballing his entire weight into Kane's torso, forcing him backward, smashing all the wind out of him. Kane crashed over two deck chairs before hitting the concrete deck and skidding several feet.

Fighting off the instinct to curl up, he shambled to his feet, only to be knocked down again by the butt of a gun that came down like a hammer on the top of his head.

The pool became a huge black hole and Kane plunged into it headfirst.

HE BECAME AWARE of a blessedly cool trickle of water on the flushed skin of his face. Kane did not open his eyes or otherwise move, trying to adjust to the fierce throbbing pain in his skull, pulsing in cadence with his heartbeat.

His thought processes were remarkably clear, and he remembered everything up to the point where he had been cold-cocked. Shame made a bitter taste at the back of his throat. He had misjudged the entire situation with Porpoise, but he couldn't have left Brigid in the man's custody while he, Grant and the other members of Cerberus Away Team Alpha staged an assault on the compound.

The thought of Brigid motivated him to open his eyes. He saw nothing but patterns of dark gray and pitch black. He tried to sit up but the effort sprayed his brain with needles and he bit back a groan. He lay back down.

"Kane?"

"Baptiste?" His whisper was a hoarse rasp.

"Right here." He felt the cool, damp touch of cloth against his forehead.

Squinting, Kane could barely make her out, kneeling over him, dabbing at his face with a wet cloth. Gingerly, he touched the crown of his head and felt the moisture, as well as a very tender lump. His scalp wasn't split, so he assumed the liquid was water. He tried to focus on Brigid again, but his blurred vision prevented him from fixing on single reference points in the darkness.

He got his hands under him and slowly pushed himself into a sitting position, silently enduring a spasm of vertigo and nausea.

"Are you all right?" Brigid asked, voice pitched very low. "That little bitch Orchid really laid one on you."

Kane started to nod, thought better of it and said, "I really hate being whacked unconscious and then waking up somewhere else."

Brigid forced a chuckle. "It's a pretty clichéd transitional device, isn't it?"

Assuming her question was rhetorical, Kane felt around him. His fingers touched damp sand. "Where are we?"

"Some sort of storage shed, about a hundred yards away from the pool."

"How long was I out?"

"About half an hour, I think."

"They didn't hurt you?"

"Not seriously. Billy-boy made some over-the-top threats about forcing me to be the bottom bitch in an offshore whorehouse. I guess he figured that would scare me into obedience."

Kane grinned, even though the motion hurt his cheeks. "Billy-boy is one enterprising bastard, isn't he?"

"He makes me want to puke for a week," Brigid shot back coldly. "Can you stand up?"

"Let's find out." Carefully, Kane heaved himself to his feet. He stumbled and Brigid put out supporting hands. He probed various aches and pains around his body, particularly his ribs. Nothing felt broken.

"What's the plan?" Brigid asked.

"In about half an hour, maybe less, Grant, Domi and CAT Alpha will come storming in here by land and by sea. I'd prefer to be out of here by then."

He walked slowly toward an area of gray, noting how threads of yellow light peeped along the lines of a door. As he touched it and rapped on the wood gently, Brigid stated, "It's locked, of course."

"Of course." Kane felt around the doorframe with his hands, touching the metal hinges and the lock.

He stepped to the left, moving slowly around the walls, his body responding sluggishly from the bruises of the beating. He ignored the pain and probed the cinder-block walls with his fingertips, scraping his nails at the mortar. Lifting his right arm, he laid the palm of his hand flat against the ceiling.

"I'd judge the size of our accommodations to be about ten by ten," he commented.

"More like twelve by twelve," Brigid corrected.

He continued moving sideways, not finding any furniture or anything of use in the storage shed. As he circled back to the door, he bumped into Brigid. His vision had cleared, adjusting to the gloom, and he could make out her face and figure, seeing a bruise on the left side of her face where someone had struck her. She was also naked to the waist.

"You don't have a top on," he said awkwardly.

Crossing her arms over her breasts, she said angrily, "Thanks for the revelation, Kane. You try fighting half a dozen scumbags wearing only a bikini sometime."

"The parts tend to fall off?"

She nodded grimly. "They do."

Quickly, Kane stripped out of his T-shirt. "There's no way you could've won. You shouldn't have mixed it up with them."

Brigid uttered a deprecating chuckle. "If I hadn't, Blister and Billy-boy would have stomped you to death, poolside."

Handing her his shirt, Kane said quietly, "Thanks."

"My pleasure, but we've got to worry about getting out of here…or signaling Grant and Domi to either hold off on the attack or launch it as scheduled."

Reaching up behind his ear, Kane fingered his Commtact. "It's not functioning. Got too stomped on, I guess."

Brigid sighed. "Figures."

Kane forced a laugh. "Doesn't it just. Well, we've relied on nothing but our fists and wits plenty of times before."

"Maybe one too many times."

Disturbed by the uncharacteristic note of resignation in Brigid's voice, he said, "I think we've still got a reservoir of luck to draw on."

She struggled to pull the shirt over her head. "Over five years of this, Kane. Five years of playing the odds, and when all else fails, placing our faith in luck. There's got to be a limit to both."

"It's not just luck that's kept us alive," he said defensively. "Not always, anyway."

"No, not always," she agreed with a wry weariness.

"Just most of the time. Face it, Kane—we're fugitives from the law of averages."

Kane knew Brigid spoke the truth, but he didn't let her know that. Lakesh had once suggested that the trinity he, Brigid and Grant formed seemed to exert an almost supernatural influence on the scales of chance, usually tipping them in their favor.

The notion had amused Kane, since he was too pragmatic to accept such an esoteric concept, but he couldn't deny that he and his two friends seemed to lead exceptionally charmed lives, particularly him and Brigid.

Kane shied away from examining the bond he shared with Brigid. On the surface, there was no bond, but they seemed linked to each other and the same destiny. He recalled another name he had for Brigid Baptiste: *anam-chara*. In the ancient Gaelic tongue it meant "soul friend."

From the very first time he met her he was affected by the energy Brigid radiated, a force intangible, yet one that triggered a melancholy longing in his soul. That strange, sad longing only deepened after a bout of jump sickness both of them suffered during the mat-trans jump to Russia, several years earlier. The main symptoms of jump sickness were vivid, almost-real hallucinations.

He and Brigid had shared the same hallucination, but both knew on a visceral, primal level it hadn't been gateway-transit-triggered delirium, but a revelation that they were joined by chains of fate, their destinies linked. The idea that he and Brigid had existed at other times in other lives had seemed preposterous at first. Perhaps it still would have if he hadn't experienced the same jump dreams as her, which symbolized the chain of fate connecting her soul to his.

It had required nearly a year before the two very different people achieved a synthesis of attitudes and styles where they could function smoothly as colleagues and parts of a team, sharing professional courtesies and respect.

Although they never spoke of it, Kane often wondered if that spiritual bond was the primary reason he had sacrificed everything he had attained as a Magistrate to save her from execution. The possibility confused him, made him feel defensive and insecure. That insecurity was one reason he always addressed her as "Baptiste," almost never by her first name, so as to maintain a certain formal distance between them. But that distance continued to shrink every day.

"I'm open for suggestions about how to get out of here," Kane said sarcastically, "even if they do rely primarily on luck."

Brigid opened her mouth, but whatever she was about to say was interrupted by the sound of footsteps and murmured voices on the other side of the door. A key rattled in the lock.

"How's that for luck?" he muttered.

"The bad kind," she retorted in an acerbic whisper.

Chapter 5

With an arm, Kane swept Brigid to one side and flattened himself against the opposite wall beside the door just as it was pulled open from the outside. The light pouring into the small building was blinding, and they averted their eyes. Billy-boy Porpoise's voice had a peculiar, petulant quality to it.

"Come out to where we can see you. Both of you!"

Kane did not stir, gazing across the open doorway toward Brigid and touching a finger to his lips. From outside came a mutter of orders. Kane recognized Orchid's icy voice, but everyone was too wary to step in through the doorway.

"We're not going to hurt you anymore, Kane," Porpoise said in a wheedling tone. "We proved our point. Just come on out."

When neither he nor Brigid responded, Porpoise commanded, "Goddammit, get your asses out here!"

"It's nice and shady in here," Kane said mockingly. "Why don't you join us?"

Billy-boy Porpoise said nothing for a long tick of time. Then, in a low, quavering tone, he demanded, "Who are they, Kane?"

"Who be who, B.B.?"

"My sentries have spotted armed men in the land-side perimeter. They're yours, right?"

"I couldn't say."

"Well, *I* can," Blister McQuade growled hoarsely. "You're coming out so they can see we have you. We can chuck tear-gas grens in there and give you the same treatment you gave the dogs last night."

"Yeah," Orchid said, a note of cruel laughter twisting around her words. "Would you like that? I would."

Swallowing a profanity-seasoned sigh, Kane exchanged a questioning glance with Brigid. Her face was expressionless, but after a thoughtful few seconds, she nodded curtly.

"All right," Kane said loudly. "Here we come."

Kane pushed himself away from the wall, set himself, then bounded through the door, head down. As he half expected, McQuade was ready to greet him. The scarred man's fists pounded a double pile-driving rhythm into his belly. Letting himself go limp, Kane fell to the ground, covering up.

"That's enough!" Porpoise squawked. "I need him mobile."

Blister uttered an animalistic snarl of disappointment and stepped away. Spitting out grit, Kane lifted his head from the sandy soil and saw Orchid pulling Brigid through the doorway, S&W revolver pressed against the side of her head. Her unbound mane glistened like a flow of molten lava in the relentless sunlight.

Porpoise, once more wearing his pink terry-cloth robe, tied shut with a long strip of cloth, prodded Kane with a sandaled foot. "Blister really, really, *really* wants to kill you, Kane."

"But you'll talk him out of it, right?"

"Not for very long. Besides, I really, really, really want you dead, too."

"Who'll sign off on your Cerberus wish list, then?" Kane demanded.

Porpoise snorted and reached out to caress Brigid's sleek thigh. "No reason why she can't. I'll keep doll-baby around for a while... I can always cut out her tongue. But for the time being, I need both of you looking healthy."

Brigid kicked at him. Porpoise immediately swung his left paw and backhanded her across the face. The gaudy, jeweled rings cut red furrows across Brigid's right cheek.

In a fury, Kane tried to rise, but a foot in the center of his back flattened him against the ground.

"You liked that love pat?" Porpoise asked, grinning at Brigid. "That's your first lesson as a slave. Kneel at my feet and kiss my dick."

Brigid didn't move. Her eyes seethed with loathing, with hatred. "Maybe you should show me where it is first. I left my magnifying glass at home."

Porpoise lifted his hand again. Kane struggled to his hands and knees, but Blister McQuade's foot came up and kicked him on the chin, snapping back his head.

Orchid grabbed Brigid's right arm and bent it

behind her, twisting sharply upward. "Kneel and kiss, bitch!"

Three distant crumps came almost together. The air shivered.

Orchid turned her head toward the house. "What was that?"

The lane that led to Porpoise's compound suddenly spewed columns of flame and smoke. A woman screamed, a sound of fear, not pain. Orchid, Blister McQuade and Porpoise stood in openmouthed, disbelieving shock, staring in the direction of the explosions.

Kane lunged up from the ground, driving his right fist into Blister McQuade's crotch. The big man roared, throwing out his arms, blunt fingers hooking around Kane's bare upper arms. For a long moment, the two men grappled, Blister's fingernails peeling away strips of skin. Orchid leveled her pistol at the back of Kane's head.

All of them heard a swishing whisper that almost instantly became a steady pressure against their eardrums. Barely twenty yards over their heads, a pattern of light twisted and shifted. Dark, ambient waves shimmered, then revealed the bronze tones of an aircraft's hull like water sluicing over a pane of dusty glass.

The craft held the general shape and configuration of a manta ray, and at first glance was little more than a flattened wedge with wings. Sheathed in bronze-hued metal, intricate geometric designs covered almost the entire exterior surface, interlocking swirling glyphs, cup and spiral symbols and even elaborate cuneiform markings. The wingspan measured out to twenty yards from tip to tip and the fuselage was fifteen feet long.

Blister stopped struggling, although he didn't release Kane. Everyone shielded their eyes as fine clouds of sand puffed up all around. Balanced on the balls of her feet, Brigid pivoted at the waist toward Orchid, her forearm slapping the girl's S&W aside while the edge of her stiffened palm slashed against the base of her delicate throat.

The electric tingling sensation in the socket of Brigid's armpit told her of the power of her blow. Orchid staggered backward, arms windmilling. She fell without uttering so much as a whimper, arms and legs flung wide. Consciousness went out of her eyes with the swiftness of a candle being blown out.

Bawling in wordless panic, Billy-boy Porpoise lunged for the pistol nestled within Orchid's slack fingers. The nose cannon of the Manta erupted with a series of stuttering thunderclaps. The short burst of explosive tungsten-carbide shells punched three-foot-high geysers of dirt into the narrow stretch of ground between Porpoise and the girl.

Brigid glanced up and waved as the Manta listed to the left and right, a waggling of the wings to let her know that Grant sat in the cockpit. The hulls of the Mantas were equipped with microcomputers that sensed the color and shade of the background and exactly mirrored the image.

Porpoise whirled and ran, big sandaled feet kicking up gouts of sand. Brigid snatched the pistol from Orchid's hand and sprinted after him, pausing only long enough to strike Blister McQuade on the back of the neck with the short barrel. She ran on, leaving the man for Kane to finish off. Her objective was Billy-boy Porpoise, and she wasn't wasting any time on underlings or guests. She knew Kane could take McQuade, even if he lost some skin and blood in the process.

The staccato hammering of subguns and the cracks of small-arms fire from two different directions reverberated against Brigid's eardrums as she ran. The sounds were punctuated by the heavier crumps of the detonating grenades launched by the H&K XM-29 assault rifles carried by Cerberus Away Team Alpha as they rushed in through breaches blown in the wall.

The dozen members of CAT Alpha wore tricolor desert-camouflage BDUs, helmets and thick-soled jump boots, as well as PASGT vests that provided protection from even .30-caliber rounds. Stuttering roars overlapped as the barrels of their autorifles spit short tongues of flame as the team spread out across the perimeter.

Porpoise's personal guard put up a disorganized counteroffensive, but they were unprepared and underarmed. CAT Alpha consisted primarily of highly trained former Magistrates, and they ruthlessly overran the defenders' positions. The high-caliber rounds fired by the XM-29s spun Porpoise's men like puppets with their strings suddenly cut. Survivors ran for cover, squalling in fear, throwing away their weapons.

Brigid glimpsed the second Manta planing along the shoreline, lancing toward the marina. She guessed Edwards sat in the cockpit. A pair of mini-Sidewinders burst from the pod sheaths under the aircraft's wings and inscribed short, descending arcs. Although she did not see where they struck, she heard the double explosions, followed instantly by mushrooming fireballs of orange and black that spewed high into the air, mixed with fragments of wood and fiberglass.

Brigid's lips compressed in a grim smile of satisfaction as Billy-boy's pirate fleet was thoroughly deep-sixed. Distantly, she heard Domi's high-pitched, forceful voice issuing orders to the team.

She saw Porpoise squeezing his bulk between a pair of palm trees, heading for the rear of the house. As Brigid followed him, long legs pumping, Shaster stepped into view, snapping up a pistol and squeezing off a hasty shot in her general direction. The bullet fanned cool air on her right cheek.

Raising the S&W, she worked the double-action trigger. The .38-caliber bullet took the man in the left leg, blowing away the kneecap in a welter of crimson and cartilage. Howling, Shaster pitched forward, dropping his pistol so he could claw at his maimed leg.

Brigid leaped over him, aware of explosions blazing orange from all points around the compound. The roof of the house erupted in a column of flame, and debris rained down, splashing into the pool. Thick smoke reeking of chemicals swirled, stung her eyes, burning the soft tissue of her throat and biting at her nostrils. A multitude of voices cried out in pain and terror.

Coughing, half-blinded by the haze, Brigid didn't see Porpoise until he loomed up behind her. Before she could lift the pistol, she felt herself imprisoned by a pair of arms that hugged her close in an agonizingly tight embrace. Lifting her from her feet, Porpoise shook her savagely from side-to-side and the revolver slipped from her fingers, clattering to the deck.

Billy-boy's hoarse voice, strained by exertion and smoke inhalation, whispered, "You're still my hostage, doll-baby. Tell these bastards to hold their fire and call off the attack."

Brigid lowered her head, then reared back, slamming the crown of her head into Porpoise's face. He cried out, stumbled backward and slipped off the curb. Still clutching Brigid, he plunged into the pool.

Fighting free of the dazed man's grasp, Brigid twisted to face the sputtering Porpoise. Blood streamed from his flattened nose and split lips. Baring red-filmed teeth, he lunged for her, thick fingers tangling in her hair.

He shoved her beneath the surface. She struggled frantically and he pulled her to him, tightly pressing her face against his belly, intending to smother her in his flab, as well as drown her in the water.

Brigid fought, fingernails raking across the fabric of the man's robe. She tore it open and clawed at his flesh. Billy-boy Porpoise's grip did not relax and with a surge of comingled horror and self-disgust, she realized all the man had to do was stand patiently for a couple of minutes and she would die a humiliating death.

Locking the muscles of her throat, lungs burning, Brigid opened her mouth as wide as she could and sank her teeth deep into a roll of Porpoise's belly fat. Despite the thunder of her pulse in her ears and the muffling effect of the water, she distinctly heard the man voice a high-pitched squeal much like the sounds emitted by his namesake.

Fingers groping over the juncture of his thighs, Brigid found and seized his testicles while she continued chewing through Porpoise's lower belly. Releasing his grip on her head, Porpoise kicked and flailed, screaming in pain.

Hovering on the fringes of unconsciousness due to lack of oxygen, Brigid shoved herself away, her head breaking the crimson-tinged surface of the pool. She spit out a mouthful of Porpoise and even over her strangulated gasps, she heard Billy-boy shrieking, "You bitch! You fucking bitch!"

He stroked toward her, water roiling and splashing in his wake, congested face contorted in a mask of homicidal rage. Brigid backed away, drinking in air, dragging her hair out of her eyes. Porpoise looped the robe's belt over Brigid's head and cinched it tight around her throat.

She managed to slide a hand between makeshift garrote and her neck, but as she strained against it and felt Porpoise's strength, she knew she was spent. She swung her free hand, knotted into a fist, against Billy-boy's chin, rocking his head back on his shoulders. But the pain of the blow was negligible compared to that of the wound she had inflicted on him with her teeth.

Through foggy eyes, Brigid glimpsed a bare-chested and scarlet-streaked Kane appear on the pool's deck. Face as expressionless as if it were carved from stone, he extended his right arm and squeezed off a single shot with the S&W revolver.

Porpoise's body jiggled and he half turned toward Kane, eyes widening in reproachful amazement. He opened his mouth as if to speak, and Kane shot him again, this time through the center of the chest. He coughed blood, and the pressure around Brigid's neck fell away.

Slowly, Billy-boy Porpoise sank beneath the surface, crimson strings stretching out from various parts of his body.

Massaging her throat, Brigid stared at Kane and demanded, "What kept you?"

Kane shrugged, gesturing with the revolver toward a Manta skimming low over the burning roof of the house. "Luck. The good kind."

KANE STOOD on the beach, smoking a self-congratulatory cigar. The Gulf of Mexico stretched away, as calm as a mirror, until the heat haze on the horizon melded it with the cloudless blue sky. He stared at the flotsam littering the sea and washing up on the shoreline. A few bodies floated amid the wreckage of the marina.

The Manta piloted by Edwards had virtually pulverized the fleet of Billy-boy Porpoise. The only seaworthy craft left were a couple of dinghies. He watched the gulls winging over the floating debris, diving down to pick up whatever offal caught their eye. Behind him, smoke boiled from many of the buildings in the compound.

Carefully, Kane rolled his shoulders, wincing at the scrape of the raw abrasions against his T-shirt. The analgesics he had taken from the medical kit blunted the sharp edges of the pain, even that in his head.

Although he had subdued Blister McQuade, he hadn't killed him. So far, the man hadn't been identified among those of Porpoise's staff who had been rounded up. Kane wasn't particularly concerned about Blister being on the loose—he had plenty of enemies on the hoof, and compared to most of them, McQuade barely rated as a nuisance, much less a genuine threat.

At the sound of feet crunching on the sand, he turned quickly, reaching for the revolver tucked into the waistband of his pants. Grant, Domi, Brigid and Edwards approached him. A patch of liquid bandage shone dully on Brigid's right cheek, covering the abrasion inflicted by Porpoise's rings.

"All of this before lunch," Grant rumbled, gesturing expansively toward the smoke rising into the sky. "What do we do before supper?"

"Go home," Brigid said curtly. She was attired in jeans, a military-gray T-shirt and low-heeled boots. "I've about had my fill of the Sunshine State."

Kane touched the lump on the top of his head and winced. "Me, too. Kind of a shame about how everything turned out. I know you had hopes of cutting a deal, Baptiste."

"Billy-boy should've believed you," Domi stated. "Fat bastard brought this on himself."

"What about the people here?" Edwards asked. "What should we do with them?"

Domi cast the big shaved-headed ex-Mag a cold stare. "Let 'em go. Not their fault Porpoise was an asshole."

"True," Grant agreed. "But they're not exactly victims, either. They benefited from Porpoise's marauding."

Edwards nodded, wiping at the sweat pebbling his brow. "We can't leave them to pick up the pieces themselves. They'll just try to take over Coral Cove."

Kane exhaled a stream of smoke. "Then we'll post CAT Alpha here, under your command, for a couple of days. Just to make sure everybody behaves."

Edwards looked as if he were on the verge of voicing an objection, then nodded. "Yes, sir."

Brigid sighed, running fingers through her tangled mane of hair. "Why is it that so many of the deals we broker are ultimately decided at the barrel of a gun?"

Grant shrugged the wide yoke of his shoulders. "That's the purest form of diplomacy, isn't it?"

Taking a final puff of the cigar, Kane flipped the butt out into the breakers. "Let's get to the Mantas. The sooner we launch, the sooner we're back in the cool mountain breezes of Montana."

Dourly, Grant said, "Not exactly."

Both Kane and Brigid eyed him challengingly. "Not what exactly?" Brigid wanted to know.

Grant hooked a thumb in the general direction of the Mantas. "I received a comm. call from Lakesh a few minutes ago. There's a situation he wants us to check out on the way back to Cerberus."

"What kind of situation?" Domi asked suspiciously, ruby eyes slitted.

"Possible overlord activity."

Kane frowned. "Where?"

Slowly, almost reluctantly, Grant intoned, "Tennessee…the former barony of Beausoleil."

Chapter 6

Alarm Klaxons warbled with a nerve-scratching rhythm, echoing through the redoubt. Personnel ran through the corridors in apparent panic, but in actuality they were racing to preappointed emergency stations as per the red-alert drills.

Farrell's voice blared from the public-address system. "Intruder alert! Sealing exterior sec door! Intruder alert!"

Mohandas Lakesh Singh dodged adroitly as he rushed to the operations center. "Coming through!" he shouted in order to be heard over the alarm.

He heard his order repeated on his left by Brewster Philboyd. Lakesh glanced toward the tall man and nodded in acknowledgment. One of the three-score refugees from the Manitius Moon colony, Philboyd was an astrophysicist. In his mid-forties, Philboyd was tall, thin and lanky, and his pale blond hair was swept back from a receding hairline that made his already high forehead seem exceptionally high. He wore black-rimmed eyeglasses, and his cheeks bore the pitted scars associated with chronic teenage acne.

"What's going on?" Philboyd demanded.

"Your guess is as good as mine at this point," Lakesh retorted, squeezing between two people clad in the white bodysuits that served as the unisex duty uniform of Cerberus personnel. "I was in the commissary, steeping my pot of lunchtime tea."

A well-built man of medium height, with thick, glossy black hair, an unlined dark-olive complexion and a long, aquiline nose, Lakesh looked no older than fifty, despite a few strands of distinguished gray streaking his temples. He resembled a middle-aged man of East Indian extraction in reasonably good health. In reality, he had recently celebrated his 251st birthday.

As a youthful genius, Lakesh had been drafted into the web of conspiracy the architects of the Totality Concept had spun during the last couple of decades of the twentieth century. A multidegreed physicist and cyberneticist, he served as the administrator for Project Cerberus, a position that had earned him survival during the global megacull of January 2001. Like the Manitius Moonbase refugees, he had spent most of the intervening two hundred years in cryostasis.

The central command complex of the Cerberus redoubt was a long, high-ceilinged room divided by two aisles of computer stations. Half a dozen people sat before the terminals. Monitor screens flashed incomprehensible images and streams of data in machine talk.

The operations center had five dedicated and eight shared subprocessors, all linked to the mainframe computer behind the far wall. Two centuries earlier, it had been one of the most advanced models ever built, carrying experimental, error-correcting microchips of such a tiny size that they even reacted to quantum fluctuations. Biochip technology had been employed when it was built, using protein molecules sandwiched between microscopic glass-and-metal circuits.

The information contained in the main database may not have been the sum total of all humankind's knowledge, but not for lack of trying. Any bit, byte or shred of intelligence that had ever been digitized was only a few keystrokes and mouse clicks away.

A huge Mercator relief map of the world spanned the entire wall above the door. Pinpoints of light shone steadily in almost every country, connected by a thin glowing pattern of lines. They represented the Cerberus network, the locations of all functioning gateway units across the planet. As they entered, Philboyd and Lakesh cast quick over-the-shoulder glances at the map. No lights blinked, so none of the gateway units were in use.

On the opposite side of the operations center, an anteroom held the eight-foot-tall mat-trans chamber. Rising from an elevated platform, six upright slabs of brown-hued armaglass formed a translucent wall around it.

Armaglass was manufactured in the last decades of the twentieth century from a special compound and process that plasticized and combined the properties of steel and glass. It was used as walls in the jump chambers to confine quantum-energy overspills.

Lakesh and Philboyd moved swiftly to the main ops console. Two people sat before it, gazing fixedly at the VGA monitor that rose above the keyboard. A flat LCD screen nearly four feet square, it flickered with icons and colors.

Farrell, a shaved-headed man who affected a goatee and a gold hoop earring, rolled his chair back from the console on squeaking casters. The brown eyes he turned toward Lakesh were anxious. "About time you got here."

Lakesh stepped up beside him and saw that the top half of the screen glowed with a CGI grid pattern. A drop-down window displayed scrolling numbers that he quickly recognized as measurements of speed and positional coordinates. "Status."

"A radar hit," Donald Bry answered, inclining his copper-curled head toward a bead of light inching across the gridwork. A round-shouldered man of small stature, Bry acted as Lakesh's lieutenant and apprentice in all matters technological. His expression was always one of consternation, no matter his true mood.

Electronic chimes sounded each time the bead of light left one glowing square of the grid and entered another. "When did you get the first hit?" Lakesh asked.

"About five minutes ago," Farrell said. "Whatever the bogey is, it's not traveling very fast."

Philboyd eyed the numbers on the drop-down window. "About two hundred klicks per hour. Could it be a Deathbird?"

Bry shook his head. "When it first appeared, the altitude was around thirty thousand feet. The maximum flight ceiling of a Deathbird is about three."

"It's not that high now," Lakesh pointed out.

"No," Farrell agreed. "And the bogey is slowing down the closer it comes. Straightforward course, too."

Philboyd adjusted his eyeglasses. "Almost like it's trying to catch our attention, not evade it."

Lakesh opened his mouth to reply, grimaced, then said to Farrell, "Turn off the alarms, but lower the security shields. Lock us down in here."

The man's hands tapped a series of buttons on the keyboard. The alarm fell silent, and the warbling was replaced by the pneumatic hissing of compressed air, the squeak of gears and a sequence of heavy, booming thuds resounding from the corridor. Four-inch-thick vanadium alloy bulkheads dropped from the ceiling and sealed off the living quarters, engineering level and main sec door from the operations center, completely isolating it from the rest of the installation.

Constructed in the mid-1990s, no expense had been spared to make the redoubt, the seat of Project Cerberus, a masterpiece of concealment and impenetrability. The researches to which Project Cerberus and its personnel had been devoted were locating and traveling hyperdimensional pathways through the quantum stream. Once that had been accomplished, the redoubt became, from the end of one millennium to the beginning of another, a manufacturing facility. The quantum interphase mat-trans inducers, known colloquially as "gateways," were built in modular form and shipped to other redoubts.

On the few existing records, the Cerberus installation was listed as Redoubt Bravo, but the handful of people had who made the facility their home for the past few years never referred to it as such.

The thirty-acre, three-level installation had come through the nukecaust with its operating systems and radiation shielding in good condition. The redoubt contained two dozen self-contained apartments, a cafeteria, a frightfully well-equipped armory, a medical infirmary, a gymnasium complete with a swimming pool and even holding cells on the bottom level.

When Lakesh had secretly reactivated the installation some thirty years earlier, the repairs he made had been minor, primarily cosmetic in nature. Over a period of time, he had added an elaborate system of heat-sensing warning devices, night-vision vid cameras and motion-trigger alarms to the surrounding plateau.

He had been forced to work completely alone, so the upgrades had taken several years to complete. However, the location of the redoubt in Montana's Bitterroot Range had kept his work from being discovered by the baronial authorities.

In the generations since the nukecaust, a sinister mythology had been ascribed to the mountains, with their mysteriously shadowed forests and hell-deep, dangerous ravines. The wilderness area was virtually unpopulated. The nearest settlement was located in the flatlands, and it consisted of a small band of Indians, Sioux and Cheyenne, led by a shaman named Sky Dog.

Concealed within rocky clefts of the mountain peak beneath camouflage netting were the uplinks from an orbiting Vela-class reconnaissance satellite and a Comsat. A radar array had been installed along the crags and cliffs of the peak.

The road leading down from Cerberus to the foothills was little more than a cracked and twisted asphalt ribbon, skirting yawning chasms and cliffs. Acres of the mountainsides had collapsed during the nuke-triggered earthquakes nearly two centuries ago.

Following an attack staged by Overlord Enlil, a network of motion and thermal sensors had planted all around the Cerberus redoubt, expanding in a six-mile radius from the plateau.

Although a truce had been struck, a pact of non-interference agreed upon by Cerberus and the nine overlords, no one—least of all Lakesh—trusted Enlil's word, and so the security network and protocols had been upgraded over the past couple of years. One of the protocols involved safeguarding the irreplaceable equipment within the op center.

"The bogey is within visual range now," Farrell said. "Switching to exterior scanners."

A second drop-down window appeared in the left-hand corner of the VGA screen. It displayed a view of the azure early-afternoon Montana sky, with only a few wispy cirrus clouds floating within the limitless expanse of blue. A section of the dark granite peak bulked up on the right.

"There it is," Bry murmured.

A disk-shape skimmer came swooping through the sky, the bright sunlight glistening from the hull as if it were brightly polished mirror. Although Lakesh was not surprised to see the Annunaki craft, he felt a cold tickle of dread at the base of his spine. The silver disk was one of the small fleet of scout vessels carried by *Tiamat*, the inestimably ancient, mind-staggeringly enormous Annunaki starship in Earth orbit.

The skimmer wheeled gracefully several hundred feet above the surface of the plateau, orbiting the peak, approaching one rocky outcrop, then darting away again almost playfully.

"What the hell is it doing?" Philboyd asked, voice tight with tension.

"I have no idea," Lakesh replied frankly. "It's almost as if the pilot is teasing us...daring us to fire on him."

"Maybe to test our defenses," Farrell ventured. "To see what kind of weapons we'll deploy against him."

Lakesh frowned. "Possibly, but I doubt it. We'd get a better idea of motives if we knew which overlord is responsible for this sortie."

"Maybe the same one who is responsible for the mess in Tennessee," Bry declared. "This can't be a coincidence."

Lakesh nodded but didn't respond. Only a few hours earlier, he had studied telemetry downloaded from the Vela satellite's photographic relay system. A year's worth of hard work on the part of Bry allowed Cerberus to gain control of the Vela and the Keyhole satellites. The Vela was programmed to transmit any imagery from the former baronies that fit a preselected parameter, such as signs of civil strife or war.

That morning, Lakesh watched a telemetric sequence that showed an object resembling a silver disk skimming over the ville of Beausoleil and hovering over the Administrative Monolith. A short time later it shot out of sight—right before the entire walled city seemed to explode in flame. Computer enhancement of the images proved what Lakesh feared— that the skimmer had laid waste to the barony with its on-board energy weapons.

On the VGA screen, the disk stopped dead in midair. Lakesh knew if the craft had not been equipped with inertial dampers like the Mantas, human crew members would have been seriously injured, regardless of whether they were strapped into shock couches.

The bottom portion of the hull suddenly bulged outward, as if it were a flexible membrane being pushed from within.

"What the hell—?"Philboyd rasped, his shoulders stiffening.

"I haven't seen anything like that before," Bry said matter-of-factly, although his eyes were so wide Lakesh worried for a fraction of second that they might fall out of his head.

A small gleaming orb popped down and out from the skimmer's hull. Lakesh gauged its size to be about that of a basketball. The sphere spun, revolved and darted around the disk, lunged toward the peak and then away from it, acting much like a fish cautiously investigating a new coral reef.

"Is that ship giving birth or taking a dump or what?" Farrell growled, trying to cover his confusion and fear with crude bravado.

As the four men stared at the screen, the sphere pirouetted around the plateau with eye-blurring speed, dropping in altitude with every revolution. It came to an abrupt halt, directly in front of the massive vanadium alloy security door. The orb floated a few feet above the surface, then three stalk-like legs extended out from beneath it, the tips growing splayed hooks that dug into tarmac, anchoring it in place.

The skimmer hovered overhead for a few more seconds, then shot straight up so swiftly it almost seemed to vanish.

Brewster Philboyd leaned forward, squinting through the lenses of his eyeglasses at the tripodal silver ball. "Whoever the overlord is, they've left us a pretty damn ugly lawn ornament."

Folding his arms over his chest, Lakesh scowled at the screen. "I'd prefer a gnome or a pink flamingo myself."

Bry and Farrell cast him confused, irritated glances but Lakesh was in no mood to clarify his cryptic comment. "Someone is going to have to go out and take a closer look at the package," he declared.

Philboyd cleared his throat. "Are you asking for volunteers or just making a generalized observation?"

Lakesh angled challenging eyebrows at the three men. "What do you think?"

Chapter 7

Lakesh glanced diffidently at the blazing red eyes of the three-headed hound and murmured, "Don't give me that look. Where were you when we needed you?"

The heads of the slavering Cerberus painted on the wall did not respond to his reproachful question. The three snarling heads stretched out from a single, exaggeratedly muscled neck, their jaws wide open, blood and flame gushing from between great fangs. Beneath the image, written in exaggerated Gothic script was inscribed one word: Cerberus.

He grasped the lever positioned on the vanadium bulkhead directly above the middle head of Cerberus, pulling it down to the midpoint position. With a whine and rumble of pneumatics and buried gears, the massive sec door began folding aside, opening like an accordion. The individual panels of vanadium alloy were so heavy, it took nearly half a minute for the door to open wide enough to allow one person to step through.

In this instance, eight people were prepared to step out. Lakesh turned to face the members of CAT Beta assembled in the twenty-foot-wide corridor behind him. All of them wore helmets, yellow-lensed shooter's glasses and dark BDUs with ballistic-resistant armor plate interwoven throughout. They were armed with M-249 automatic rifles.

"Are you sure you feel up to this, Colonel Sinclair?" he asked quietly.

A wiry, lean-muscled black woman in her mid-thirties, Sela Sinclair scowled in reaction to Lakesh's question, despite his solicitous tone.

"Dr. DeFore gave me a clean bill of health," she retorted curtly. "If you have doubts about my recovery, you should talk to her."

Lakesh shook his head. "No need. I trust her medical opinion."

Sinclair nodded sharply and focused her attention on what lay beyond the opening sec door. Unlike most of her fellow Manitius scientists, Sela Sinclair served in the United States Air Force and had earned the rank of lieutenant colonel shortly before being assigned to the Moon base. Although she held a doctorate, her military bearing was more akin to the demeanors of the former Magistrates in the CAT squad than the lunar colony personnel.

Lakesh had initially opposed the formation of the three Cerberus Away Teams, made uncomfortable by the concept of the redoubt's own version of the Magistrate Divisions, ironically composed of former Magistrates. However, as the scope of their operations broadened, the personnel situation at the installation also changed.

No longer could Kane, Grant, Brigid Baptiste and Domi undertake the majority of the ops and therefore shoulder the lion's share of the risks. Over the past year, Kane and Grant had set up Cerberus Away Teams Alpha, Beta and Delta. CAT Delta was semipermanently stationed at Redoubt Yankee at Thunder Isle, rotating duty shifts with New Edo's Tigers of Heaven, and CAT Beta was charged with the security of the redoubt and surrounding territory.

Generally, Domi commanded Beta Team while Sela Sinclair was the officer in charge of CAT Delta. A short while before, Sinclair had suffered an injury while defending Redoubt Yankee and spent her convalescence at Cerberus. With Domi out in the field, Sinclair was the logical choice to take command of Beta.

"All right," Lakesh said loudly, addressing the other members of the team. "Do not fire unless fired upon. We want this thing—whatever it is—intact."

"My people know their duties," Sinclair reminded him coldly. "Sir."

Lakesh repressed a smile and stepped aside, making a grand, sweeping gesture toward the sec door. "Then have them hop to it, Colonel."

"Yes, sir," she drawled, stepping forward.

When three of the door panels had folded completely aside, Sinclair announced to her team, "I'll take point. You'll deploy by twos and establish a triangulated firing pattern. On my mark."

The woman set herself, took a deep breath, then kicked herself forward. "Go!"

She rushed over the threshold, followed by the members of CAT Beta, moving with a swift, efficient grace.

Lakesh glanced back to see Philboyd standing several yards away, an anxious look on his face and a heavy tarpaulin folded under his arm. They exchanged nods and with a studied nonchalance, Lakesh strolled out of the installation.

The sprawling plateau was broad enough for the entire population of the redoubt to gather without getting near the rusted remains of the chain-link fence enclosing it. On Lakesh's left, the plateau debouched into grassy, wildflower-carpeted slopes, and the bright sun gleamed on the white headstones marking more than a dozen grave sites. The fabricated markers bore only last names: Avery, Cotta, Dylan, Adrian and many more.

Ten of them were only a couple of years old, inscribed with the names of the Moon base émigrés who had died defending Cerberus from the assault staged by Overlord Enlil. The surface of the plateau itself was still pockmarked by the craters inflicted by that attack, even though efforts had been undertaken to fill them in with gravel.

On the far side of the plateau, the asphalt dropped away into an abyss nearly a thousand feet deep, plunging down to a riverbed. Lakesh gratefully inhaled the fresh air. He had spent most of his adult life cloistered in installations like the Cerberus redoubt, and he couldn't help but sourly note that it was only after Earth had become a nuke-blasted shockscape that he had come to appreciate the small things about it.

CAT Beta, the stocks of their M-249s braced against their shoulders, were in wide V formation around the three-legged orb, the bores of the weapons positioned to catch it in a cross fire. As Lakesh warily approached it, he thought the surface looked disturbingly dark, more like old pewter than quicksilver.

He knew it was composed of smart metal, a liquid alloy that responded to a sequence of commands programmed into an extruder. A miniature cohesive binding field metallicized it from liquid to solid. Over the past couple of years, the Cerberus personnel had learned that the smart metal was a fundamental building block of Annunaki technology.

Lakesh inspected the sphere, appreciating its smooth, seamless appearance but experiencing a mounting frustration because of the mystery it posed. He reached out to touch it with a forefinger.

"Dr. Singh—" Sinclair warned.

"Yes, yes," he retorted irritably. "You have your job, Colonel, and I have mine."

He ran a tentative fingertip over the top of the orb, pinged it with a fingernail, then carefully laid his right hand against it. The metal was cool, slick and he felt no mechanical or electronic vibrations from within it.

"For a Trojan horse," he commented to no one in particular, "this thing seems singularly ineffective."

Philboyd stepped out onto the tarmac, squinting

against the sunlight. "Lakesh," he called, "let's wrap it up and cart it inside for examination."

Lakesh cast the man a crooked smile. "I thought you would have learned your lesson about bringing home cybernetic strays after the last time, friend Brewster."

Philboyd's cheek muscles knotted in embarrassment, but he did not respond to Lakesh's gibe. Over a year earlier, Philboyd had insisted there was nothing threatening about a severely damaged piece of Annunaki technology and brought into the redoubt for study. He still bore a small scar on the back of his neck as reminder of how thoroughly wrong his assessment had been.

Returning his attention to the sphere, Lakesh prodded one of the tripodal legs with a foot, noting how deeply the claws were sunk into the tarmac. He absently tugged at his nose, then gestured. "Bring it up, friend Brewster."

Philboyd crossed the plateau, unfurling the canvas as he came. He and Lakesh quickly stretched it out and draped it over the tripod.

"Now what?" asked Sela Sinclair, a note of impatience in her voice. "It doesn't look like you can uproot it without tools."

"Very true," Lakesh agreed. "Nor do I think we should try."

Philboyd's eyebrows lifted above the rims of his glasses. "Why not?"

"Assuming that this is some sort of monitoring or observation device, preventing it from performing its designed function may be the best way to either elicit a response from the overlord who left it here or to minimize the danger it presents."

"So far," Philboyd remarked, "it's about as dangerous as a birdbath."

"The operative term is 'so far'—"

"Hey!" cried Alvarez, one of the Beta team. "Something is happening!"

Lakesh stared at the canvas-concealed sphere with a mixture of confusion and apprehension crowding into his mind. He reached out, his fingers brushing the tarp, and he jerked his hand back in pain. The fabric was like fire.

He felt a wave of heat radiating from the shrouded shape, and faint tendrils of gray smoke curled up from it. Blackened scorch marks appeared and the odor of burning cloth stung his nostrils.

Alarmed, he blurted, "Everyone back away! Quickly now!"

CAT Beta didn't move until Sinclair snapped, "You heard the man. Fall back!"

As the squad hastily complied, rifles still trained on the sphere, heat waves shimmered in a wavery aura, as if they rose from a sun-baked desert. Lakesh felt the searing temperature against his skin and he recoiled, pushing Philboyd back with him. The heat within a three-foot radius around the tripod went from uncomfortable to unbearable inside of ten seconds.

The canvas covering suddenly burst into flame, dissolving magically, burning scraps falling away to smolder on the tarmac. Red-glowing embers corkscrewed into the air, eddied by the breeze.

For a long, awkward moment, no one spoke. Philboyd broke the silence by husking out, "Guess it doesn't like being covered up."

Lakesh nodded, lips compressing in a tight, grim line. "We should find out what else it doesn't like. Colonel, if you would be so kind—"

Sinclair sighted down the length of her autorifle. "Squad, fire at will."

She squeezed off a long staccato burst. Bright brass arced out of the smoking ejector port, tinkling down at her feet. The other seven members of CAT Beta triggered simultaneous, full-auto fusillades. Lakesh and Philboyd clapped hands to their ears.

Sparks flew from the multiple impact points on the tripod. The keening whines of ricochets echoed over the plateau. The hailstorm of bullets struck bell-like chimes from the orb but did not penetrate. They bounced off with angry, buzzing whines without leaving so much as a dimple.

Sela Sinclair released her pressure on the M-249's trigger and shouted, "Cease-fire! We're not having an effect! Cease-fire!"

Lowering her weapon, Sinclair snatched away her shooter's glasses and glowered angrily at the unmarred surface of the globe. "I don't believe it."

Lakesh stepped up beside her. "Believe it. Apparently the smart metal can increase or decrease its density, as well as control its surface temperature depending on the stimuli."

Sinclair hefted her rifle. "We've got a lot more ordnance to draw upon than these."

Lakesh nodded thoughtfully. The Cerberus armory was quite likely the best stocked and outfitted arsenal in postnuke America. Glass-fronted cases held racks of automatic assault rifles. There were many makes and models of subguns, as well as dozens of semiautomatic pistols and revolvers, complete with holsters and belts.

The armory also housed heavy-assault weaponry like bazookas, tripod-mounted 20 mm cannons, mortars and rocket launchers. All the ordnance had been laid down in hermetically sealed Continuity of Government installations before the nukecaust. Protected from the ravages of the outside environment, nearly every piece of munitions and hardware was as pristine as the day it was first manufactured.

Lakesh himself had put the arsenal together over several decades, envisioning it as the major supply depot for a rebel army. The army never materialized—at least, not in the fashion Lakesh hoped it would. Therefore, Cerberus was blessed with a surplus of death-dealing equipment that would have turned the most militaristic overlord green with envy, or given the most pacifistic of them heart failure—if they indeed possessed hearts.

New additions to the arsenal included a handful of rail pistols and pulse plasma rifles, experimental weapons salvaged from the Moon base.

"The objective isn't to destroy the thing," Philboyd interjected testily.

Sinclair gave him a level stare. "Isn't it?"

Philboyd approached the tripod with a swift, purposeful gait. "No. I'd like to finally have a chance to examine working Annunaki tech instead of wreckage. If we can actually subject it to testing, then we can retroengineer—"

One of the three legs suddenly whipped free of the asphalt and curled upward like a tentacle. Philboyd rocked to an unsteady stop, his mouth falling open in surprise.

Stretching out toward Philboyd, the tentacle waved back and forth in a chilling and unmistakable imitation of a wagging warning finger.

Swallowing hard, Philboyd stepped backward. "I guess it's not going to allow us to study it, either."

Lakesh tried to tamp down the fear rising in his mind, like lengthening shadows. He gazed at the tripod and stated calmly, "It's here for the duration."

"Duration of what?" Sela Sinclair demanded.

"The duration of its mission," Lakesh replied bleakly. "Whatever that might be."

Chapter 8

Spread out below the wings of the Mantas were great vistas of pastureland, rolling hills and forests, forming a mosaic of bright green, yellow and dark green.

The mist-shrouded Smoky Mountains were on the horizon as Kane banked the Transatmospheric Vehicle in a gradual turn, leveling off at four thousand feet. The sky was a sea of unbroken blue on which the Mantas piloted by Kane and Grant sailed gracefully.

Kane commented to no one in particular, "Even if an overlord burned Beausoleil's barony to the ground, I don't understand why that's of any interest to us."

"Me, either," Grant replied gruffly, his voice echoing within the walls of Kane's helmet. "Unless the baroness burned with it."

"Little chance of that," said Brigid from the jump seat behind Grant. She adjusted her headset. "There hasn't been a Baroness Beausoleil for quite some time."

"Even so," Domi spoke up from the small seat in the cockpit of the Manta piloted by Kane.

She did not elaborate, and no one requested that she did. All of them remembered how long it had taken

Grant to recover from the injuries he received after being captured and tortured by the sadistic Baroness Beausoleil several years earlier.

As fields, farms and the occasional settlement rolled by beneath them, the two Mantas soared at slightly under Mach 1, flying wing to wing. The maximum cruising speed of the Transatmospheric Vehicles was Mach 25, but neither Kane nor Grant had seen the necessity to boom through the sky from Florida to Tennessee at such air-scorching velocities.

Inside the cockpits, both Grant and Kane wore a bronze-colored helmet with a full-face visor. The helmet attached to the headrest of the pilot's chair. A pair of tubes stretched from the rear to an oxygen tank behind the seat. The helmet and chair were of one piece, a self-contained unit.

The CGI inventory of all the dials, switches, gauges and fire controls flashed across the inner curve of the helmet's visor. All of them showed green. At altitudes of one thousand feet, neither Kane nor Grant was too concerned with accidentally overshooting their objective or colliding with another aircraft.

Because of the 250-mile-per-hour winds that once swept regularly over the rad-ravaged face of America, aerial travel had been very slow to make a comeback. Unpredictable geothermals in the hellzones and chem storms quadrupled the hazards of flying. Even the Deathbirds gunships in use by the Mag Divisions had only been pressed into service in the past thirty-five years.

Although the composition of the TAV hulls appeared to be of a burnished bronze alloy, it was actually a material far tougher and more resilient. The craft had no external apparatus at all, no ailerons, no fins and no airfoils. The cockpits were almost invisible, little more than elongated oval humps in the exact center of the sleek topside fuselages.

A small fleet of the transatmospheric craft had been found on the Manitius Moon base. Of Annunaki manufacture, they were in pristine condition, despite their great age. Powered by two different kinds of engines, a ramjet and solid-fuel pulse detonation air spikes, the Manta ships could fly in both a vacuum and in an atmosphere. The Manta TAV was not an experimental craft, but an example of a technology that was mastered by a race when humanity still cowered in trees from saber-toothed tigers.

Grant and Kane had easily learned to pilot the ships, since they handled superficially like the Deathbirds the two men had flown when they were Cobaltville Magistrates. But as they learned when they flew the TAVs down from the Moon, the ships could not be piloted like winged aircraft within an atmosphere while in space.

A pilot could select velocity, angle, attitude and other complex factors dictated by standard avionics, but space flight relied on a completely different set of principles. It called for the maximum manipulation of gravity, trajectory, relative velocities and plain old luck. Despite all the computer-calculated course programming, both men discovered quickly that successfully piloting the TAV through space was more by God than by grace. Skill had almost nothing to do with it.

Tidy orchards of trees laid out in neat, geometrical order appeared, giving way to wild woodland. Ahead, the blue ribbon of the Tennessee River cut through a grass-carpeted valley. A group of people in fishing boats stared upward as the Mantas winged overhead.

"Seems like a very agrarian area," Brigid observed, a wistful note underscoring her voice. "A simple life."

"Simple because you have to fight for every crumb of food, every stitch of clothing," Domi retorted. "If you're not fighting animals, coldhearts or the weather, then you're fighting your own body, to keep it from getting sick and quitting on you."

Domi paused, then added in a bitter whisper, "That's the simple life in the Outlands."

No one disagreed with her, since the girl knew whereof she spoke far more than her three friends, but they knew enough. In the Outlands, people were divided into small regional clans, communication with other groups was stifled, education impeded and rivalries bred. The internecine struggles in the Outlands had not only been condoned by the baronial authorities, but encouraged.

Outlanders, or anyone who chose to live outside ville society or had that fate chosen for them, were of a different breed. Born into a raw, wild world, accustomed to living on the edge of death, grim necessity had taught them the skills to survive, even thrive in the postnuke environment. They may have been the great-great-great-grandchildren of civilized men and women, but they had no choice but to embrace lives of semibarbarism.

The people who lived outside the direct influence of the baronies, who worked the farms, toiled in the fields or simply roamed from place to place, were reviled and hated. No one worried about an Outlander or even cared. They were the outcasts of the new feudalism, the cheap, expendable labor forces, even the cannon fodder when circumstances warranted.

Domi had decided at a very young age she would not settle for the short, brutal life of a serf. She had sold herself into slavery in an effort to get a piece of the good life available to ville dwellers, but she had never risen any further than Cobaltville's Tartarus Pits.

Since baronial society was strictly class and caste-based, the higher a citizen's standing, the higher he or she might live in one of the residential towers. At the bottom level of the villes was the servant class, who lived in abject squalor in consciously designed ghettos known as the Tartarus Pits, named after the abyss below Hell where Zeus confined the Titans.

Tartarus swarmed with a heterogeneous population of serfs, cheap labor and slaves like Domi. She ended her period of slavery by cutting the monstrous Guana Teague's throat with the blade and saved Grant's life in the same impulsive act.

Like so many others, Teague had dismissed her as semimindless Outlander. The average life expectancy of an Outlander was around forty, and the few who reached that age possessed both an animal's cunning and vitality. Domi was nowhere near that age, and in fact had no true idea of how old she actually was, but she possessed more than her share of both cunning and vitality.

After another five minutes of flying over great stretches of pastureland broken by random ravines and patches of forest, a long intestine of black smoke, shading to gray at the end, uncoiled from behind a range of hills.

"I think that might be the place," Kane said.

He and Grant throttled back on the airspeed and dropped the altitude. The LARC—or low-altitude-ride-control—subsystem fed them turbulence data. The controls automatically damped the effects of turbulent air pockets by the deflection of two small fins extending down from beneath the cockpit areas of the Mantas.

The two ships glided over the walls of the former barony of Beausoleil, punching holes in the wavering curtains of smoke.

Silently, the four people looked down at the ruined streets of the ville. All the villes in the nine-barony network were standardized, so the architecture and layout were familiar.

The walls rose fifty feet high and at each intersecting corner, a watchtower protruded, housing Vulcan-Phalanx gun emplacements that supplied a clear field of fire on the road leading up to the main gate. One of the official reasons for fortifying the baronies was a century-old fear—or paranoid delusion—of a foreign invasion from other nuke-scarred nations.

In Beusoleil ville, there were no longer any checkpoints on the road, no "dragon's-teeth" vehicle obstacles, no armed patrols, but inside the walls still stretched the complex of spired Enclaves. Each of the four towers was joined to the others by pedestrian bridges.

The Enclaves formed a latticework of intersected circles, all connected to the center, from which rose the tower known in baronial days as the Administrative Monolith. But the massive round column of white stone no longer jutted proud and haughty three hundred feet into the sky. The structure looked as if it had been broken in two by titanic blows combining fire and shock.

At the base of the monolith were heaps of rubble that had fallen from the high ramparts. Most of the surrounding buildings were nearly invisible in rolling plumes of dark smoke. The walls themselves showed huge breaches and in places had collapsed altogether. All of the streets were littered with corpses and debris. Vapor curled from black-edged craters.

"Holy God," Kane said in a whisper.

"Aerial bombardment," Brigid stated crisply.

"But why?" Grant rasped.

"Set down," Domi suggested. "Mebbe find out."

The Mantas circled the city, Kane and Grant searching for signs of life and when they saw none, they looked for relatively clear places on which to land. The best areas were outside of the walls.

Grant and Kane engaged the vectored-thrust ramjets of the Mantas and dropped the TAVs straight down, bringing them gracefully to rest facing the gate. Fine clouds of dust puffed up all around.

The two men switched off the engines, and they cycled down to low-pitched whines. Opening the seals of their helmets, Kane and Grant unlatched the opaque cockpit canopies and slid them back. Everyone disembarked, sliding down the wings to the ground.

Domi unholstered her Combat Master and Brigid checked her TP-9 autopistol. Grant and Kane made sure their Sin Eaters were secure in the rather bulky holsters strapped to their forearms. The Sin Eaters were big-bored automatic handblasters, less than fourteen inches in length at full extension, the magazines carrying twenty 9 mm rounds. When not in use, the stock folded over the top of the pistols, lying perpendicular to the frame, reducing its holstered length to ten inches.

When the weapons were needed, by tensing their wrist tendons, sensitive actuators activated flexible cables within the holsters and snapped the pistols smoothly into their waiting hands, the butts unfolding in the same motion. Since the Sin Eaters had no trigger guards or safeties, the blasters fired immediately upon touching their crooked index fingers.

"Let's go in slow," Kane announced. "Standard deployment. Baptiste, you've got our six."

With that, Kane strode purposefully toward the gate, taking the point. In his dozen or so years serving as a Magistrate, he almost always assumed the position of point man. When stealth was required, Kane could be a silent, almost graceful wraith. In a dangerous setting, his senses became uncannily acute, sharply tuned to every nuance of any environment. It was a prerequisite for survival he had learned in a hard school.

When the Cerberus warriors entered the walls of the barony, they had to blink repeatedly, not just because of the drifting planes of eye-stinging smoke, but also in an effort to reconcile the panorama of devastation with their memories of identical cities they had visited.

Smoldering craters pockmarked the narrow lanes, and all of the buildings were shattered heaps of flaming kindling. The sky was hidden by a dense pall of black, choking smoke. The oppressive heat from the multiple fires drew perspiration from all of them. To Kane, the air had felt cooler in Florida.

The smell of roasted pork rose thick and strong from the rubble, and they recognized it as the odor of seared human flesh, known in Magistrate vernacular as "barbecued long pig." Blackened bodies lay everywhere, outflung limbs lending them a sickening resemblance to charred starfish. They heard no sound other than the crackle of flames. A shared aura of nightmarish unreality numbed them.

"There wasn't a battle here," Grant growled. "This was a slaughter. A massacre."

"But why?" Brigid asked. "It makes no sense. The villes mean nothing to the Supreme Council."

Domi jerked to such a sudden halt, Grant nearly trod on her heels. She gestured for her companions to do the same. "Hear something," she whispered.

Kane, Brigid and Grant didn't question her, placing the utmost faith in the wilderness-honed senses of the Outlander girl. They strained their hearing and a faint, groaning gasp reached their ears: "…mouthy bitch…"

Grant and Kane flexed their wrist tendons. Sin Eaters popped up from their holsters, the butts slapping solidly into the waiting palms of the two men. Brigid and Domi leveled their pistols, peering through the twists of smoke.

"Just some mouthy bitch…"

A figure crept into view through the haze, a filthy, battered, bleeding, burned and blinded man. He crawled on his hands and knees, slowly, painfully, like a half-crushed beetle. The man's face was a peeling mask of raw, red flesh. The ruins of his nose, lips and eyes were a nauseating testimony to his agony. Charred stubble sprouted from his blistered scalp in patches.

As he crawled forward, he gasped, "….mouthy bitch…Team Phoenix for America, fuck yeah…"

Stiffening at the man's barely intelligible words, Domi stepped toward him, followed by Brigid, Grant and Kane.

"Team Phoenix?" Grant murmured. "What the hell would they be doing here?"

The man stopped crawling and swung his ravaged face toward the sound of Grant's voice. "Who's there?"

Eyeing him closely, Brigid answered, "We're from Cerberus."

The man gaped with empty, sightless eye sockets in her direction and after a few seconds, he croaked, "Is that you, Baptiste? Brigid Baptiste?"

"Yes," Brigid said, stepping up beside him. "Who are you?"

"Weaver, Joe Weaver. Remember me?"

Domi's ruby eyes narrowed for an instant, either in relief or disappointment. Her companions knew the girl bore a Team Phoenix member named Sean Reichert a considerable grudge.

"I remember," Weaver whispered, then he lay down on his right side. "I'm still alive, right?"

Brigid kneeled next to him, giving him a swift visual examination. "Yes, but not for much longer. I'm sorry."

"Weaver," Kane said, leaning over him, "can you tell us what happened here?"

The man's blistered lips writhed. "Mouthy bitch happened here."

"What does that mean?" Domi demanded.

A gurgling, rattle came from Weaver's mouth. It took the Cerberus warriors a few seconds to recognize the sound as bitter laughter. "Happened yesterday…came in a flying saucer…landed on that big dildo of a building you folks called an Admin Monolith. Then there was a saucer that walked…"

Lines of confusion appeared on Brigid's smooth forehead. "What? A flying saucer?"

"It grew three legs, like something out of the *War of the Worlds*, then a weird-looking bimbo in a kind of silver-and-blue body armor showed up…not bad-looking if you like them with bald and with scales. She had an attitude, tell you that—"

"What happened next?" Kane broke in impatiently.

Weaver shifted position, grunting in pain. "She started giving orders…pissed Major Mike off. I told him to be careful, but he tried to blow her away anyhow."

He paused, swallowed painfully and gasped out, "Didn't work. Blew us all away instead with some sort of energy weapon…Major Mike, Reichert, Robison…blew them all away. I ducked, but not fast enough. Guess they thought I was dead."

He paused, coughed rackingly and added, "Weren't too far wrong were they, huh?"

Not replying to his question, Brigid asked, "Then what?"

"I couldn't see, but they started shelling the place from the air…no, not shelling. Some kind of explosive plasma charges…I found a hole and stayed in it."

Weaver choked, blood welling up in his throat and spilling over his lips. "Don't know why this happened, but I don't mind it."

His body shook in a spasm and he whispered, "Don't mind it. Time to leave…go back to the past where I came from…"

Joe Weaver laid his head down, smiled and died.

Brigid Baptiste, Domi, Grant and Kane stood for a

silent few moments, staring down at the dead man. All of them knew that even an ersatz soldier like Weaver did not expect tears at his passing.

Brigid stood up, automatically brushing off the knees of her jeans. "It's a shame he had to die like this, but he's right. He and Team Phoenix definitely didn't belong in this time and place. I'm surprised they managed to live this long."

Grant grunted, gazing toward the broken off stump of the Administrative Monolith. "Lilitu did that."

Kane nodded. "She seems the most likely suspect."

"Suspect?" Grant snapped. "Hell, she advertised it."

Domi frowned. "Why? This used to be her ville. Why destroy it? Make no sense."

Under stress, Domi reverted to the curt, abbreviated mode of outlander speech.

Grimly, Brigid said, "Makes no sense to us, perhaps. I imagine it does to Lilitu. Destroying her own ville must be part of a plan."

Kane coughed into his fist. "If it is, I don't get it."

Chapter 9

Kane looked at the distorted reflection of his face in the orb and said, "Now I get it."

"Oh, really?" Philboyd inquired, not even trying to warm the cold edge of sarcasm in his voice. "Explain it to the rest of the class, will you?"

"Lilitu dropped this off," Kane replied, straightening up.

Lakesh, Philboyd, Sela Sinclair and even Brigid Baptiste regarded him doubtfully. The Cerberus warriors had arrived back at the redoubt only a few minutes before, landing the Mantas in a field atop a nearby knoll. They had exchanged stories, but no questions had been conclusively answered on the topics of Coral Cove, the barony of Beausoleil or the mysterious tripod.

"Assuming it was Lilitu who dropped this off," Philboyd ventured, "why would she give us this bulletproof conversation piece?"

A breeze gusted over the plateau and stirred the spent cartridge cases, rolling them over the tarmac with semimusical tinkles.

"I don't know," Kane said frankly. "But this is the

first major overlord activity in about five months. It's something important."

"I agree Lilitu is behind this," Brigid stated, stepping forward to inspect the three-legged globe. "Occam's razor is in full force here if you ask me."

Domi slitted her eyes. "What's that mean?"

Lakesh smiled at the girl fondly. "It means, darlingest one, that the simplest solution is most often the correct one."

Domi's porcelain lips crooked in a smile. "Buy that."

Sweeping his disapproving stare over the litter of cartridge cases, he said, "Looks like a lot of ammo was burned through."

Sinclair, still holding her autorifle, said defensively, "Ammo normally gets burned through before we get an idea of what we're up against."

Brigid bent before the sphere, her face only six inches away from it. "I don't understand this at all. Why drop it off and fly away?"

"I thought it might be a bomb or a monitoring device," Philboyd said. "But it doesn't fit the functionality of either. We can't move it, so we can't take it inside so it can spy on us or blow us up."

Pursing her lips, Brigid blew gently, fogging the orb's surface. "There's only two other possibilities. It's either malfunctioning, or it's supposed to serve an entirely different purpose. Therefore—"

A section of the sphere suddenly swirled and Brigid took a hasty step back, not able to completely suppress a cry of surprise.

Gun barrels snapped up as the forepart of the globe wavered like water in a violently shaken glass container. It seemed to pulse and throb as smoky waves of changing color passed over its smooth surface.

Kane felt his nape hairs tingle, his skin prickling with a shiver. The smart metal of the sphere molded itself into a three-dimensional female face, one of cold, classic beauty. Neither the capacity for mercy or kindness, nor any other human emotion could be found in the high-planed, aristocratic features. The face might have been a sculpted mask of an ancient goddess, but the eyes moved, the lips stirred and a voice spoke.

"All of you are aware of who addresses you."

The rich, vibrant tone had not asked a question. The voice was fluid, but underscored by a machinelike cadence. Grant uttered a muffled curse and leveled his Sin Eater at the face on the sphere. He growled, "Lilitu."

The smart-metal visage said, "We may converse in this fashion. It is a more secure method than dealing with you personally, given our history, and it is less likely that the transmission can be intercepted by any other member of the Supreme Council."

"Do they make a habit of eavesdropping on you?" Lakesh asked.

"We habitually spy on one another," Lilitu answered diffidently. The voice held a faint harsh echo as if metal struck metal somewhere within the sphere. "Part and parcel of power. When you have it, you must constantly guard against it being taken away."

"Not to mention," Kane commented offhandedly, "when you have it, you always want more."

Shielding his eyes beneath a hand, Philboyd scanned the skies. "Where are you really?"

"Immaterial," came the curt response.

"I don't think so," Sinclair countered. "We're under no obligation to do more than make sure this installation is secure. I vote for planting a pound or two of C4 around that thing and blowing it off our mountain."

A hint of a smile ghosted over the metallic mask of Lilitu's face. "You would not have the chance, woman."

"Why not?" Grant asked.

With a faint whir of electronics, the three legs uprooted themselves from the asphalt and the tripod rose, the sphere towering twelve feet above the plateau. It took a sideways step toward Sinclair.

"This device is more than just a means of communication," Lilitu stated. "It has defensive and offensive capabilities."

"I can vouch for the latter," Lakesh muttered. In a louder voice, he demanded, "Are you guiding it from a remote location?"

"I have not undertaken this effort to communicate with you in order to answer your questions."

"Then why did you?" Brigid inquired. "We just returned from the barony of Beausoleil. You apparently weren't interested in fielding questions there, either."

"No," replied the likeness of Lilitu, the three legs

sliding into the bottom half of the sphere so it was the same height as Brigid. "This device has been waiting for your physiognomical signature to register on its sensors so we may begin our talks."

"*My* signature?" Brigid asked, a note of surprise in her voice. "Why me?"

"You are a woman and you successfully faced me down in the past." Lilitu's tone was matter-of-fact. "I can respect your capabilities, if not your arrogance. Therefore, I seek your help."

The statement paralyzed everyone's vocal cords for a long moment. Lakesh was the first to recover. "Why should we even consider helping you? You're a betrayer, a murderer, an archfoe of humankind, going all the way back to prehistory."

"By helping me, you would not only be helping yourself but humankind, as well."

"Next question," Kane said, with a studied nonchalance. "Why should we believe anything you say? The Annunaki hate us apekin and we apekin hate the Annunaki overlords. Pretty much case closed."

"Not to mention," Domi spit, voice hitting a high pitch of contempt, "you wiped out your own ville and everybody in it for no damn reason!"

Although it was hard to tell, the countenance of Lilitu expressed anger. "I always have a reason for everything I do, although those reasons are rarely understood by the apekin."

"Which pretty much makes my point for me," Kane declared.

"The Annunaki and humanity struck many alliances of convenience throughout the history of your race."

"Which primarily consisted of using ambitious men and women as pawns," Brigid said curtly. "Once the alliances served your purpose, they were discarded."

Grant took a menacing step forward. "Why are we even having this conversation?"

His voice was so guttural with rage, his words came out as a bestial snarl. "This psychotic bitch needs to be killed, not talked to like a diplomatic envoy!"

Everyone knew the reason for Grant's hatred of Lilitu, and not all of it stemmed from memories of the torture he had suffered when a prisoner of Baroness Beausoleil. Until he had been captured by her, it had been Grant's intent to leave Cerberus and live in the little island monarchy of New Edo with Shizuka.

But after being rescued from the sadistic ministrations of the baroness, Grant realized he couldn't stand down from the struggle. When the barons evolved into their true forms as overlords, he realized the conflict remained essentially the same, only now with new players on the field. The war itself would go on and would never end, unless he took an active hand in it, regardless of his love for Shizuka.

"Friend Grant," Lakesh murmured, "let us choose our words with more discretion."

Sighting down his Sin Eater at the face on the sphere, Grant growled, "I'm not discreet when I'm face-to-face with someone who did her damnedest to torture me to death."

"Face-to-face," Lilitu echoed, tone purring with amusement. "Very whimsical."

Grant's jaw muscles bunched in anger and Brigid interjected hastily, "Let's hear her out."

"Why?" Grant demanded. "No matter what name she travels under now, that's still Baroness fucking Beausoleil."

"No, she isn't," Lakesh retorted firmly, but sympathetically. "Nor is she really here, so your bullets will be as wasted as all the others fired at that machine today."

Brigid said quietly, "Let's maintain our perspective, Grant. We always need intel on the overlords, regardless of the source."

Grant continued glaring at the metallic mask, then with a wordless snort of disgust, he wheeled away, toward the sec door.

The face of Lilitu intoned, "I knew I could expect reason from you, Brigid Baptiste."

"Just tell us what you want," Brigid snapped impatiently.

Lilitu said flatly, "I want your help to keep Enlil from either killing or enslaving the other members of the Supreme Council…which would then result in the killing or enslavement of the human race."

Kane brayed out a scornful laugh. "Hell, that's exactly what all of you overdressed snake-faces want. Why should we believe a single word that comes out of your lying alien mouth—figuratively speaking, of course."

"Alien," Lilitu said, sneering. "The Supreme Council is all that is left of the oldest race on Earth. We knew your kind before you walked erect. We built our cities when you lived in holes and were still trying to understand fire."

"But," Domi said between clenched teeth, "we still beat you."

"You bred faster than we," Lilitu retorted dismissively. "And we grew old. We built our strongholds in the wild places and for many centuries we were not troubled by the rebellious apelings. But then, over the course of millennia, we abandoned our cities, our fortresses. After my people fled back to the stars, there was no one left to live in them and they fell into ruin and were lost. But one stronghold remained."

Lilitu paused, then imperiously she said, "It was our greatest port city and the eternal sands of the desert drowned it. Now I have found Nippur again. For the past two years, I and a faction of overlords loyal to me have been engaged in excavating it. Within Nippur are the vaults that contain all the secrets of the Annunaki, forgotten for many thousands of years."

Lakesh shifted his feet uncomfortably. "Why do you think we care about that?"

The image of Lilitu seemed almost to smirk. "Because one of those secrets is the method to take complete and permanent control of *Tiamat*. I suggest you discuss my request before rejecting it out of hand."

Brigid and Kane exchanged swift, startled glances.

"We've heard that talk before," Brigid said. "From none other than Overlord Nergal."

"That arrogant fool did not know what he was talking about."

"But you do, my lady?" Lakesh challenged.

Lilitu's response was calm and confident. "I do indeed."

"You're going to have to prove it," Brigid said.

"That's why I'm communicating through this device," Lilitu replied enigmatically. "Return to it when you've reached a decision."

The face of Lilitu flattened, lost detail and was absorbed back into the smooth surface of the sphere.

After an awkward moment of silence, Philboyd said, "Well, if nothing else, at least now we know what the damn thing is."

Gazing at the tripod, Kane inquired, "Where's this Nippur place supposed to be?"

"The Sinai desert," Lakesh answered.

Kane cast him a suspicious, surprised stare. "How can there be a port city in a desert?"

"Easy," Brigid replied. "A spaceport can be anywhere."

Chapter 10

Inside Cerberus, the alert level was downgraded to yellow and the interior security shields raised, but a contingent of armed guards was posted around the tripod. Only authorized Cerberus security personnel were allowed to venture out onto the plateau, a decision that raised few complaints.

Most of the time briefings were convened in the dining hall, but under the current circumstances, Brigid needed access to the database.

Seated at a keyboard, Brigid nodded toward an image on the monitor screen of the computer station. It showed a bas-relief stone carving of a woman's lissome form but whose legs terminated in splayed, ea-glelike talons. The carving looked very old.

"Lilitu or Lilith has been identified with a female demon in the Sumerian prologue to the Gilgamesh epic," Brigid said. "This particular piece is known as the Burney relief and dates to roughly 2000 B.C."

Kane narrowed his eyes. "How'd you find this information so quickly?"

Brigid regarded him soberly over the rims of her former badge of office as an archivist—wire-frame, rectangular-lens spectacles. "Once I learned the names of the Supreme Council, I compiled a dossier on all of them…or at least their place in legend and lore. Lilitu's is one of the most interesting and complex."

"How so?" Philboyd asked.

"Mainly because versions of her appeared all over the Mideast. Her myth is found in over one hundred different religions and has numerous variations on her name. In Mesopotamian legend, she was the chief demoness of vampirelike spirits called the Lilu who roamed during the hours of darkness, hunting and killing newborn babies and pregnant women."

"Sounds about right," Grant rumbled, his furrowed brow casting his eyes into deep pools of shadow.

Not responding to the observation, Brigid went on, "Jewish exiles in Babylon claimed that Lilith was a goddess of the night. And of course, the Talmudic references to Lilith provide the most comprehensive insight into her character as a demoness, particularly her carnality."

Domi frowned. "Her what?"

Lakesh's lips quirked in a half smile. "Her horniness, darlingest one."

Domi nodded. "Oh."

"Lilith was reputed to sexually take men by force while they slept," Brigid continued, "and of course, in Talmudic lore, she is believed to be the first wife of Adam. She's described as refusing to assume a subservient role to Adam during sexual intercourse and so deserted him, leaving the Garden of Eden and settling on the Red Sea coast."

"They have resort towns like Coral Cove in those days?" Kane asked.

Brigid smiled slightly. "Who knows, but the citizens of the seaside town Lilith settled in were full of demons, Asmodeus for one."

Kane stiffened in surprise, remembering that Overlord Enlil had been known as Asmodeus.

Brigid stroked a key on the board and the image on the screen changed to a lurid illustration of leering, horned, malformed creatures clutching terrified women. She said, "Lilith mated with Asmodeus and various other demons she found there and created countless demon-spawn, known as *lilin*.

"Adam urged God to bring Lilith back, so three angels were dispatched after her. When the angels, Senoy, Sansenoy and Semangelof, made threats to kill one hundred of Lilith's demonic children for each day she stayed away, she countered that she would prey eternally upon the descendants of Adam and Eve, who could be saved only by invoking the names of the three angels. She did not return to Adam."

"What about her connection to the Annunaki Supreme Council?" Grant asked impatiently.

"That's a little more difficult to establish. The Sumerian mythographies portray Lilitu as being a terrible harlot-goddess. Some historians described her clergy as being temple prostitutes."

Brigid paused and added wryly, "That could be an example of male historians expressing their obvious fear of being powerless against women and controlled by them, of course."

"Of course," Grant commented sourly. "Can we get on with this? I promised Shizuka I'd make dinner for her… She'll be gating in from Redoubt Yankee in a couple of hours."

Everyone was aware that Grant and Shizuka were determined to spend a couple of days together a month, despite their respective duties that kept them apart most of the time. Still, to accommodate that determination often resulted in awkward timing.

Kane directed a challenging stare at Grant. "What would she have done if the Coral Cove op had really taken a southernly turn, no pun intended?"

Grant lifted the massive yoke of his shoulders in a shrug. "Eaten alone, I guess."

Kane rolled his eyes in good-natured exasperation and returned his attention to Brigid. "You were saying?"

"In the Sumerian pantheon, Lilitu's position isn't easy to pin down conclusively. She was often confused with Ishtar, Isis and even Enlil's mate, Ninlil. I think that confusion arose due to the garbled legends about Lilith being the consort of Asmodeus. However, I imagine Lilitu was an influential member of the royal family and as such served as a confidant and counselor to both Enlil and his half brother, Enki. She could have been their lovers, too."

"Why, that naughty little minx," Kane murmured.

Brigid gave him a fleeting, appreciative smile. "Scholars theorized that the fabled Queen of Sheba with whom King Solomon was so smitten was none other than Lilitu."

Domi's face twisted in disgust. "Ew. Didn't he notice she was a snake with legs?"

Lakesh chuckled. "Perhaps the origins of cosmetic surgery can be attributed to Lilitu on top of all her other accomplishments."

"What about the spaceport?" Grant broke in impatiently.

Brigid half turned in her chair and tapped a key. On the monitor screen appeared a sweeping vista of barren desert and rocky outcrops. "We know the Annunaki built their first settlements in the Mesopotamian Valley area—Larsa, Bad-Tibira, Larak, Shurupak Lagash and Nippur. All of these settlements were constructed in such a manner as to form a flight corridor for shuttle craft from *Tiamat*, with Nippur serving as the central mission control and cargo port."

The original Annunaki had arrived on Earth nearly half a million years before from an extrasolar planet known as Nibiru, traveling in a mile-long spaceship named *Tiamat*.

For aeons, the sentient *Tiamat* floated in a region of dead space called Kurnugi by the Annunaki. She awaited the time when she would be summoned to fulfill her role as a Magan, a repository where the souls of the dead slumbered between incarnations, preparing for rebirth. A blending of inorganic and organic, composed of an incredibly ancient, incredibly complex genetic code, *Tiamat*'s countless neuronic subsystems that constituted her programming made her self-aware.

When the physical bodies of the Annunaki Supreme

Council ceased to function, the electromagnetic pattern of their individuality broke free of the organic receptacle and was downloaded into a vast data storage bank aboard the ship. *Tiamat* maintained them until they could be uploaded into new organic receptacles—the bodies of the hybrid barons.

"We also know that the Annunaki fought among themselves on more than one occasion," Brigid said. "Their last major civil war involved Overlord Marduk and his faction battling Enlil for supremacy of the planet. Marduk's main objective was to secure and occupy the Nippur spaceport in the Sinai Peninsula. Rather than allow it to fall into his hands, Nergal saw to its destruction, circa 2025 B.C."

"Those are just legends and myths," Philboyd ventured uncertainly. "Right?"

"You should know better than that by now," Lakesh said sternly.

According to information gathered by the Cerberus personnel over the past few years, most myths regarding gods and aliens derived from a race known in ancient Sumerian texts as the Annunaki but also known in legend as the Dragon Kings and the Serpent Lords.

A species of bipedal reptile that appeared on Earth at the dawn of humanity's development, the Annunaki used their advanced technology and great organizational skills to conquer the Mideast, most of Europe and the African continent.

They built cities and spaceports and influenced the evolution of Homo sapiens. They were also consumed by abounding pride, arrogance and more than a few maintained an insatiable appetite for conquest and control. The Annunaki faction led by Enlil had developed and imposed complex, oppressive caste and gender systems on early human cultures to tighten that control.

Brigid shrugged. "Physical evidence of some sort of catastrophe can be found all over the Sinai. There is an immense cavity in the center of the peninsula with fracture lines stretching away from it all the way to the Dead Sea. It was theorized the Dead Sea became dead because of the war between the overlords."

"The cities of Sodom and Gomorrah were located in that region, too," put in Lakesh.

"If Nippur was destroyed," Kane asked, "what's left to be excavated?"

"More than likely most of the actual control systems were underground," Brigid replied. "Much like Area 51. So, it's possible that enough of the original Annunaki technology is intact enough to be used to interface with *Tiamat*, since that's what it was initially designed to do."

Grant grunted skeptically. "Yeah, well, that's what old Nergal thought about the tech in the Xibalba pyramid. I'm sure you don't need a reminder of how that turned out."

Grant made oblique references to events in the recent past as well as a tongue-in-cheek comment about Brigid Baptiste's ability to produce eidetic images. Centuries ago, it had been called a photographic memory. Brigid could, after viewing an object or scanning a document, retain exceptionally vivid and detailed visual memories.

When she was growing up, she feared she was a mutant, but she later learned that the ability was relatively common among children, and usually disappeared by adolescence. It was supposedly very rare among adults, but Brigid was one of the exceptions.

Since her forced exile from ville society, she had taken full advantage of the Cerberus redoubt's vast database, and as an intellectual omnivore she grazed in all fields. Coupled with her eidetic memory, her profound knowledge of an extensive and eclectic number of topics made her something of an ambulatory encyclopedia. This trait often irritated Kane, but just as often it had tipped the scales between life and death, so he couldn't in good conscience become too annoyed with her.

"The other factor in this is finding out which over-lords are siding with Lilitu," Brigid stated.

"Why?" Kane asked bluntly.

Philboyd's brow furrowed. "Why what?"

Kane gestured in the general direction of the plateau. "No matter what Lilitu tells us, we wouldn't believe her, we wouldn't trust her."

Grant's grim, locked face relaxed a trifle. "So you think she's lying?"

"Hell, yes."

"Of *course* she's lying," Brigid said crossly. "But I'm interested in finding out why."

"Even if she really is digging out an old Annunaki spaceport," Kane argued, "she needs something from us. So why should we play into her claws, further her own agenda, just so we can find out what she's really up to?"

"What do you suggest, friend Kane?" Lakesh asked.

"I suggest we tell her to shove her talking tripod up her ass and get the hell off this mountain."

Brigid's eyebrows rose. "That's quite a tactic."

"It's my suggestion, too," Grant growled.

"Mine three," Domi piped up. "Can't trust those snake-faces any further than we can piss into windstorm."

Lakesh winced at the girl's vulgar simile but said dryly, "I seriously doubt Lilitu will accept that suggestion with good grace and merely go on her way. Whatever game she has in mind, she wants us on the field and on her side."

"Then," said Kane flatly, "my next suggestion is to stall her long enough to find out what game she really does have in mind."

Philboyd shuffled his feet uncomfortably. "Lilitu doesn't strike me as particularly patient."

"Neither am I," Kane stated. "So we have that in common at least. Maybe I can use that to open a dialogue."

Grant speared him with an incredulous stare. "A dialogue?"

"Isn't that what we've been trained to do the last couple of years?" Kane's voice held a mocking note. He looked directly at Brigid. "We can always hope the dialogue we open with Lilitu has the same satisfactory results as the one we enjoyed with Billy-boy Porpoise. That was pretty much diplomacy in its purest form."

Chapter 11

Shizuka eyed the case of *shippo*, a Japanese cloisonné enamel featuring bees, flowers and birds. She glanced at the pair of Noh masks affixed to the wall and the wooden panel of miniature swords with their *muyuki* ornaments on the hilts.

She said softly, "You've brought much of New Edo here."

Grant nodded, lit the final tea candle floating in a bowl of water and blew out the match. "It keeps me from missing you too much."

Shizuka smiled. "How much is too much?"

A little over five feet tall, Shizuka wore her luxuriant blue-black hair piled high. The tumble of glossy black hair framed a smoothly sculpted face of extraordinary beauty. Her complexion was a very pale gold with peach and milk for an accent. Beneath a snub nose, her petaled lips were full. She wore a billowy, pale green *kamishimo*, the formal attire of a daimyo's retainer, with both a *katana* and shorter *tanto* sword thrust through the bright red silk sash tied around her narrow waist.

Usually, her dark almond-shaped eyes glinted with

the fierce, proud gleam of a young eagle, but this night, in Grant's dimly lit quarters, they held a peaceful inner light.

Grant, dressed in a traditional kimono of black silk, said, "Too much is when I need constant reminders of New Edo."

"And those reminders extend to this meal you have prepared," Shizuka replied, sniffing the fragrant aromas rising from the dishes laid out on the long, low table. She glanced with approval at the *kani* salad, hot noodles and a saucer filled with *shitake ryori*.

"I understood you took cooking lessons at the palace," she went on, a teasing smile touching her lips. "While I was otherwise occupied."

"What other kind of instruction should I have taken?" Grant asked with mock gruffness. "How to be a ninja or something equally idiotic for a man of my age?"

"You prepared all of this food yourself?" she asked skeptically.

"I sense a lack of faith in my abilities," he retorted, sliding his arms around her waist.

Bending his head, he kissed her full lips, then nuzzled her ear. "I wanted to show you I have skills other than just weapons. I can't paint pictures or write haiku poetry, but I can at least prepare a meal that won't put us in the infirmary."

"You've shown me your various skills many times," Shizuka said softly, standing on her tiptoes to hungrily return his kiss.

Reluctantly, he disengaged himself. "Maybe we should eat first."

Shizuka laughed, a surprisingly girlish sound. "As you wish, Grant-san."

They seated themselves on cushions on opposite sides of the low table, crossing their legs. Shizuka removed her scabbarded weapons from her sash, placing them on the floor close at hand.

Despite her laughter and demure demeanor, Shizuka never allowed her blades out of arm's length. She could not have survived the political turmoil of New Edo and become the captain of the Tigers of Heaven by letting her guard down completely.

Although New Edo was certainly better than most of the Western Isles, it was still a dangerous place, but she considered the little island empire her home. Moreover, she considered the well-being of its citizens her responsibility.

A few years earlier during an attempted insurrection, New Edo's daimyo, Lord Takaun, was grievously injured and Kiyomasa, the former captain of the Tigers of Heaven, was slain. It fell upon Shizuka's slender shoulders to end the rebellion and she did it in the only way that would satisfy the honor of both factions—by killing the seditionist leader in single combat, literally slicing him in two with her *katana*.

The rebels saw only two options—to continue to press their faltering coup and die to a man, or to swear loyalty to the samurai who had slain their leader. They decided to swear loyalty and to live. Ironically, many

of them did not live long after making their oaths.
They perished repulsing the invaders dispatched from
Baron Snakefish. Despite the losses New Edo suffered,
it was Shizuka who had led them to victory over a tac-
tically superior force.

After that New Edoans obeyed her every command,
appeased her every whim with a kind of devotion different, yet more powerful than that they would have
given to a man. Shizuka was not viewed as a woman
or even a Tiger of Heaven—she was revered almost as
a goddess.

Grant poured Shizuka a cup of sake, then one for
himself. They toasted each other and began eating.
Chopsticks were provided for Shizuka, but Grant chose
the more conventional fork. Shizuka smiled wanly but
said nothing. Even after three-plus years of regular
visits to New Edo, Grant had yet to completely master
the art of chopsticks. More food ended up on him or
his companions than in his stomach.

"Things are under control on the island?" he asked.

"Which one?" Shizuka inquired. "Ikazuchi Kojima
or New Edo?"

"Both. Either."

New Edo and its companion islet, known as Ikazuchi
Kojima, Thunder Isle, were part of the Santa Barbara,
or Channel Island, chain. Many of the other Western
Isles were overrun by pirates and Asian criminal or-
ganizations known as tongs and triads. Thunder Isle had
played host to the Totality Concept's most daring and
dangerous undertaking, the seat of Operation Chronos.

"On Ikazuchi Kojima the repairs to the perimeter wall have been completed. As for the rest—"

Shizuka spoke of the matters she dealt with in her capacity of commander of the Tigers of Heaven, and she related gossip of minor court intrigues. To Grant's surprise, he found himself enjoying the stories. It felt like a very long time since he had engaged in simple conversation with anyone, much less the woman he loved. He took a keen pleasure in talking about everyday concerns that had nothing to do with Annunaki overlords or imminent threats from elsewhere.

Grant knew that the lives of him and his friends were filled with high strangeness, the bizarre almost commonplace. He was sensitive to the possibility that his own personality didn't become so far removed from normal that he would be unable to relate to ordinary issues and people.

"How is Tshaya getting along?" he inquired.

"Actually, she appears to be thriving with the family who adopted her. She misses you, though."

Grant smiled crookedly. "Kind of hard to tell, isn't it?"

Shizuka returned his smile. Tshaya was an eight-year-old gypsy girl who had been pulled through the temporal dilator of Operation Chronos a short time before. Although blind, deaf and essentially mute, she possessed extraordinary psionic abilities. She had bonded to Grant after he found her on Thunder Isle.

"What about here?" Shizuka asked. "The last time

I visited you were monitoring a revolution in Cambodia, trying to find two of your people who had been kidnapped by Roamers and dealing with a plan by the Millennial Consortium to build a base on the polar ice cap."

"Oh, right," he said, deadpan. "That was the day I took off because nothing much was happening."

Shizuka chuckled. "I did not see Kane, Brigid or Lakesh when I arrived. Are they not present?"

"They're here: They're just…" He trailed off, groping for the proper word. "Preoccupied."

"With what?"

He sighed. "Nothing urgent."

Her eyes narrowed. "I know you well enough to realize when you're being evasive."

Grant busied himself refilling their cups with sake. "While we were off in Florida, one of the overlords came calling. They left a package outside."

Shizuka's eyebrows lifted like dark wings over jet almond eyes. "A package? What was in it?"

"Actually, the package was a comm device. We talked to an overlord."

Eyes widening, Shizuka asked, "Which overlord?"

Grant stared directly into her face and intoned, "Lilitu."

Even in the flickering candlelight, Grant saw how Shizuka's complexion paled by a shade. She shared his hatred of the creature, for what Lilitu had done to him in her former identity as Baroness Beausoleil. A few years before, Shizuka had accompanied Brigid

Baptiste and Domi to Australia to rescue the hybrid woman Quavell, whom the baroness had abducted.

Although she had not dealt with the baroness personally, she had nursed Grant back to health after the injuries inflicted on him with an infrasound wand had come near to crippling him.

"Why is Lilitu seeking to communicate with Cerberus?" Shizuka demanded, her voice acquiring a sharp edge.

"She claims she wants our help."

"For what?"

"To overthrow Enlil and gain control of *Tiamat* so it's no longer a threat."

Shizuka's nostrils flared in angry incredulity. "And you are considering it?"

"No!" he blurted. "Hell, no. None of us believe her. But—"

He broke off, took a deep breath and said in a rush, "We can't continue to have *Tiamat* hanging over our heads, ready to destroy the planet whenever we go up against one of the Supreme Council. The overlords know it, too. Really cramps their style during their family squabbles."

Shizuka made a spitting sound of derision. "They're a family of megalomaniacs who just want to be able to cut one another's throats without reprisal from the great mother goddess in orbit. They're outnumbered by humanity as it is, so of course they want all the advantages they can arrange, even if that means striking alliances with Cerberus."

Grant nodded in agreement. "Trouble is, what they lack in quantity, they more than make up for in quality. Even a quarter of a million years ago, Annunaki science and technology made ours at our height look like the knowledge of Tasmanian aborigines."

"No matter how godlike they think their technology makes them," Shizuka argued, "they're just as petty as human beings…worse, actually. Each one played the part of a little god in a little part of the world and came to believe in their role. That egocentricity makes them vulnerable."

"We know," Grant replied. "But by the same token, we can't go out into the field against the overlords without risking destruction ourselves."

With *Tiamat* in permanent orbit, hanging over the world like a dark angel of doom, the Cerberus warriors had resigned themselves to the realization that they had no chance of emerging victorious from a head-on confrontation with the overlords, even if they managed to kill all of them.

The giant ship was capable of dispatching remote probes, essentially smaller versions of itself, to blanket the planet with fusion bombs, biological and chemical weapons and defoliants of all kinds.

If the Supreme Council were killed, then *Tiamat* would engage its program of punitive action. The seas would be rendered toxic, the atmosphere contaminated, and starvation and exposure to radiation would kill anyone who was unlucky enough to survive the initial onslaughts. Within two weeks, humanity as the dominant species on Earth would cease to exist.

Shizuka considered Grant's words for a silent few seconds, her gaze downcast. When she lifted her eyes again, they held the anthracite-hard glint of the warrior, the samurai. He felt his throat constrict.

"I wish to see this communication device." She rose from the table, uncrossing her ankles, rocking forward on her knees and then on her heels. She came to her feet in one smooth, flowing motion.

"Why?" Grant asked.

Shizuka picked up her scabbarded *katana*. "It is an emissary of an enemy, not just yours or mine, but all of humanity. Please show it to me."

Grant glowered at her, picked up the cup and swallowed the sake in one gulp. The liquor was still scorching a path to his stomach when he got to his feet. The two people went out into the corridor. As it was after nightfall, the overhead lighting was diffused. For most of the permanent residents of the redoubt, the passage of time was measured by the controlled dimming and brightening of lights to simulate sunrise and sunset.

Side by side, Shizuka and Grant strode down the passageway, turned right at a T junction and continued on down the twenty-foot-wide main corridor. The floors and walls were sheathed by dully gleaming vanadium alloy. The high rock roof was supported by curving arches of thick metal.

As they reached the entrance, Grant saw Kane leaning against one of the door panels. He smoked a cigar with a single-minded intensity. At the sound of their footfalls, he turned toward Grant and Shizuka, eyebrows lifting in surprise.

"That was a short and sweet dinner," he remarked. "You guys on a diet or what?"

"Leather it," Grant grunted as he and Shizuka squeezed past him to step out onto the plateau.

The touch of the wind was cool, with just a hint of winter's frigidity underlying it. The constellations wheeled overhead, the stars burning frostily in the vast, blue-black canopy of the night sky. Two spotlights mounted on wheeled platforms cast brilliant beams of incandescence on the dull gray orb. It did not reflect the light.

Four members of CAT Beta walked sentry, M-249 autorifles cradled in their arms. Brigid stood before the tripod, peering over the rims of her spectacles as she consulted the LCD gauge of the power analyzer in her right hand. The rectangular device was designed to measure, record and analyze energy emissions, quality and harmonics. She swept the extended sensor stem back and forth in short left-to-right arcs.

When Shizuka stepped toward the tripod, one of the guardsmen moved forward to intercept her. "Sorry, ma'am, we're under orders to keep the zone secure."

Brigid glanced up, taking notice of her for the first time. "You can let Captain Shizuka through."

The man hesitated and Grant rumbled, "It's all right. Stand down."

"Yes, sir," the man replied, stepping aside to allow Shizuka to pass.

Shizuka stalked around the tripod, examining the globe and the three legs. Her face was expressionless.

"It's not a very interesting item, actually," Brigid said.

Shizuka nodded. "What are you doing?"

Brigid waggled the sensor stem and said wryly, "Trying to pick up energy readings. I don't know whether the power core is just shielded or whether the whole machine is currently inactive."

Grant glanced toward Kane and asked, "How long do you figure to study this damn thing before you open that dialogue of yours?"

Before Kane could answer, Shizuka's hand closed around the hilt of her *katana* and she swiftly drew it from the scabbard of black, lacquered wood. She whipped the sword up and held it over her head. The blade gleamed with a mirror brightness.

Alarmed, Brigid asked, "What are you doing?"

Brigid, Grant and Kane had all been witness to Shizuka's prowess with a *katana* many times before, so they weren't surprised when she slashed with it in a semicircle, wheeling around on the heel of her left foot.

However, they were shocked into speechlessness when the blade cleanly severed the center leg of the tripod. The machine remained immobile, the tip of the cut leg still sunk into the tarmac. Although the Cerberus warriors were aware of the New Edoan sword-smithing process that employed a laser to sharpen blades to only a few molecules in thickness, they hadn't expected edged weapons to be effective against smart metal.

Grant and Kane moved forward to examine the damage and Shizuka cast them an over-the-shoulder glance, eyes glinting with triumph. "Shall I continue?" she asked, tapping the globe with the point of the *katana*. "Shall I split this in two like a melon?"

She did not wait for a response. Her impulsiveness surprised and disturbed all three people, but Grant understood her actions were an outward manifestation of the profound rage she felt toward Lilitu.

Balancing on the balls of her feet, Shizuka lifted and dropped her sword in the space of an eye blink, shouting, "*Ketsu no ana!*"

As the blade touched the top of the sphere, a popping, pinpoint white flash flared from the contact point. Shizuka flew backward, arms and legs flailing. The *katana* fell from her nerveless fingers and clanged against the tarmac.

Grant managed to catch Shizuka before she fell. The thick odor of ozone hung in the air. As CAT Beta surrounded the tripod, leveling their rifles at it, Kane and Brigid gathered around Shizuka and Grant. Brigid winced at the sight of reddened flesh that surrounded leaking blisters at the base of Shizuka's fingers.

Although in pain from the terrible, stunning shock, Shizuka remained conscious. "I am all right," she said between clenched teeth.

"Commander Kane—!" came the urgent cry from a Beta team member.

Kane spun just as Lilitu's face formed in the center of the orb. Even though it was only a simulacrum of her features, the expression exuded contempt and anger.

"Consider yourselves fortunate," stated Lilitu's cold voice. "This unit could kill all of you where you stand so foolishly gaping. I extend mercy this one time. Do not expect it again. As for a decision regarding my proposal, if I do not receive an answer by midmorning tomorrow, I will waste no more of my time with you. But be warned—there will not be another invitation to join me. If you refuse me, the next time you speak my name will be to beg me to spare your lives."

The face of Lilitu vanished, absorbed back into the surface of the sphere. The sword slash in the leg of the tripod vanished, as well, as the two halves were bridged by a flow of alloy.

Slowly, Shizuka rose to her feet, flexing her fingers and grimacing.

"Are you sure you're all right?" Brigid asked.

"Except for my profound embarrassment," she replied, "*hai*. Yes."

Grant glared at the featureless orb, then shifted his dark gaze to Kane. "I think the dialogue has been opened. Now where are you going to take it?"

Shizuka reached down and picked up her *katana* with her left hand, swiftly examining it for damage. "Wherever you take it," she intoned grimly, "I'm going with you."

Chapter 12

Sunrise flooded the broad plateau with a golden radiance, striking highlights from the scraps of the chain-link fence enclosing the perimeter. The snow-capped peaks of the Beaverhead range shone with a rosy brilliance as the rising sun touched their summits. Despite the sunlight, the air still carried the nighttime chill.

"All right," Kane said, his breath pluming before his face. "We're inclined to go along with you."

The alloyed lips of Lilitu creased in a satisfied smile. "That is wise."

"But," Kane went on as if he hadn't heard, "we need to know who the overlords are who've thrown in with you."

Lilitu's smile vanished. "Don't be a fool. Do you think I shall reveal anything specific that you could use against me?"

Lakesh and Brigid stood on either side of Kane. The CAT Beta guards had been dismissed. Grant and Shizuka stood in front of the sec door. Shizuka's second-degree burns had been treated the night before by the redoubt's resident medic, Reba DeFore. She had diagnosed them as inconveniences rather than incapacitating.

DeFore made the comment during an emergency war council. The eight-member senior command staff of Cerberus had been involved in a meeting that had lasted until well after midnight. The often contentious discussion finally resulted in a provisional plan of action.

Flatly, Lakesh said, "Madam, surely you understand that with the paucity of information you provided, Cerberus cannot make an official agreement with you."

"You officious, pompous idiot," Lilitu hissed. "Cerberus is a gang of criminals, of seditionists hiding out in a high-tech hole. Drop the pretense that your acts of anarchy and rebellion have any real influence on the rest of the world. You've never been more than annoyances to us."

Despite a surge of anger and the chilly temperatures, Kane felt cold sweat break out at his hairline. The results of their past encounters with the overlords had been little more than cruel stalemates. Although the Supreme Council was not omnipotent, Lilitu's reputation for ruthlessness was unmatched by any of her brethren, even the monstrous Enlil.

"How do we know we can trust *you?*" Brigid asked.

"How do I know I can trust you?" Lilitu shot back. "Could you not take what you learn from me to Enlil?"

"Couldn't the other overlords you've enlisted do the same?" Lakesh demanded.

"We have all sworn to abide by a common-front truce. We need one another, so we put aside our differences and work together. It is the only way it will be possible to defeat Enlil, and a truce is what I am proposing to you."

"We have a truce with Enlil ourselves," Kane remarked. "Why should we break ours with him and make one with you?"

Lilitu glared at Kane and he stared back with a studiedly neutral expression. He was sure that Lilitu knew that the agreement observed by the Supreme Council and the Cerberus personnel had been made under duress and Enlil would use any excuse to consider it void. If not for Balam acting as mediator, a state of open war would have existed between the reborn Annunaki and Cerberus.

Only the fact that Balam held an infant hostage prevented such a catastrophe from coming to pass. The baby, carried to term by the hybrid female Quavell, had been bred to carry the memories and personality of Enlil's mate, Ninlil.

In actuality, Quavell had given birth to an empty vessel waiting to be filled. Although the child carried the Anunnaki genetic profile, she was born in an intermediate state of development. Certain segments of her DNA, strands of her genetic material, were inactive and needed to be encoded aboard *Tiamat*.

Once there, through a biotechnological interface, she would receive the full mental and biological imprint of Ninlil. Then the Supreme Council would be as complete as it had been thousands of years before and *Tiamat* could set into motion the rebirth of the entire Annunaki pantheon. Enlil would not be pleased with any overlord who put Ninlil, and thus the long-range plan to remake Earth, at risk.

"The term is enlightened self-interest," Lilitu said icily.

Kane snorted. "You can't rely on the other overlords not to betray you if they think it's their best self-interest, enlightened or not."

"No," Lilitu admitted. "They trust me no more than I trust them. But this is quite likely our only opportunity to break the oppression of Enlil and *Tiamat*. It is not probable any of them would lightly violate the truce."

"What do you expect from us?" Brigid inquired.

"To come to Nippur," Lilitu answered. "Once there, you will learn everything."

Lakesh uttered a scoffing laugh of derision. "You can't be serious. You expect us to voluntarily put our people in your hands?"

In a low, intense voice, Lilitu said, "Don't you know I could destroy this place, kill everyone here, if that's what I actually wanted? If that was my true goal, you would even now be on your knees before me, pleading for your lives. You are aware of the anger I feel toward Cerberus. But I will not permit myself the luxury of gratified emotions when my own, far more important objectives have yet to be reached."

Kane, Lakesh and Brigid exchanged swift speculative glances. Then Kane asked, "How do we get to Nippur?"

"This unit will provide you with the coordinates with which to program the transportation device you call the interphaser."

As Lakesh's eyebrows rose in surprise, Lilitu chuckled. "Oh, yes. The Supreme Council is aware of your machine and the uses you put it to. In this instance, you will use it to travel to Nippur."

"How many of us?" Brigid wanted to know.

"As many as you care to bring with you," Lilitu replied negligently. "All I require is the presence of you, Grant and Kane. Any others are superfluous, but if you feel more secure traveling in a pack, I promise safe passage."

Lakesh gazed contemplatively at the likeness of Lilitu. "How do we know the coordinates you give us will take us to Nippur?"

"You may match them up with the vortex node index I'm certain you have in your database."

Two red-glowing numerical sequences suddenly flashed onto the surface of the orb, or just beneath it. Brigid stared at the longitude and latitude, committing the coordinates to her memory.

Tugging absently at his nose, Lakesh said, "Please give us a moment to confer."

He turned and strode toward the sec door. Stepping into the redoubt, he gestured for Kane, Brigid, Grant and Shizuka to join him.

Once out of the tripod's range of vision, Lakesh spoke softly but grimly. "This is a trap."

"Obviously," Brigid said dryly. "But what's the point of it?"

"Do we really care to find out?" Lakesh inquired.

Kane smiled crookedly, glancing over at the three snarling heads of Cerberus on the wall. "I think we should. Lilitu as much as claimed she'd launch an attack against us if we didn't go along."

"A bluff," Shizuka stated. "If she wants your help for this undertaking of hers, then she considers you very valuable."

"It could be she considers us so valuable," Kane said, "that she prefers us dead rather than running around as wild cards on the game board."

Lakesh's dark face creased in a frown. "If we help her to achieve her goal, the fate of Cerberus will be intertwined with hers forever."

"Not necessarily," Brigid interjected. "If we can end the threat of *Tiamat*, the scope of our operations will be expanded considerably."

"And if Lilitu *isn't* successful," Lakesh argued, "and our complicity in her attempted coup is discovered by Enlil, we can expect no mercy, his concern for Ninlil notwithstanding."

Kane nodded in grudging agreement. "Very true."

Even a couple of years after learning the truth behind the baronies and the Program of Unification that put them into power, the Cerberus warriors were still trying to come to terms with the full implications of the maneuvers and countermaneuvers undertaken by Enlil.

In his various guises, the overlord had moved his chess pieces over a vast board of power plays that stretched across the world and through the millennia. Enlil assumed many names and adopted many physical vessels in order to manipulate events and human belief systems to best fit the Annunaki agenda.

He felt completely justified in setting into motion the atomic megacull, because the Annunaki lived on Earth long before modern man. The world that emerged from the nuclear holocaust of 2001 fit the Nibiruan model.

As far as Enlil was concerned, the nukecaust was a radical form of remodeling and fumigation. The extreme depopulation, as well as the subsequent atmospheric and geological changes approximated Nibiruan conditions.

"But if she *is* successful," Brigid retorted, "we can go right into overlord territory if we need to, without worrying about breaking the pact or drawing down the wrath of *Tiamat* by killing one of them. Who knows, we might even be able to make Lilitu an ally."

Grant stared at with her disbelieving eyes. "Lilitu enjoys absolute power too much to ever have allies she couldn't kill whenever they became nuisances."

Lakesh nodded. "I agree—therefore I'm four-square solid against this. I vote we act on Kane's earlier suggestion about how to deal with Lilitu."

Kane sighed. "I might've been a bit too hasty."

Lakesh's frown deepened to a scowl. "How so?"

"The fact is, we've been playing a game of bluff and

counterbluff ever since the barons turned into overlords." He glanced over at Brigid. "Like someone said to me yesterday, we're fugitives from the law of averages."

The sunset-haired scholar smiled wanly but said nothing.

"Bottom line," Kane continued, "we've run out of high cards to play. We're the ones who've been bluffing, playing poker with empty hands. What's saved us from being called out until now is that the overlords were too busy reestablishing their empires to think about us."

Lakesh drew in a breath, then exhaled through his nostrils. "You may be right. You may not be. Regardless, I vote no." He cut his eyes toward Brigid. "You?"

Brigid ran nervous fingers through her mane. "I think it's a risk we're going to have to take. It was inevitable that we were going to have to cut a deal with one of the overlords at some point."

Lakesh looked at Grant. "And you?"

Slowly, almost hesitantly, Grant said, "The world would be a hell of a lot safer if Lilitu were dead. It would be even safer if a goddamn monster Annunaki spaceship wasn't in permanent orbit around it. As much as I hate to say it, I'm with Kane and Brigid on this one."

Lakesh's eyes shone bright with anger. "That still leaves the rest of the command staff to approve this insane operation, and I'll do whatever I can to veto it."

Kane regarded him bleakly. "Don't waste your time, old man. We'll always have one more vote than you."

Kane stared into Lakesh's bright blue gaze, but the man never flinched. He had finally grown accustomed to dealing with a robust—relatively speaking—Lakesh, whose eyes weren't covered by thick lenses and whose voice no longer rose to a reedy rasp. But he still had to consciously catch himself from addressing Lakesh as "old man." It had become a habit over the past few years, and he found it was a hard one to break.

Lakesh's lips compressed in barely repressed fury. He instantly understood Kane's oblique reference. When he, Domi, Grant and Kane first arrived at the Cerberus redoubt five years before, Lakesh held the position as the primary authority figure in the redoubt. Within a few months, the staging of a minicoup dramatically changed the situation.

Lakesh hadn't been totally unseated from his position of authority, but he became answerable to a more democratic process. At first, he bitterly resented what he construed as the usurping of his power by ingrates, but he grew to appreciate how the burden of responsibility had been lifted from his shoulders. With the removal of that burden, the risk that his recruitment methods would be exposed also diminished.

Before the arrival of the Manitius personnel, almost every exile in the redoubt had joined the resistance movement as a convicted criminal—after Lakesh had set them up, framing them for crimes against their respective villes. He admitted it was a cruel, heartless plan with a barely acceptable risk factor, but it was the only way to spirit them out of their villes, turn them against the barons and make them feel indebted to him.

This bit of explosive and potentially fatal knowledge had not been shared with anyone other than Grant, Kane, Domi and Brigid. Grant's grim prediction of what the others might do to Lakesh if they learned of it still echoed in all their memories: "I think they'd lynch you."

"Go, then," Lakesh grated in an unsteady voice. "Go tell that inhuman bitch that you're willing to throw your lives away on a madman's mission. I no longer have the reservoir of energy to worry about you."

He spun and stalked down the corridor, in the direction of the command center. The four people watched him go, standing in perplexed silence.

After a few uncomfortable moments, Kane cleared his throat and turned toward the plateau. "Well, I guess we'd better go and do what he says, tell the inhuman bitch what we've decided."

None of them laughed, but Shizuka's lips creased in a smile. It did not reach her eyes. "*Hai*," she said softly. "Go tell her. Tell her also that I will be accompanying you."

She gingerly flexed the fingers of her right hand, the palm glistening with liquid bandage. "You could even mention that I am very much looking forward to meeting her in the flesh. We have much unfinished business, she and I."

Chapter 13

They felt themselves diving through an alternately brightly lit and shadow-shrouded abyss, an endless free fall into infinity. Time and space were confused. They could find no tactile connection between their bodies of flesh and bone and their minds. They were conscious of a half instant of whirling vertigo as if they hurtled a vast distance at blinding speed.

Then the sensation of an uncontrolled plunge lessened. Massed whiteness dissolved into flickering yellow light. Carefully, Brigid, Kane, Grant and Shizuka stepped out of the energy field radiated by the interphaser.

· A cascade of light whirled and spun around it like a diminishing cyclone, shedding sparks and thread-thin static discharges. As quickly as it appeared, the glowing cone vanished, as if it had been sucked back into the apex of the gleaming pyramidion. The small device rested upon the raised center of a giant altar stone.

Deeply engraved into the rock was an elaborate geometric design, a complex series of interlocking cuneiforms that formed a spiral of concentric rings over twelve feet in diameter. A plinth and pedestal supported the thick disk of stone.

"We're here," Brigid husked out.

"Wherever 'here' is," Shizuka murmured, her eyes darting back and forth apprehensively.

They stood within a chamber apparently chiseled out of solid rock, carved from a cliff face. Torches cast a strobing firelight from wrought-iron wall sconces. High overhead, seventy to eighty feet up, a narrow crack of stone showed a scrap of bright blue afternoon sky. The air was hot.

"Let's get down and see where we are," Kane said, moving toward the edge.

He knew the design cut into the stone was an ancient geodetic marker, carved into the naked rock as a two-dimensional representation of the multidimensional geomantic vortex points that comprised the natural electromagnetic grid of Earth energies. He and his friends had seen similar markers in the past, in diverse places such as Iraq, China and even South America.

Kane didn't completely understand the scientific principles of geomantic vortex points, but he respected their power, as had the ancient peoples who engraved the rock floor with the symbols. He had no idea of how old it was, but the chamber itself exuded a brooding aura of ancient menace. His point man's sense tingled and the hairs of his nape prickled. A quick glance into the faces of his friends showed him they shared his uneasiness.

All of them were attired in tricolor desert camouflage BDUs and thick-soled, tan jump boots. The BDUs were departures from the skintight shadow suits they usually preferred to wear on away missions. They knew from experience that more conventional clothing made them appear less sinister than the formfitting black garments. However, the three Cerberus warriors carried the suits rolled up in their backpacks.

Grant and Kane carried war bags full of assorted odds and ends taken from the armory, some brought along due to their maximum destructive capabilities and others that served altogether different functions. They were experienced enough to know they could not plan for all contingencies and were always prepared to improvise.

All four people carried abbreviated Copperhead subguns attached to combat webbing over their field jackets. Under two feet long, with a 700-round-per-minute rate of fire, the extended magazines held thirty-five 4.85 mm steel-jacketed rounds. The grip and trigger units were placed in front of the breech in the bull pup design, allowing one-handed use.

Optical image intensifier scopes and laser autotargeters were mounted on the top of the frames. Low recoil allowed the Copperheads to be fired in long, devastating, full-auto bursts.

A TP-9 autopistol rode in a paddle holster rode high on Brigid's hip. Shizuka, although she had accepted the Copperhead, refused the offer of another firearm. Her *katana* and *tanto* swords were scabbarded at her back.

Grant and Kane instinctively made sure their Sin Eaters were secure in the bulky holsters strapped to their forearms. The right sleeves of their jackets were just a bit larger than the left to accommodate the weapons. Long combat knives, the razor-keen blades forged of dark blued steel, hung from canvas sheaths at their hips.

Brigid bent and disengaged the power pack from the interphaser and carefully placed the device within its cushioned and watertight carrying case. Her movements were swift, practiced and deliberate. If the interphaser was damaged, they would be stranded on the far side of the world. However, the current version of the machine was far sturdier than its predecessors.

Standing before the altar stone, Kane nodded at the dust on the floor and the two sets of footprints clearly visible. "Someone has been here recently. One person."

Grant visually followed the tracks. "Whoever it was came in, lit the torches and went away."

"Considerate of them," Brigid commented, adjusting the strap of the interphaser case.

Shizuka's eyes narrowed. "You think it was done for our benefit?"

Brigid nodded. "I do. Lilitu claimed she'd make preparations for our arrival."

Only a few hours earlier, they had informed Lilitu via the tripod of their decision to travel to Nippur. She had reacted with neither surprise nor happiness, but only with a smug, "You are wise. I will prepare for your arrival."

Then the legs of the tripod were withdrawn into the orb and it shot straight up into the sky, as if pulled by a celestial magnet.

Kane wet a forefinger, tested the air currents, then pointed ahead of them. "Thataway."

He went forward, walking heel-to-toe the way he had been trained to do when in a potential kill zone. Kane's sixth sense was on high alert. The skin between his shoulder blades seemed to tighten and he heard every whisper of sound, every flicker of movement, smelled every errant odor. His point man's sense was really a combined manifestation of the five he had trained to the epitome of keenness.

The four people had not walked far before they came to a litter of bones and human skulls scattered over the rock floor. Ancient armor glinted among the grinning jawbones, broken rib cages and splintered femurs. It was like blundering into an ancient charnel house, a crypt that had burst open and spilled the tumbled-together skeletons of what had once been human warriors.

"What the hell is this, Baptiste?" Kane wanted to know.

"I couldn't tell you," she replied quietly. "The Sinai was the scene of countless wars over the centuries. Jabal Musa, also called Mount Sinai, is significant in Christian, Judaic and Islamic tradition."

"Why?" Grant asked, interested in spite of himself.

"It's allegedly the site where Moses received the Ten Commandments. The Israelites made one of their camps during the Exodus at the foot of Mount Sinai, in an unspecified part of the Sinai desert."

"Could this be the camp?" Shizuka inquired.

Brigid considered the woman's question for a thoughtful few seconds, then shook her head. "I don't know. Whatever happened here happened a very long time ago."

A few battered bronze helmets and bucklers could be seen in the shadows, swords and spearheads melted into the mass of bones. The wood had long rotted from the spears, leaving only the notched blades of bronze.

"Bronze weapons weren't used much after the time of Alexander, were they?" Grant asked.

Brigid and Kane eyed him with surprise. "No, they weren't," Brigid said. "Good call."

"Try not to faint," Grant growled. "I occasionally read other things than just gun specs, you know."

The four outlanders picked their way carefully among the skeletons and skulls staring up at them, some with helmets tilted rakishly over an empty eye socket.

The chamber was vast and and echoing. Every rustle of sound was answered from the high, vaulted ceiling. The walls were tiled in Arabian patterns, with shocking pinks and bright blues.

"The original name for the Sinai was Mafkat, or the Country of Turquoise," Brigid commented. "Since so much of it was mined here."

The chamber narrowed, then opened into a broad foyer, bracketed on either side by crumbling collonades. Beyond the pillars they saw high cliffs, the rims ablaze with the white light of midday. The sky beyond the canyon was alive with reflected desert colors.

A hot wind whined, pushing eddies of sand before it. A collection of ruins rose like vague dreams from the foot of the sandstone cliffs. They saw several walls, a few broken columns and a fallen monument in the shape of headless, winged bull. All the detail work had been eroded by millennia of exposure to wind, baking heat and sand.

"So, that's Nippur?" Grant grunted sourly.

"A little less grand than I pictured an Annunaki spaceport," Kane intoned.

Brigid opened her mouth to speak, but the sudden stutter of automatic rifle fire cut her off.

Chapter 14

The four outlanders swiftly took up defensive positions at the bases of the sandstone pillars, unlimbering their Copperheads. They gazed out into the canyon, but except for wind-driven puffs of sand, nothing stirred.

They waited, straining their ears. Then the rattle of automatic-weapons fire reached them again. Grant and Kane tensed, slowly easing their bodies around the columns, staring out, slitting their eyes against the bright blast of sunlight.

They saw the figures of four mounted men, cantering down the throat of the gorge. The distance was too great to pick out specific details, but they wore white burnooses and girdled caftans. They rode their horses expertly, spread out in an orderly formation between the canyon walls.

"They're hunters," Kane declared matter-of-factly.

"Hunting what?" Brigid asked, staring out from beneath a shading hand.

"I don't know," he replied. "Just a suspicion I have."

Kane's suspicions suddenly crystallized into an ugly certainty when he glimpsed the small figure of a woman emerge from the ruins. She ran with the grace, if not the speed, of a gazelle toward the sheltering colonnade. The voices of the riders rose, shrill and strident. The horses came clattering down the canyon in pursuit.

The woman ran in a full-out sprint, head back and legs pumping. Kane received an impression of a slender, gracile build. Her face was small, high-cheeked, even elfin, and her eyes were enormous, wide and black. Her hair, streaming out behind her, was equally black and glossy, holding dark copper highlights.

Stomach turning a cold flip-flop, Kane recognized the type. She was a hybrid, a mixture of Archon and human genetic material. Since the advent of the overlords, he had not expected to see one again.

Impulsively, Kane stepped out from behind the column and gestured to the woman, shouting, "Come on!"

The hybrid female turned upon him eyes shining with fear. The fear was almost instantly replaced by determination. She increased the length of her stride, not looking behind her at the horsemen.

"What the hell are you doing?" Grant demanded angrily. "Why are you getting us mixed up in this? We don't know what's going on here."

Kane checked the action of the subgun. "No better way to find out. The rest of you stay out of sight. I'll see if these guys can't give me some information."

"Or some bullets," Brigid commented dourly.

"Is this what Lilitu meant by preparing for our arrival?" Shizuka asked.

No one answered.

Kane settled the stock of the Copperhead into the hollow of his right shoulder and squinted through the top-mounted sight, focusing on the faces of the pursuers. They were all swarthy, their expressions uniformly feral and ferocious. They wore the typical attire of the desert nomad—baggy trousers tucked into well-worn boots, robes and burnooses. To his surprise, he saw they were armed with Copperheads, but the weapons weren't equipped with the extended magazines.

As the drumming of hooves grew loud in Kane's ears, the hybrid woman swept past him and fell, uttering a strangulated cry of relief or resignation. Brigid pulled the gasping woman to her feet, leading her behind a pillar. Absently, Kane noted she was considerably shorter than Brigid, barely as tall as Shizuka. She wore a one-piece tan coverall, the zipper pulled down past her clavicle. Her face glistened with a film of perspiration.

Small breasts rising and falling, she husked out two words, "I'm sorry."

When the huntsmen caught sight of Kane, they reined their mounts down and pointed the bores of their subguns skyward. Kane wasn't inclined to follow their example. He kept his Copperhead planted firmly against his shoulder, finger resting on the trigger. The men rode closer, eyeing him with a mixture of caution and anger.

"That's far enough," Kane called, although he had no reason to believe they understood English.

The riders halted their horses. The animals did not look particularly sweaty, so Kane guessed they hadn't been running in the heat of the day for very long.

"Where is the woman?" one the men demanded in accented but perfectly comprehensible English.

Kane pegged him as the leader—tall, rangy and one-eyed, his left eye socket disfigured by a cicatrix scar. He affected a drooping mustache beneath his eagle's beak of a nose. His mouth was as thin as the slash of a razor.

"Why were you hunting her?" Kane asked.

"Because she was running away," the man retorted, a touch of arrogance underscoring his voice.

"Fair to say," Kane replied. "Why was she running away? And from whom? Or is it a what?"

The man kneed his horse several paces forward, saddle leather creaking. Even in the shadows cast by the folds of his burnoose, his one eye glittered with a fanatic's scorn for life, both his own and any others.

"She disobeyed the goddess," the man said flatly. "That is all you need to know."

"I can't help but disagree about that," Kane stated. "What *you* need to know is that your goddess is expecting me."

"Expecting you and several others, Kane," the man replied gruffly. "We were sent to escort you to her."

"But you decided it was more to fun to chase a woman instead?"

"Bring her forth."

"If you know who I am," Kane said, letting a steel

edge slip into his voice, "you know damn well I'm not going to do that just on your say-so. Who are you?"

"I am Ibrahim el-Amid. No matter what I and my men may seem to you outwardly, you must accept that we are servants of the goddess of this land. She has charged us to bring you and your companions to her, so I ask that the others show themselves."

"You haven't gotten to the part about meaning us no harm."

"We mean you no harm," Ibrahim el-Amid said automatically, as if by rote. "We were sent as guides, not as assassins."

Kane considered the Arab's words for a few thoughtful seconds, then backstepped into the temple foyer, glancing over at the hybrid woman. Her respiration was less labored now. He asked, "What's your name?"

"Rhea." Unlike other hybrid women, her voice was not a soft, breathy half whisper but a rich contralto.

"You want to tell us what's going on here?"

In an odd, slow voice, as if she were thinking of something else, Rhea said, "I came to warn you, but as you have no doubt deduced, I was a trifle too late."

"Warn us of what?" Grant demanded.

Rhea did not remove her unblinking gaze from Kane. He felt the intensity of her stare, as if she were committing to memory the color of his hair and the hue of his skin. "I came to warn you that you must return to where you came from. It is too late to do so now, and I'm sorry."

Kane gave Rhea a swift visual examination and felt

his heart clench in his chest due to her resemblance to Quavell. Still, that was not unusual. She looked much like most other female hybrids he had seen. Although she was small, she was perfectly proportioned with a face composed of sharp planes and fine-complexioned skin stretched taut over prominent shelves of cheekbones. Her flesh was of marble whiteness, but with a faint olive undertone.

Her cranium was high, the forehead smooth, the ears small and set low on the head. Her back-slanting eyes were large, shadowed by sweeping supraorbital ridges. All in all, the female hybrids were beautiful to look upon, almost too perfect to be real, and Rhea was one of the most lovely Kane had ever seen. She looked no more than eighteen years old, but he knew more than likely she was twice, perhaps three times his own age.

Rhea's face, for all of its appearance of youthfulness—a characteristic of most hybrids, male and female alike—was not the face of a girl. She was a woman who had experienced the full gamut of emotions in her life, from passion, to bitterness, pain and loss.

Kane found himself unable to hold her gaze and he wondered if the hybrid woman had been one of the many ordered to participate in the breeding experiment several years before in Area 51.

El-Amid called impatiently, autocratically, "You will come with us. It is the will of the goddess."

"And if we refuse?" Kane countered.

"Then there is only one alternative."

The voice that spoke from behind them was like a crashing of metallic echoes, but strangely toneless. As one, Kane, Shizuka, Grant and Brigid whirled, lifting their weapons but not firing upon the figure looming in the murk.

A broadly built man with a look of utter impassivity about him strode forward with a single-minded gait, like the march of an unstoppable automaton. Sand crunched under his heavy boots.

Beneath jutting brow ridges, the deep-set white eyes of the Nephilim did not blink, nor did his craggy, scale-pebbled face register emotion. The Cerberus warriors knew why. From the undersides of the ovoid shells that enclosed the back and top of the creature's hairless head, thread-thin filaments extended down to pierce both temples. It was a bioelectronic interface that for all intents and purposes turned all of the Nephilim into mind-controlled drones.

From neck to toe tip, the Nephilim's body was encased in silver-blue armor. From raised pods on the gauntlets rose three S-curved flanges, the ends flaring out like adder's hoods. Little balls of red energy pulsed in the gaping mouths of the stylized serpent heads that comprised the actual emitters of the accelerated stream of protons.

The Nephilim served as the foot soldiers of the overlords. When the barons reached their final stage of evolution as the overlords, so, too, had the Quad-Vees, the rank-and-file servant class of hybrids. According to ancient legend, the hybrid offspring of the cursed fornications between fallen angels and human women were called the Nephilim. They were believed to be soldiers in the armies of darkness.

Like soldiers, they wore armor but it was composed of smart metal, a liquid alloy that responded to a sequence of commands programmed into an extruder. A miniature cohesive binding field metallicized it from liquid to solid.

"I am Quarlo, the strong right fist of the goddess Lilitu," the Nephilim announced, raising his right arm and extending it toward them. "You will obey me as you would obey her."

Although the outlanders had encountered the Nephilim of several overlords, they had never heard one speak. They assumed the creatures were without the thought processes to be able to talk.

After a few seconds of wide-eyed staring, Grant challenged, "You're the torch lighter, aren't you?"

Quarlo did not respond to the question. "You do not have to surrender your weapons, but I insist you come with me."

Brigid inclined her head toward Rhea. "We will if she will."

Kane kept his eyes on the pulsing glow within the serpent heads rising from Quarlo's wrists. He knew a direct strike from an ASP bolt was almost instantly fatal, regardless of what part of the body it struck.

Quarlo said, "I have no orders regarding this woman.

Whether she accompanies you or not is irrelevant to the mission I have been charged with completing."

Grant, Brigid and Kane exchanged questioning glances. Rhea interjected calmly, "If I go back with you, I will most probably be killed."

"And if you stay here?" Shizuka inquired.

"I will most probably be killed here, too." The hybrid woman smiled ruefully. "However, if I return in your company, at least I will live long enough to fall under Lilitu's judgment."

"We'll see if we can intervene on your behalf," Brigid said uncertainly. "But Lilitu has never struck me as being particularly lenient with those who have crossed her."

"Your assessment is quite accurate," Rhea said crisply. "She has always been this way. Vindictive and short-tempered."

"How long have you been in her service?" Grant asked, eyeing Quarlo but not wanting to appear too obvious about it.

"All of my life, in one way or another."

"So you know her well," Kane ventured.

Rhea turned toward him, her onyx eyes revealing nothing. "As well as one sister knows another, I surmise."

Chapter 15

The dry, baking heat, although not unbearable, was distinctly uncomfortable. The air felt parched of all moisture. Grant began to sweat profusely, globes of perspiration springing to his brow and body. Within moments of leaving the temple, he felt like a walking swamp.

The Cerberus group slipped on sunglasses as they followed Ibrahim el-Amid and his men along the canyon. Quarlo brought up the rear, a dark giant with a face as expressionless as if it had been carved from the stone upon which he trod. He marched a few yards behind them, heavy boots crushing the gravel beneath the metal soles.

The outlanders carried canteens of distilled water, so they didn't suffer from thirst but none of them enjoyed the hike, either. The canyon seemed like the half-healed wound cut into the flesh of Earth.

Rock walls, raw and barren, rose high above them on either side, the streaks of exposed strata showing the white of marbleized granite and even the dark blue hue of turquoise deposits.

The ravine narrowed, widened and twisted among

the ruins. The structures were square, and were not tall, all of them graceless and even sullen looking, but they were old, perhaps as ancient as the Sinai Peninsula itself. Undecipherable hieroglyphs were visible on a few of the walls, chiseled deep into the stone.

Brigid said quietly, "The Mamluks of Egypt controlled the Sinai from 1260 to 1518, when the Ottoman sultan, Selim the Grim destroyed them at the Battles of Marj Dabiq and al-Raydaniyya. From then until the early twentieth century, the Sinai, as part of the Pashalik of Egypt, was under the control of the Ottoman Empire. We'll probably see a very strange mixture of styles."

"If I pay attention," Kane replied darkly. "At the moment, I'm too hot to care about Mamluks or sultans."

Rhea seemed the most uncomfortable under the brutal sun, panting and wiping at the perspiration glistening on her face.

"I'm guessing you're not native to these parts," Brigid said, handing the hybrid woman a canteen.

Rhea sipped at it out of politeness and handed it back. "You would guess correctly. Until three days ago, I lived in the barony of Beausoleil."

Kane and Grant whipped their heads toward her in surprise. "We were there two days ago," Grant rumbled. "The place had been leveled."

Rhea nodded. "I'm quite aware of that. I witnessed it. I was in Lilitu's skimmer when the ville was razed."

"Where were you before that?" Kane asked.

"In the Admin Monolith, where I had worked since my sister's…" Her words trailed off as she groped for the proper term. "Transformation."

"We've been operating under the assumption that the barons were the creations of cloning procedures," Brigid said, a hint of a challenge in her tone. "Selected human DNA blended with that of the race called the Archons. So how can Lilitu be your sister?"

Rhea regarded her haughtily. "Obviously we sprang from the same base genetic material at roughly the same time."

Grant grunted. "I met Lilitu when she was Baroness Beausoleil. You resemble her, but you're not her twin."

"Nor was I intended to be. Adjustments and minor modifications were made in our individual DNA sequences. We are not identical, but we are by blood related."

"I thought the entire baronial hierarchy was related," Shizuka said. "Since your Archon genes were supplied by one provider."

Rhea smiled slightly. "Balam."

"I never heard of any other barons having siblings," Grant commented.

"As far as I know, they did not," Rhea retorted. "I am unique."

"Why?" Kane asked bluntly. "Why make a sister for Lilitu? So she wouldn't get lonely while pulling the wings off flies?"

Long lashes veiled Rhea's eyes for an instant as she pondered Kane's question. "Would you believe me if

I told you I have no idea? I lived with her in the Administrative Monolith for most of my life. When I was not ignored, I was used as the brunt of her wrath."

For the first time Rhea's voice was edged with an emotion other than resignation. "She delighted in humiliating me…I, who came of the same blood as her, the blood of the barons, the lords of the Earth. And now she claims to be a goddess."

She inhaled a steadying breath. "As the so-called imperial mother, Erica van Sloan, she left the barony. Then, months later, when she reached her developmental peak as Lilitu, she abandoned the ville altogether. I administered it for over two years. And then…" She broke off, the tip of her pink tongue touching her dry lips. Finally she added in a whisper, "And then she came back."

Brigid scrutinized her over the rims of her sunglasses. "Which brings us around to the big question…if you're truly her sister, why didn't you make the changeover to an Annunaki overlord, too?"

Rhea met her gaze with her dark, inscrutable eyes. "I can only speculate. My DNA was missing the genetic trigger that responded to the signal transmitted from *Tiamat*. I do not have that specific marker, the imprint that *Tiamat* could locate and essentially upgrade."

The Cerberus warriors knew about the process to which Rhea referred. The fragile hybrid barons, despite being close to a century old, were only in a larval or chrysalis stage of their development. Exposed to an activation code beamed from *Tiamat* in synchronous orbit, the barons changed. When that happened, the war against the baronies themselves ended, but a new one, far greater in scope, began.

The baronies had not fallen in the conventional sense through attrition, war or rebellions. The barons had simply walked away from their villes, their territories and their subjects. When they reached the final stage in their development, they saw no need for the trappings of semidivinity, nor were they content to rule such minor kingdoms. When they evolved into their true forms, incarnations of the ancient Annunaki overlords, their avaricious scope expanded to encompass the entire world and every thinking creature upon it.

"Why the hell did Lilitu return to her old barony?" Kane asked skeptically.

"To fetch me," Rhea answered. "To loot the armory. And to destroy what I accomplished there in her absence. I had disbanded the Magistrate Division and made self-sufficiency the barony's first priority. We had almost attained it."

"She must have wanted to bring you here for some reason," Shizuka commented.

"I'm still waiting to find that out. However, I do know she intends to use you for her own ends and then discard you."

Grant snorted. "We don't need you to tell us that."

"Whatever promises she made you," Rhea continued, "my sister will not keep. As it is, she has angered a couple of her allies by allowing you to come here. They do not think highly of you."

"Do you know why that might be?" Brigid asked with feigned innocence.

The corners of Rhea's small mouth curved in a wry smile. "Please. The Cerberus warriors are possibly the most famous—or infamous—group of human beings who have lived in the past two centuries. Your enemies are many. My sister confided to me how deeply all of you are hated by some members of the Supreme Council…and how some members fear you just as deeply."

"Should we assume this is all a trap, then?" Shizuka inquired as calmly if she were asking the time of day.

Rhea frowned. "I cannot be certain. Lilitu wants you for more than either vengeance or simply to kill you. There is some task she feels only you can fulfill, some objective only you can reach. If nothing else, you have that knowledge with which to bargain."

"That's comforting," Kane remarked inanely.

"Isn't it, just?" Grant said, palming away sweat from his forehead. "How long until we get out of this heat so we can start the bargaining?"

Rhea only shrugged.

They continued following the horsemen for another hundred yards. The ravine declined gradually, turning into a path that was partly natural and partly roughly hewed out of naked stone. It angled to the right toward the cliff-face and at its end yawned a wide hole. The

Outlanders heard voices and the clink of tools echoing in a great hollow space.

Ibrahim el-Amid and his mounted party led them into a huge cave. Once inside, the relief from the sun's assault was immediate. The air was still stifling, but in contrast to the hammering heat of the canyon, the sudden change felt as refreshing as plunging into a stream fed by mountain meltwater.

Shafts of sunlight pierced the domed ceiling and they saw dark-skinned men and women crouched upon high ledges, working among heaps of piled stone. They chipped away at the rock walls with hammers, chisels and pickaxes. None of them wore much more than a ragged loincloth and they all bore the same unmistakable stamp of hardship.

They were tethered together by thick leather collars and lengths of slender chain. Several men wearing burnooses oversaw their labors, occasionally urging them on with curses and cracking strokes of long whips that raised blood-edged weals with every flail.

Looking around with slitted eyes, Kane asked, "What's going on here?"

"Excavation, or so I've been told," Rhea replied. "This is the day shift."

"Slave labor," Brigid stated, voice frosty with disgust. "Strong backs and primitive hand tools."

"The more primitive the tool," Shizuka said softly, "the more primal the inevitable revolt."

Grant glanced over his shoulder to make sure Quarlo was still there. He was, his white gaze fixed on them expectantly. Turning back around, he commented, "I don't think it's going to work that way this time."

Kane smiled grimly. "Remember our record."

Wherever the Cerberus team went, it always seemed that violence and death followed. It was rarely planned that way, but terrible and bloody events always happened and the body count soared. Brigid had once opined that they were avatars, catalysts, triggering revolutions and explosions of savagery that had simmered at a low boil for a long time.

Ibrahim el-Amid reined his horse to a halt and gestured expansively. "Go there."

"Go where?" Brigid asked.

The Arab thrust his arm toward a bastion of basalt. "Go that way."

Quarlo stepped up close. "The goddess awaits."

The cave floor inclined, winding around boulders. It led up to a stone stairway with risers too high for normal human legs to climb easily. The stairs led to a great rectangle in the rock wall. On either side of it stood four ten-foot tall statues depicting male and female creatures that were manlike and womanlike, but not quite either.

They stood solemn and naked, their hands folded over their chests, their fathomless eyes fashioned of turquoise. Although their features were composed and even regal, there was no mistaking their reptilian cast and the pattern of scales sculpted by a master's hand that covered their bodies. Grant, Brigid and Kane had seen similar statues before.

Still, Kane felt his stomach turn a slow flip-flop and Grant's scalp tightened. Both men involuntarily reached for their weapons.

Brigid spoke only one whispered word, but it sent chills of dread dancing up and down their spines: "Annunaki."

Chapter 16

At the top of the staircase, just inside the archway, loomed a pair of statues of a brassy metal, both about twelve feet tall. The figures stood, each with a slender arm raised, pointing outward, as if they were signposts. Upon the pedestal of each statue was a lengthy inscription in cuneiform characters.

The necks of the Annunaki were longer than those of humans, the heads blunt of feature with wide, lipless mouths. The narrow, elongated skulls held large, almond-shaped eyes that were almost invisible under knobbed brow ridges.

Kane, Brigid, Grant, Shizuka and Rhea stood upon a broad shelf of basalt thrusting out over a space so vast their eyes couldn't perceive its true proportions. All of them stared down into a bowl-shape depression that held an entire city. Kane stared, squeezed his eyes shut and stared again, too overwhelmed by astonishment to even breathe deeply.

The city rose up starkly from a rocky plain. The buildings stretched up like a series of streamlined cliffs, dark, massive and foreboding, set along a continuous square front. Entire quarters of the city lay crumbling in ruin. Sand had drifted down to choke wide avenues lined with the shattered eidolons of long-forgotten gods.

The structures hid everything on their far side but the top of one tall tower—a titanic black bulk dominating the surrounding structures like a giant column among a scattering of dominoes.

The tower rose arrogantly, the stonework tapering in close at the top. On its highest point glinted a globe-tipped spire. Rods of crystal projected from the sphere and it revolved slowly, glowing with a phosphorescent white flame. Far back, crowning a rocky hillock, a pile of rubble that had once been a sprawling complex slumped in acres of wreckage.

Clearing his throat, Grant commented offhandedly, "Does that tower look the slightest bit familiar?"

"The slightest bit," Kane replied. "We might have seen one exactly like it on the Moon."

"There's no 'might' about it," Brigid declared. "It's identical to the citadel of Enki."

Rhea swept them with a searching stare bordering on incredulity. "You have been to the Moon?"

"More than once, over the past three years," Kane admitted. "On our first trip, we toured the cemetery of the Annunaki royal family." He gestured to the sculptures. "We saw statues very much like these."

From the ledge, the ground sloped gently downward. Quarlo lumbered past them. "You will follow."

The Outlanders hesitated a moment, then with a resigned shrug, Brigid fell into step behind the Nephilim. "We will follow."

They walked down the slope to a narrow, elevated causeway that intersected with a paved road. On either side pylons of black marble rose like fifty-foot-tall obelisks, with hieroglyphs still visible upon their faces. The passage of centuries had worn and pitted the sleek marble until the glyphs could scarcely be seen.

"So this is the Nippur spaceport?" Shizuka inquired.

"Once, apparently," Rhea replied. "I've been told very little about this place…only that it once was a thriving commerce center for the Annunaki."

Noting lights gleaming within the slit windows of many of the buildings, Brigid commented, "The power is on, at least."

The avenue they followed was wide. The lights in the windows burned with a multicolored rainbow radiance. The walls of the inner buildings were inlaid with elaborate turquoise mosaics. They heard no sound as they walked, only the scuff of their own feet. There air hung heavily with the utter silence of dead places.

Rhea hunched her shoulders and murmured, "I do not like this place much."

"We've been to cheerier spots ourselves," Kane agreed absently, eyes darting from one wedge of shadow to another.

Quarlo led them into a great plaza, where six avenues met around the tall tower. They hesitated a moment, looking down one lane and then another. Quarlo strode toward a portal at the base of the tower. He did not glance behind him to see if the outlanders followed. Carefully they did so.

The doorway led into a large chamber, with a flagstone floor the color of midnight and slender fluted pillars holding up an arching roof. The colors of the frescoes on the walls had dimmed, faded by the passage of inestimable centuries. Quarlo was nowhere in sight.

Monolithic slabs of stone stood in two rows, arranged to curve around and meet in a circle. They were hung with tapestries worked in multicolored threads that depicted scenes from ancient times—ziggurats from which sprouted terraced gardens, animals long extinct, human and inhuman faces. They offered brief glimpses into a world lost millennia ago, when the Annunaki were the gods of the Earth.

"This is almost an exact duplicate of Enki's quarters in his citadel on the Moon," Brigid said quietly.

"Maybe the snake-faces all bought their furniture from the same place," Grant rumbled.

Kane grinned crookedly. "From what we've seen of their cribs so far, interior decorating doesn't seem to be their strong suit."

Shizuka sighed at the banter but did not voice an objection.

Abruptly, amplified tinnily, they heard a voice say, "Please. Don't stop the brittle byplay. We were enjoying it no end."

The voice was feminine, but as sharp as a steel blade. "Come forward."

Kane, Brigid, Grant, Shizuka and Rhea strode in the direction of Lilitu's voice. The chamber was like a cathedral in its loftiness. Most of it was draped in darkness but the polished black stone under their feet shone with a dim translucence. Ahead of them in the shadows gleamed a collection of round lights, like a miniature cluster of stars that cast a yellow light upon the overlords lounging upon their thrones.

There were four of them, all sitting in identical, high-backed chairs and wearing white mesh robes that shimmered like sun-touched water. Sitting on either side of Lilitu were two overlords the Cerberus warriors had only glimpsed in the past. Flipping through the index file of her eidetic memory, Brigid identified them as overlords Zu and Ishkur.

Although Zu and Ishkur were not identical to each other or to Lilith, they shared the same protuberant bony brow ridges overhanging shadow-pooled eyes, their finely pored skin stretched tight over sharp-boned jaws and high cheekbones. There was no hair, not even any eyelashes. Their faces were dusted all over with minute, glistening scales.

A crest of back-curving spines sprouted from their skulls, shimmering iridescently with different colors— leaf green for Ishkur and deep purple for Zu. Once again, Kane struggled to reconcile the sight of the tall, regal aristocrats with the memories of the small, fragile creatures who had ruled the baronies from the shadows of their high, isolated aeries.

As the hybrid barons, they had been a beautiful folk and as the overlords they still were, but now there was something disturbing, even revolting in their beauty.

With their gracefully arrogant postures and glistening skins, they were like of a group of depraved aristocratic children. Their fierce, lusting eyes put Kane in mind of snakes—cold, impenetrable, without heart or warmth or soul.

But a mocking wisdom beyond humanity glinted there, as well as a terrible strength. The eyes exuded age, but not weakness. They gleamed with an awareness of their own antiquity, of memories of a time that stretched back into a past so dim that even the most ancient of human civilizations was but a yesterday in comparison.

The Annunaki were a very old race by the time they left Nibiru, and for all intents and purposes they had reached the upper limit of their development as both a people and a civilization. Although their collective knowledge was immeasurable, they were losing the capacity to learn new things, and that rigidity of thought was passed on to their offspring. Children were born possessing in full the memories and knowledge of not only their parents, but also the entire history of the race. There was no singularity—what one knew, all knew.

Only when the Annunaki arrived on the small, watery planet of Earth did they undergo a great surge of excitement and a zest for new experiences. That zest expressed itself in a competition of how best to exploit the abundant resources of the new world, and over the centuries of colonization, the competition led to strife and eventually to war, the first of many between the overlords.

These conflicts were often noted in mythology as wars of the gods, even though the Annunaki were more demonic than divine by nature.

Kane easily recalled the conditioning undergone by the Magistrates that instilled in them the belief the barons were kings, demigods, their personal deities and thus deserving of their unquestioning obedience. Even learning the barons were products of synthetic wombs and recombinant DNA had not completely stripped them of their semisacred mystique.

The figure in the fourth throne did not resemble anything of the sacred, but rather of the damned. His face was disfigured by the scars of third-degree burns. Flames had swept over his features, scorching away his inhuman beauty and leaving only a livid mask in which his mouth and nose were dark spots in a swatch of raw, red flesh.

Dark, round-lensed goggles covered his eyes, but they gave him a form of sight because he fixed a blank, glassy stare on Grant. The thick metal rims emitted the faint drone of electronics. In his right hand he held a staff of black metal with a round ball on top. The ball blazed bright silver in the overhead glare.

The Cerberus warriors had wondered what became of Overlord Utu after Grant caused the Mirror of Prester John to literally explode in his face. Now they knew.

Lilitu surveyed them with disdain, not speaking. Kane met her gaze, sensing how a coldness of spirit radiated from her, from all of the overlords, like the dank breath from a glacial tomb. Her garment covered her upper body in a tight, contoured sheath, clinging to her waist, hips and breasts with a luminescent sheen. Her headband of platinum inset with turquoise, sapphire and beryl gave off a twinkling glow.

She reached out a hand toward Rhea. "Come here, sister. Face me."

Slowly, Rhea obeyed, walking to stand before Lilitu, her head bowed but with an expression on her face that was anything but contrite. Lilitu rose from the throne and putting one long-nailed finger under her chin, she lifted the woman's head so they stared directly into each other's eyes.

"You betrayed me," Lilitu whispered, her voice sibilant with spite. "Why?"

"You destroyed the ville," Rhea replied in the same sibilant hiss. "You killed my advisers, you murdered hundreds of people…on a whim."

Lilitu cocked her head quizzically. "What difference do a few lives make in the span of eternity? Were they not my subjects to do with as I willed?"

"No," Rhea countered, her voice acid with hate and rage. "They were *mine!*"

They gazed at each other in silence for a long moment, then Lilitu whipped her hand from beneath Rhea's chin and slapped her face. She went staggering toward Utu.

Utu's lean left arm shot and secured a grip on Rhea's wrist, preventing her from falling into his lap. His long fingers cut savagely into the firm muscle of her forearm, but she did not wince. He shoved her roughly away, as if the very act of touching her had contaminated him.

A bruise darkened the side of her face, but Rhea did not touch it. She glared at Lilitu. "Kill me if that's your intent."

Lilitu's eyes glittered. "Why did you go to intercept the party from Cerberus? Did you not know you were risking your life?"

"I risked warning them because I think they are my only hope of stopping you."

In a whisper full of menace, Lilitu said, "You do not know what you are talking about. I will hear no more of it."

Staring at the Outlanders, she demanded, "What has she been telling you?"

"Nothing we hadn't already figured out for ourselves," Grant rumbled. "That you plan to use, abuse and discard us."

A half smirk creased Lilitu's face. "But you came anyway."

"Well," Kane drawled, "you asked so nice and all."

He turned toward Utu. "Yo, Utu. Looks like you've lost weight."

Utu's lips writhed back over his discolored teeth in either a grimace or a grin. "You'd be the one to tell me about that, Kane."

His voice was a raspy, rusty croak. "Did you think to ever confront me again, after you left me for dead?"

"Actually, no," Grant said flatly. "But we didn't devote a whole lot of thought to it, either."

"You should have. We of the Supreme Council have long memories."

"And very short dicks," Kane snapped.

Ishkur half rose from his chair. "Silence!"

"Hey, that's what I heard," Kane said defensively.

He stared at Lilitu. "So these three are all you could talk into joining up with you? The halt, the lame and the blind?"

Zu's molten eyes glared at him out of face twisted with fury. "We can call upon resources that you've never dreamed of, Kane."

"If that's the truth," Brigid said, tone hard with suspicion, "then why do you need us?"

Lilith regarded them contemplatively. "Because you have access to the one item Overlord Enlil wants most in the world but cannot reach."

Shizuka frowned. "What might that be?"

Lilitu smiled. It was a sincere smile and it had no humor or warmth in it, only pride and a mocking cruelty. "Shall I tell her, or will one of you enlighten her?"

Slowly, as if he begrudged each syllable that left his mouth, Grant muttered, "Ninlil…the mate of Enlil."

Chapter 17

Sunlight penetrated the inner chambers of the vast hollow beneath the Sinai only in refracted rays. Lilitu led them along the winding walkways of the subterranean settlement, affecting a hip-swinging swagger that at once irritated and attracted Kane. Overlord Zu walked beside her. Rhea had been ordered to stay behind, and she hadn't argued. Quarlo brought up the rear.

"Once Nippur was an immense metropolis," Zu declared matter-of-factly. "Babylon and Ur paled beside it. But that was a very, very, *very* long time ago."

"Where are you taking us?" Grant demanded harshly.

"Where we want to take you," Lilitu replied with a dismissive toss of her head. She did not deign to look at him. "Be patient."

Grant's jaw muscles knotted and his hand reflexively closed around his Copperhead. Shizuka caught his eye and shook her head warningly.

Zu suddenly swung his head around, spearing the big man with a molten glare of accusation. "I know what you're thinking… What all of you are thinking."

"Oh, do you?" Kane inquired patronizingly. "Share it with *all* of us."

Keeping his eyes fixed on Grant's face, Zu said slowly, "You think you and your friends may never have a better opportunity to kill us, to cut down on future opposition, so you won't have to fight us in the future."

Grant's brows curved down toward the bridge of his nose, but he did not otherwise respond.

"I understand the temptation," Zu went on conversationally, "but all of you would die within seconds of the attempt."

He nodded in the direction of Quarlo. "The exchange would not be an equitable one."

"Just the same," Grant bit out between clenched teeth, "I enjoy thinking about it."

"As long as that is all you do," Zu said contemptuously, turning back around.

Enormous grottos opened out above them. Indirect lighting formed bizarre shadows on the ceilings of the caverns through which they passed. Torches burned here and there along the walls, and by their smoky glare they saw that the passageway was faced with quarried smooth black rock. There were no carvings or frescoes, no furnishings.

"This looks man-made," Brigid said.

Lilitu snorted. "Hardly. It was built by Igigi, with tools supplied by the House of Anu."

"Igigi?" echoed Kane. "Who the hell was that?"

"They," Brigid corrected. "Igigi is the plural,

singular is Igigu. According to Sumerian myth, they were the three hundred lesser gods without individual names who remained in Heaven after six hundred greater gods left Heaven to grow food for the gods living on Earth."

She paused for a second, then added, "In the demythologized version, they were the servant class who stayed aboard *Tiamat* while the Annunaki royal family set up the first colony on Earth. When the Annunaki found the actual process of building a colony a tiresome and difficult occupation, they ordered the Igigi to come down to Earth and do all the heavy lifting. But the Igigi found farming fully as wearying as the Annunaki and quickly returned to Heaven, where they stayed forever after.

"I imagine they were prototypes of the Nephilim… they were worked too hard by the royal family and started thinking about staging rebellion. But they feared a confrontation with both Enki and Enlil and persuaded Zu to make their request known to the House of Anu."

"So the ancient Annunaki had labor-relation problems even way back then," Kane said sarcastically.

"True," Lilitu said tauntingly. "That was why we created humanity…so they could be our dray animals and slave labor. But I'm sure you know that story."

No one responded. Reluctantly and grudgingly, they knew they could not refute Lilitu. After several years of clue sifting, historical detective work and life-risk, the core group of Cerberus exiles had finally accepted as fact, not speculation, the involvement of the Annunaki in the development of human culture on Earth. The true full extent of that involvement was still open to conjecture, however.

The Outlanders knew that the ancient Annunaki set about maximizing the potentials of Earth's indigenous hominids by redesigning them. The first generation of slaves was only a step above the primitive protohumans. They were encouraged to breed so each successive descendant might be superior to the first.

Their brains improved and technical, manual skills expanded. So did cogent thoughts and the ability to deal with abstract concepts. One of these abstract concepts was that of freedom to choose their own destiny.

One faction of the overlords agreed that their creations, the humans, should be set free and allowed to develop independently. Another group, by far the most vocal, opposed them. This opposition led to full-scale hostilities among the Annunaki.

Enlil, who commanded lordship over Earth, wanted humankind to be kept in as primitive a state as possible. The opposing group, led by his half brother, Enki, disagreed with this stance.

The ruling council of the Annunaki delayed making a final decision and decreed that intermediaries were needed between themselves and the masses of humanity. A hierarchy was clearly defined and for many millennia the Annunaki oversaw the welfare and fate of humankind. All the while they remained apart from the people, approachable only by the high priests and kings on specified dates, communicating only with their plenipotentiaries.

A fierce rivalry arose between opposing factions of the Annunaki for the hearts and minds of people, partly because they had come to depend increasingly on human kings and their armies to achieve their ends. When this situation became too unwieldy, the Annunaki chose to create a new dynasty of rulers, known as demigods or god-kings, because of their exalted bloodlines.

As a bridge between themselves, a pantheon of gods and humankind, they introduced the concept of the god-king on Earth. They appointed human rulers who would assure humankind's service to the deities and channel their teachings and laws to the people.

Sumerian texts described how, although the Annunaki retained lordship over the lands and humankind was viewed as little more than a tenant farmer, humanity grew arrogant. Fearing a unified human race, both in culture and purpose, the Annunaki adopted the imperial policy of divide and rule. For while humankind reached higher cultural levels and the populations expanded, the Annunaki themselves fell into decline.

King Anu returned to Nibiru after arranging a division of powers and territories on Earth between his feuding sons, Enlil and Enki. Civilizations such as Egypt, Sumer and the Rama Empire were created by the two half brothers. Wars were fought by the extended families of Enki and Enlil, and the nations changed hands back and forth through different conflicts.

After one such war, following the declaration of an uneasy peace, Enlil tried to force his brethren to make a decision about what to do about humanity.

As humankind procreated and their numbers increased, while those of the Annunaki lessened, Enlil grew fearful and prevailed upon the Supreme Council to allow a deluge to wipe humanity off the face of the earth. But Enki was not happy about the decision to commit genocide and sought ways to frustrate the plan. He managed to do so to a point; his efforts were immortalized as the story of Noah and the ark.

The Annunaki agreed to wipe the slate clean and start again. They departed from Earth, journeying back to Nibiru, intending to return one day in the future.

Lilitu and Zu walked along an elevated causeway that was little more than a channel filled with rubble. Shadowed, yawning cracks bisected the sheer walls on either side of them. Bright streaks of metallic ores and mineral deposits gleamed dully.

The causeway plunged into a round shaft quarried out of the rock. Beams and girders of metal shored up the ceiling and from these hung little round lights. The people walked past a collection of picks and shovels.

"Almost there," Lilitu announced breezily.

"And where the hell is there?" Grant growled.

"Here," Zu said.

They led the way through a huge pair of bronze doors bearing the images of winged bulls in bas-relief. Inside, the Cerberus warriors found themselves in total darkness. A motorized whine filled their ears, and the giant doors swung shut with a ponderous thud. Dazzling light sprang from an overhead fixture.

The Outlanders glanced around a spacious, marble-floored chamber with colorful tapestries on the walls. The room was as tight as a box, and despite its size, Kane experienced a brief surge of claustrophobia. Before he could half grasp all the details of their surroundings, the floor began to sink beneath their feet. The tapestries slowly rose.

"An elevator," Brigid murmured. "The ancient Annunaki didn't like stairs, either."

Zu faced her, a smirk lifting the right corner of his mouth. "You pride yourself on your knowledge of my people."

She lifted a shoulder in a negligent shrug. "Know thy enemy."

"What do you know about me?"

Narrowing her eyes and gazing at him steadily as if she were scrutinizing a germ culture through a microscope, Brigid stated, "Zu was a servant of Enlil, from whom he stole the Tablets of Destiny, so hoping to determine the fate of all things.

"Zu was an orphan, and the old texts mention that his family were enemies of Anu and his clan on Nibiru. Only Enki was aware of this, and he chose to keep the matter secret. Zu was adopted by the Igigi, and lived as one of them. He was not their equal, but he was their kind, of common birth. He became their spokesman, their advocate. The Supreme Council did not respect him because of this."

Zu's face darkened, but the smirk remained although it looked forced. Brigid continued, "Enlil wasn't too interested in the Igigi's grievances. He preferred to kill them and replace them. Enki suggested that the whole matter could be delayed indefinitely if Enlil would reassign Zu to his own personal service. Service to either brother would supercede any other commitments.

"The suggestion was made to have Zu guard the most sensitive area, in the secret chamber where the Tablets of Destiny were kept. This position was considered important enough to delay making a decision about the Igigi. Enlil agreed and made it so.

"Zu envied the Tablets of Destiny and the power that they could bring to him. He perhaps even realized the tactics of Enlil were not in the best interest of the Annunaki as a whole. He stole the tablets and escaped back to 'the heavens,' from where he began to utilize their power.

"Anu and the royal family were shocked. The entire planet was in a state of crisis over this violation of trust. Anu ordered Zu to restore the tablets to Enlil, but the Supreme Council was worried that no one could fight Zu with the power of the tablets at his command."

The floor continued to descend, and they saw smooth walls of alloy set with recessed white lights behind rectangular panes of frosted glass. The air took on a still and stale taste.

"It was decided that Enlil's firstborn son, Ninurta, would do battle with Zu," Brigid went on calmly. "Ultimately, the battle was won and Ninurta restored the tablets to their sacred chamber. There was a dramatic trial in which all of the godhead sat in judgment and condemnation of Zu. He was handed over to Ninurta, who cut his throat."

Brigid eyed Zu keenly. "This myth was so meaningful to the Sumerians that it was depicted on countless clay seals and artistic impressions. Zu was often depicted as a bird, with feathers and wings, to represent his allegiance to the Igigi.

"The epic was remembered in Babylonian and Assyrian rituals where a winged bull, representing the evil Zu, was sacrificed in the presence of the godhead. To Sumerians, Zu represented the ultimate personification of betrayal, and he served as a metaphor of deception and affliction."

"Nice reliable guy, this Zu," Kane commented snidely. "I'll bet I can guess the real story."

Zu cast him a venomous stare. "Mind your tongue."

As if he hadn't heard, Kane declared, "The Tablets of Destiny were computer control disks for *Tiamat*. Zu was some sort of navigator for the Annunaki space program. He hijacked *Tiamat* and sent her running around the solar system, waging war on his own kind. He incited a mutiny among the Igigi, too. Probably got most of them killed, too."

"I told you to mind your tongue," Zu barked.

"Blow it out your ass," Kane retorted. "I'm not one of your Igigi."

With a grinding of gears and a barely perceptible lurch, the marble floor stopped descending. Double stainless-steel pneumatic doors hissed back, revealing a corridor with alloy-sheathed walls.

An Arab sat inside a wire-enclosed booth, cleaning a wickedly curved throwing knife with a scrap of cloth. Seeing Lilitu and Zu, he sprang up, crossed his arms over his chest and bowed from the waist. Even though he stayed bent over until they passed, the Cerberus warriors glimpsed the fanatic luster in his dark eyes.

As they walked by the security checkpoint, Brigid glanced back and noticed the man eyeing her like a slab of succulent meat. He ran the ball of his thumb up and down the edge of his blade.

"How many of the locals do you have working for you?" Grant asked.

The explanation was interrupted by the hissing open of another pair of doors at the corridor's end. Beyond, in a huge chamber, a collection of electronic equipment towered up at least two floors. On a low balcony stretching all around the alloy-walled room, banks of computers hummed. The other items of bizarre appartus were ranged around the stone floor, but the centerpiece was a stainless-steel shaft mounted in a drum-shape socket raised from the floor.

The shaft shot upward thirty feet or more, a hoop

of pure crystal balanced atop it. Nearby were several control board consoles. A number of people gathered around them.

Lilitu paused before the open door and made a mock bow, indicating that the Outlanders should go ahead. Kane stopped and asked distrustfully, "What's in there?"

Zu chuckled lowly, a sound like dry bones being clicked together. "You claimed that in my first incarnation I was a navigator?"

"So?"

Zu gestured toward the room. "I believe you would call this place mission control."

Chapter 18

The Cerberus warriors stepped cautiously into the room. A confusion of noises filled their ears. They could barely distinguish the humming of generators, voices, engines revving and a whole series of rhythmic tappings.

As they entered, the personnel manning the control consoles cast them quick, unemotional glances. They were a mixed lot—two appeared to be of Middle Eastern extraction, one European and three Asians. All of them wore one-piece bodysuits like that of Rhea.

"Who are they?" Grant asked.

"Technicians, drawn from various places around the world," Lilitu answered curtly. "They needn't concern you."

Zu gestured toward a wide embrasure, set chest high in the wall. "Have a look at mission control, if you've a mind to."

The Outlanders looked over the barrier and down into the interior of a huge cavern. Lined up in an orderly row were ten circular crafts made of dully gleaming metal, a fleet of Annunaki sky skimmers.

Objects and machines they couldn't identify cluttered the cavern floor—large and small, of metal, glass and crystal. Some were of the sleek simplicity of a minimalist sculpture and others were of a design so complex, they could scarcely determine top from bottom. However, they all shared the appearance of alien instruments of an unknown and extraterrestrial science.

While they watched, a saucer shape floated in from the far end of the immense hangar. It settled down gently and a vertical seam appeared in its smooth surface.

A ramp slid out and Overlord Marduk, resplendent in his elaborate cobalt-blue body armor came striding out, voluminous cloak belling out behind him.

"Marduk!" Brigid exclaimed, turning to look at Zu. "Why is he here?"

Zu smiled. "He has invested a great deal of his own resources in this excavation project."

A chill finger of dread stroked the base of Kane's spine, but he continued staring down into the huge hangar. He heard a rhythmic, familiar drone. Following the sound with his eyes, he saw what he expected— enclosed within slabs of transparent armaglass stood a fusion generator. More than twenty feet tall, it resembled two solid black cubes, a slightly smaller one balanced atop the other. The top cube rotated slowly, producing the steady drone.

All of them had seen generators of that type before in various and unlikely places around the world. Lakesh had put forth the initial speculation they were fusion reactors, the energy output held in a delicately balanced magnetic matrix within the cubes. When the matrix was breached, an explosion of apocalyptic proportions resulted. A swarm of personnel worked around a broad console at the base of the generator. Far above, movable cranes slid to and fro on rails set in the roof of the cave.

"This way please," Lilitu called out.

They turned. A dozen monitor screens cast a pale light over the vaulted chamber. Most them displayed scenes of desert desolation, but two of them showed exceptionally dissimilar views: a flat and barren plain from which a pitted, wind-eroded megalithic structure rose. All of them recognized Egypt's great pyramid, half-buried by drifting sand dunes. In the background, the vague outline of smaller structures could be discerned.

The second screen showed a disquietingly familiar image, that of a crater on the Moon. Black, square structures were built into the regolith, the inner wall of the giant depression in Luna's surface.

The collection of ruined buildings looked eerie in the eternal twilight. Less than a quarter of a mile southward towered the citadel of the Enki, a titanic black bulk dominating the buildings like a thundercloud. The stonework of the tower tapered in close at the top and on its highest point came a glinting of a reflective object, like a captive star.

"They're interested in Egypt and the Moon for some reason," Brigid whispered to Kane.

Lilitu turned toward her, eyes glittering. "The reason is simple. After nearly two years of back-breaking labor, we have succeeded in excavating the main ground-control nexus to the navigational computer on the Moon. We were barely able to do so. The damage was extensive."

"That's a shame," Kane said inanely.

Lilitu's right hand suddenly lashed out with the eye-blurring speed of a striking serpent. Her claw-tipped fingers dug viciously into his flesh. He flexed his wrist tendons and with the faint whine of a tiny electric motor, an actuator popped the Sin Eater from its forearm holsters into his waiting hand. At the same time, his companions made motions to draw their own weapons.

With a swift scutter of metal-shod feet, shapes seemed to materialize out of the shadows. A half-dozen miniature snake heads reared back, open jaws crackling and emitting tiny sparks. The armor-sheathed arms of three Nephilim were attached to them. More of the green and silver-blue armored soldiers were assembled on either side of the door. They moved in a semi-circle around Kane, Brigid and Shizuka, ASP emitters extended, faces impassive, white eyes unblinking. Quarlo was among them.

Kane fought as hard to keep from triggering his pistol as he did to keep the pain from registering on his face. "This will get you nowhere," he husked out.

"Perhaps not," Lilitu hissed, "but it was you and your associates who disrupted much of the Annunaki technology we left on the Moon. Your destructive actions doubled our difficulties."

"Unintentional," Kane said. "But I can't say I'm sorry."

"I can *make* you sorry." Baring her teeth, Lilitu increased the pressure of her hand around his neck, cutting off his ability to breathe normally.

Kane's head swam, his vision blurring on the edges. His finger hovered over the Sin Eater's trigger stud. He managed to say hoarsely, "Let me go or you'll be dead in about three seconds."

Lilitu chuckled, a savage grin creasing her face. "As will you and your friends. I know how you apelings think… You will fight against great odds, but you are not suicidal."

Recognizing Kane's plight, Brigid said, "How does it happen, Lilitu, that lowly apelings like us can disrupt the ambitions of the Supreme Council?"

Lilitu suddenly released Kane, who rocked back on the balls of his feet. Threads of blood inched from the shallow lacerations on his neck. "Put up your weapon," she commanded.

Slowly, Kane retracted the Sin Eater into the holster. "Tell your zombies to do the same."

"No," she snapped, turning to Brigid. "Shortly after my resurrection, I realized that the so-called plans of the Supreme Council to reestablish the Annunaki empire were ill conceived, doomed to failure. Enlil would realize it, as well, except he is a vain fool surrounded by weaklings and sycophants. He has not learned from the past."

"How is your plan any different?" Grant demanded, pretending that the sparking viper head inches away from his face didn't disturb him.

"The past rebellions against Enlil and his faction failed because they relied almost entirely on force of arms," Zu said. He gestured expansively. "The fact that this port was virtually buried is proof of the last failed effort to unseat Enlil."

"What do you mean?" Shizuka asked.

"You wanted to know why Marduk has a vested interest in this place?" Lilitu asked.

"Only if you want to tell us," Brigid said. "But I think I know. He was the only Annunaki overlord who nearly unseated Enlil, wasn't he?"

"Marduk was almost successful," Zu conceded, "around the year 4000 B.C. He rose up and contended with Nergal and Enlil for control of all Mesopotamia. But Enlil faced him down with a scorched policy. Enki tried to intervene as a peacekeeper, but Nergal hated Marduk. He destroyed the temples and shrines of other members of the Supreme Council and blamed it on Marduk's followers. The greatest sacrilege was the defilement of Enlil's temple in Nippur…all of his priests, priestesses and worshipers were executed and he believed it was Marduk's doing."

Kane began to say something, thought better of it and shook his head in disgust.

"When Enlil heard that even his Holy of Holies was not spared," Zu continued, "he ordered that Marduk be seized and brought before the Supreme Council.

Ninurta and Nergal were given the assignment, but they couldn't find him, although they knew his ultimate goal was to take control of the Nippur spaceport."

"Enlil decided to deny Marduk the spaceport by the simple expedient of destroying it. So, with one powerful blow, it was obliterated. He used what you would call IRBMs—intermediate range ballistic missiles."

Zu gestured with both arms in all directions. "The mountain within which the mission controls were hidden was pulverized, the plain that served as the runways and launch platforms completely destroyed. Not even a tree was left standing."

"When the air finally cleared," put in Lilitu, "all of southern Mesopotamia lay prostrate. The nuclear firestorm crushed the land, wiped out everything. The cities known as Sodom and Gomorrah were no longer the seats of learning they had once been, and the Dead Sea became truly dead—lying at the bottom of a great hole in the earth."

"Do the skeletons we saw in the temple date back to that time?" Shizuka asked.

Zu nodded. "More than likely. Life only began to stir anew seven years later. Backed by Elamite and Gutian troops loyal to Enlil, a semblance of organized society returned to Sumer under human rulers seated in former provincial centers such as Isin and Larsa. It was only after the passage of seventy years that Enlil's temple in Nippur was restored. But by this time, the

Supreme Council saw no purpose in resurrecting the past and shortly thereafter came the flood, the deluge."

Lilitu showed the edges of her teeth in a predatory grin. "But you know about all of that, don't you?"

"As a point of fact," Brigid said coldly, "we do. So why did you come back here, nearly seven thousand years later?"

Zu ran his hand up and down the shaft of metal. "From here, we can alter *Tiamat*'s navigational systems. That's just the first step of freeing her from Enlil's control."

"Freeing her of his control," Kane asked, "or taking it away from him so you can impose your own?"

"Does it make any difference?" Lilitu countered.

"If it doesn't," Grant growled, "what do you need us for?"

"To put in place the final component of the plan," Lilitu retorted, turning toward Kane. "You were quite correct when you identified the Tablets of Destiny with data cards. You may recall that each member of the Supreme Council used a tablet to upload our neuronic signatures into *Tiamat*'s memory nexus."

"Yes," Brigid said, recollecting the ritualistic event aboard the giant ship.

"One was not uploaded," Zu announced.

"Let me guess," Kane said with feigned weariness. "Enlil's."

"Exactly." Lilitu's white teeth flashed in a triumphant grin. "Nor was it necessary at the time."

"But now it is?" Shizuka inquired.

"To achieve our goals, yes," Zu answered. "Unlike

my brethren on the council, I am the only member of the royal family qualified to pilot *Tiamat*. However, without Enlil's express, specific instructions to override the security protocols, *Tiamat* will not recognize my authority."

"And for some insane reason," Grant rumbled menacingly, "you think we can steal Enlil's Tablet of Destiny and bring it back to you?"

"Of course not." Lilitu's tone dripped with scorn. "You can, however, obtain an item that he would be willing to barter for."

Skin flushing first cold and then hot, Kane asked the question, even though he knew the answer in advance. "What item is that?"

Voice purring with amusement, Lilitu replied, "His darling baby Ninlil. You know where she is and how to reach her."

"And you," Brigid asked incredulously, "actually expect us to travel to Agartha, abduct a baby and turn her over just so you can blackmail Enlil into abdicating?"

"No." All the humor vanished from Lilitu's tone, bearing and eyes. "I expect you to do it to not only save yourselves, but everyone you hold dear in Cerberus and New Edo. Make no mistake. Neither refusal nor failure is an option. You will do as I bid or you will watch everyone you love die before I allow you the release of death."

Chapter 19

"Disarm them," Lilitu snapped to the Nephilim.

As a metal-shod hand reached for the Copperhead clipped to her vest, Brigid asked, "Why didn't you do this before?"

"I wanted you to think you were safe," Lilitu retorted. "Guests, not prisoners."

"You took quite a risk," Grant said sourly as a Nephilim began working at the straps and buckles of his Sin Eater's holster.

"It was worth it," Zu commented. "We've got you, don't we?"

Kane smiled inanely. "You do. I should point out that lot of assholes have said the same thing. In fact, one of them said it to me only a couple of days ago."

While he spoke, he observed that only two of the Nephilim had their ASP emitters held at a ready position and only one of them had it aligned with his head. Slowly, carefully, he gathered his legs under him.

Before he could move, Shizuka cried out, "*Aitsura!*" and sprang for Lilitu, unsheathing her *katana* in the same motion. A green-armored Nephilim extended his ASP emitter toward her. Triple streams of eyeball-searing yellow light spit from the serpent mouths, joining together to form a coruscating globule of plasma, which jetted toward Shizuka like a fireball launched from a catapult.

Her slender body instantly curved in a half crouch, and the bolt blazed well above Shizuka's head and impacted against the far wall with a multicolored burst of energy. Lilitu shouted in angry alarm, speaking in the harsh Niburuan tongue.

Shizuka drew her *tanto* sword and slid in among the Nephilim, her blades flashing. The armored men had not expected attack, and the woman had sprung into motion too quickly for them to do more than fix their attention on where she had been. Both Zu and Lilitu continued shouting, backing away toward the console.

The *katana* in Shizuka's right hand sliced through a Nephilim's neck As he reeled away, clutching at his throat, blood spraying from between his alloy-coated fingers, Shizuka performed a half pirouette on the ball of one foot. An ASP blast missed her by a margin and struck one of Lilitu's Nephilim square in the chest, the plasma interacting violently with the alloy of the armor. Sparks showered in a dazzling display of pyrotechnics.

Recovering from the surprise of Shizuka's actions, Kane moved with the eye-blurring speed and an explosion of near superhuman reflexes that had made him something of a legend in the Cobaltville Magistrate Division. Hurling himself forward, he shoulder-smashed his way between a pair of Nephilim, his Sin Eater slapping solidly into his hand.

His first two shots were fired at Lilitu and Zu, but a green-armored Nephilim jostled his arm and spoiled his aim. The subsonic 9 mm rounds ricocheted off the control consoles with flares of blue sparks and keening whines. Bleating in fear, the technicians took cover behind their chairs. Bullets struck the metal shaft stretching up to the ceiling, crashing into it with a metallic clangor and ricocheting away.

Brigid triggered a short snare-drum rattle from her Copperhead, and bullets struck one of Zu's soldiers in the chest. Little sparks burst up at the multiple points of impact, driving him backward.

Grant fired his Copperhead in a long staccato burst. Bright brass arced out of the smoking ejector port, tinkling down at his feet. As a Nephilim wearing the colors of Lilitu was hammered off his feet, he roared, "Let's go! Move it!"

He, Shizuka, Brigid and Kane stepped back toward the double doors, peppering the Nephilim with a barrage of bullets. The gunfire was like a continuous roll of thunder in the enclosed space.

Lilitu shrieked commands in a wild frenzy. The Nephilim regrouped and two of them converged around Grant. Shizuka slashed the edge of the *katana* across a man's wrist, shearing through the viper heads of the ASP emitter.

Her twin blades wove lethal nets of flashing steel around Grant. A quick stroke with the *tanto* sent a

Nephilim tumbling backward with his throat spewing a river of blood while a downward chop of the katana split a man's hairless skull from crown to forehead.

Slashing with one sword and stabbing with another, Shizuka wrought scarlet havoc. A lightning-swift sliding side step shifted her head and body away from an ASP bolt. It struck the doors behind her with a kaleidoscopic splash of color and a halo of smoke.

The vast room was filled with a medley of angry yells and a confusing mill of rushing bodies. Autofire from the Cerberus warriors' weapons rattled, weaving a deafening stutter around single-shot cracks. The bullets struck sparks and bell-like chimes from the gleaming exoskeletons of the Nephilim, bouncing off with angry, buzzing whines.

The racket of the fusillade was almost deafening with three guns blasting all at once.

Brigid hit a switch on the wall, the double doors slid apart and the Outlanders rushed out into the corridor. The Nephilim surged out into the passageway, but they were hampered by their bulky body armor and the relative narrowness of the doorway. Only two of them could squeeze out at a time, but they fired their weapons as they did so.

A streak of energy fanned scalding-hot air on Kane's face. A flurry of ASP bolts lanced around him, striking the floor and the wall, stinging him with blizzards of white-hot sparks.

Whirling, depressing the trigger stud of his Sin Eater, he emptied the entire magazine in a thundering drumroll and whine of ricochets. The lumbering Nephilim staggered and stumbled, colliding with one another.

When the firing pin of his handgun struck the empty chamber, Kane flexed his wrist tendons to retract the Sin Eater into the holster. At the same time he unclipped his Copperhead from the combat webbing, focusing his attention on what lay ahead of them in the passageway.

The Arab guard stepped out of the security booth, an autopistol in both hands. He sighted down the barrel and squeezed off a shot. The bullet went wild, but before he could adjust his aim, Grant aligned his skull before the sights of his Copperhead. The kill dot from the laser autotargeter shone like a pinpoint of blood against the dark olive of his forehead.

Grant fired only once. The back of the man's broke open in a slurry of bone chips, hair and a misting of blood. The Arab fell limply back inside the booth, and the Cerberus warriors raced past the security checkpoint toward the stainless-steel doors of the lift.

An ASP bolt sizzled past them, impacting on the wall beside the open lift doors, imprinting a plate-size scorch mark on the alloy. Brigid swiveled at the hips, firing a prolonged burst and bowling a Nephilim armored in silver-blue off his feet.

Suddenly, the doors of the elevator began sliding shut. Gritting his teeth, Kane increased his speed, running full-out, legs pumping. He quickly outdistanced his companions, his lungs straining to pull in enough air.

He reached the pair of panels when a little over two feet separated them. Not really thinking, moving only on impulse, he slammed his Copperhead lengthwise between the doors, jamming them open. He slid into the lift, gesturing frantically toward his friends. A cluster of Nephilim jogged down the corridor behind them, trailing by a score of yards. They weren't able to aim their ASP emitters accurately while running.

One by one, Shizuka, Brigid and Grant squeezed under the Copperhead and between the edges of the two door panels. The fit was a tight one for Grant and he struggled and wriggled, uttering a breathless obscenity. Under other circumstances, the sight would have made Kane grin.

Securing a fistful of combat webbing, Kane hauled on the big man, yanking him into the elevator. Without hesitation, Brigid reached out and slammed the frame of the subgun with the heel of her right hand. The Copperhead popped out from between the doors and clattered loudly on the floor of the corridor.

Before the panels sealed, a globe of seething plasma blazed between them and impacted against the far wall with a flare of flame and a spurt of smoke. Everyone ducked, but the doors thudded shut and the elevator began to ascend. Faces damp with perspiration, panting heavily, the Cerberus warriors checked over their weapons.

"What's the damn plan?" Grant grated, reattaching his Copperhead to its clip and unholstering his Sin Eater.

"Our options are pretty limited," Brigid said grimly. She shifted the straps of the carrying case of the interphaser. "All we can do is make our way back to the canyon and the vortex point in the temple."

Grant snorted. "That's all? Let's worry about getting out of this elevator."

Brigid nodded. "Best bet is to do a Butch and Sundance."

Kane and Grant didn't request a clarification. The three people had watched the old movie together several years before.

"Too bad the interphaser doesn't work like a portable mat-trans," Kane commented with a sour half grin. "Just punch a couple of buttons, and hey, presto, we're beamed back home."

Brigid didn't return his grin. "If you're wishing for that, why not just wish that it could whisk us to a parallel reality?"

Shizuka crossed her blades before her, forming an X. She murmured tensely, "*Yabaiyo.*"

"What's that mean?" Grant inquired.

Shizuka's full lips twitched with a bitter smile. "You don't want to know."

The elevator platform continued to rise so smoothly that when the bottom edges of the wall tapestries appeared, it almost looked as if they were stretching downward.

"I assume there's a welcoming committee waiting for us," Brigid said dryly.

"I assume the same thing," Kane replied, dipping

into his war bag and bringing out a cylindrical concussion grenade of the Alsatex series, a flash-bang developed by the military two centuries ago for crowd control. "Let's get ourselves set."

"Set," Grant and Brigid responded in unison, hefting their weapons.

Kane tweaked out the pin of the flash-bang, keeping the striker depressed with his fingers. "Everybody close their eyes. Once I toss it and it goes off, we need to start running and not stop."

The elevator bumped to a gentle stop and the brass doors began sliding apart. Kane lobbed the metal-shelled grenade underhanded between them. It struck the floor and bounced. The four people squeezed their eyes shut just as the Alsatex detonated with an eardrum-compressing *bang!* The eruption of white light was so intense it registered even through their eyelids.

While the echoes of the explosion still rang in the air as if someone had pounded a bass guitar with a sledgehammer, Kane, Grant, Brigid and Shizuka kicked themselves into headlong sprints. They leaped over two whimpering Arabs writhing on the floor, hands clapped over their eyes.

Kane took the point, running low and running fast. His speed saved him. A third Arab, whose eyes were dazzled but not blinded, triggered a burst from a subgun. Bounding to one side, Kane ducked beneath the swarm of slugs as they dug long gouges in the wall. Kane shot the man down with a triburst from his Sin Eater. Then he heard a familiar crack-sizzle.

An ASP bolt flashed down the passageway and Kane dropped flat, painfully banging his elbows and knees. He heard a small, hand-clapping explosion behind him, then Shizuka cried out in surprise. Instinctively, he twisted his head.

He saw Shizuka, her back against the wall, slowly sliding toward the floor. She still held her swords crossed over a smoldering patch on her midsection. She kept her blades in place as Brigid grabbed her by the upper arms, easing her down into a sitting position.

Spinning toward her, Grant put all the power of his lungs into an anguished, wordless bellow that echoed down the corridor.

A cold fist clenching around his heart, Kane rose and made a move to join his friends but he turned his attention and pistol bore on the lean figure silhouetted at the end of the passageway.

The deep voice of Overlord Marduk floated to him. "Please oblige me by *not* surrendering, Kane."

The overlord stood with his back to the cavern opening, his armored body outlined against the pallor of the diffuse sunlight. He looked implacable, an ASP emitter trained directly on Kane.

Gritting his teeth so hard he heard them squeak, Kane glanced over his shoulder at Grant and Brigid tending to Shizuka. Brigid's eyes were jade bright in the shocklingly pale mask of her face. The reek of scorched cloth and seared flesh bit into his nostrils.

"You have to do it," Brigid whispered hoarsely. "We don't have a choice."

Throat constricting, Kane cut his eyes toward Marduk, sighting down the Sin Eater, then back toward Brigid. He said, "Baptiste—"

"Do it!"Grant roared savagely as Shizuka sagged within the cradle of his arms. The *katana* and *tanto* blades fell from her hands, chiming dully against the floor. "*Do it!*"

Chapter 20

The steel walls of the room were windowless. The narrow door was barred and cross braced. Grant stood before it, gripping the rods of metal in his big fists, straining, twisting and tugging. Brigid leaned against the far wall, arms folded over her breasts, eyes full of worry. Kane sat on the floor, hands on his knees, and struggled to control his rage.

He judged the cell to be about twelve feet wide and fifteen feet long. There was no cot or pallet to sit on, so he had to settle for the hard stone floor. The floor was obviously old, worn smooth by countless feet in an area by the door. On the other side of the bars there was nothing to see but semidarkness. Weak illumination was provided by a small neon strip inset into the ceiling.

Uttering a snarl of frustration, Grant rattled the bars and spun to glare at the steel walls, then at Brigid and finally at Kane. "What are we going to do?"

Kane assumed the question was rhetorical, so he didn't respond, but Brigid said soothingly, "Locking us up is a hopeful sign. They don't intend to kill us just yet."

Grant glowered at her. "There's the torture first."

"Try to relax," Kane said. "There's nothing we can do."

"Until Marduk decides he's let you twist in the wind long enough," Grant argued. "He hates your guts."

"He hates yours, too," Kane shot back defensively. He glanced at Brigid. "And yours."

"Yours most of all," she replied casually, combing her fingers through her tangled mane of hair. "Just accept it."

Kane had and did. As Baron Cobalt, Marduk had suffered a number of indignities and humiliations due to Kane and swore years ago he would one day arrange a reckoning.

Grant returned his attention to the bars, throwing all of his weight and considerable upper-body strength against them. He pulled, heaved and wrenched with no result other than sweat rivered from his pores.

Conversationally, Kane remarked, "This is a pretty low tech hoosegow for an advanced race like the Annunaki. But I guess you can't really improve over steel walls and iron bars."

Brigid smiled wryly. "I don't think enlightened penal theory was one of the Annunaki's favorite fields of research."

Grant growled in frustration, but continued to pull at the bars. Brigid and Kane exchanged sour glances and exasperated head shakes.

After surrendering to Marduk, the Cerberus warriors had been disarmed by the Nephilim. Lilitu ordered Shizuka to be taken to a facility so her injuries could be treated. Only the promise that she was being tended to kept Grant from attacking the overlords and Nephilim bare-handed.

Although they hadn't been mistreated, Kane's thirst had grown from the intense to the painful. It felt as if the dry desert air had sucked every drop of moisture from his body.

Grant released the bars, leaning against them wearily. "I shouldn't have believed anything Lilitu said. I should have broken her fucking neck when I had the chance."

"I think you can take her at her word that she'll do what she can to save Shizuka's life," Brigid replied calmly.

Kane angled a questioning eyebrow at her. "What makes you think that?"

"It's to her benefit."

Grant turned around to face her. "How so?"

"She threatened to attack New Edo and Cerberus if we didn't agree to her terms, but instead we went on the offensive and tried to escape, right?"

"Right," Kane drawled. "Me and Grant were there, remember?"

Musingly, Grant said, "So you figure that Lilitu will save Shizuka so she can use her as a hostage, promising to release her once we come back from Agartha with Ninlil?"

Brigid nodded. "Exactly."

Kane shifted position on the floor. "Why does Lilitu think Balam will give up the baby to us?"

"She doesn't care one way or the other if Balam gives her up," Brigid stated grimly. "I would imagine she prefers him dead at this juncture…one less wild card to factor in, one less reminder of the time the Annunaki's children turned on them."

In a low tone, Grant said, "They'll be taking us out of here eventually. It would be nice to have some kind of plan before then."

"I don't think jumping the Nephilim is a sound one," Kane said, pushing himself to his feet.

"Neither do I," Brigid agreed. "We don't have the element of surprise."

"What the hell do we have?" Grant demanded harshly.

"We'll have to let the overlords think we'll do what they want."

Grant's brow creased. "If it means saving Shizuka, then we'll do it."

Kane stared at his partner in disbelief. "You're not serious."

Grant met his stare, unblinking and defiant. "Why wouldn't I be?"

Before Kane or Brigid could respond, they heard the quick scuff of footfalls in the passageway outside the cell.

"Here we go," Brigid whispered, pressing herself against the wall.

Grant turned to gaze out into the gloom. "That doesn't sound like the pitter-patter of Nephilim feet."

"No," replied the brusque voice of Rhea. "They sound like my feet."

The hybrid woman appeared at the door, expression and bearing very grave. "Are you well?"

"I hope you've brought us something to drink," Kane said. "We're parched."

Rhea did not address his comment. "My sister has sent me to fetch you."

Brigid's eyebrows rose. "Only you? Why?"

"Lilitu seems to think that whenever you are faced with threats of physical violence, you invariably react with violence yourself…the exact opposite of the way she thinks you should. So she assigned me this task, to come to you, unarmed."

Her gaze flitted to Grant. "Lilitu wants you to know that if you wish to see the woman you call Shizuka again, you will cooperate with me."

Grant nodded. "Of course."

Rhea produced a cylindrical metal key from the breast pocket of her bodysuit and inserted it into the lock. Tumblers clicked and she pulled the door open, swinging it wide.

Grant took a swift forward step, his right hand stabbing out and closing around the slender column of her throat. She gasped loudly, her mouth opening and closing like a landed fish.

"Why don't I bring you to Lilitu like this?" Grant rumbled. "Force her to trade your life for Shizuka's?"

"Grant—" Brigid said warningly.

"Answer me, you inhuman little bitch," Grant growled, leaning down and staring straight into her eyes.

Rhea gagged and fumbled at Grant's fingers. Her eyes were wide and full of fear. "She cares nothing for me," she said, her lips working. "Using me as a hostage, trading me for Shizuka wouldn't work. Believe me, I hate her as much as you do."

Kane stepped forward and said in a level voice, "Let her go, Grant. This won't get you, us or Shizuka anything but dead."

Grant's face remained as immobile as a mask carved from mahogany, then he opened his hand and Rhea stumbled backward, breathing hard, rubbing her throat, blinking repeatedly. The red imprint of his fingers showed against the pale flesh of her neck. The big man glanced behind him at Kane and Brigid and rasped, "Let's go."

For most of his adult life, Grant had been the ultimate Magistrate in attitude, behavior and thought processes. Over the past ninety-odd years, both the oligarchy of barons and the Mags that served them had taken on a fearful, almost legendary aspect. Both Grant and Kane had been part of that legend, cogs in a merciless machine. Although they had been through the dehumanizing cruelty of Magistrate training, they had somehow, almost miraculously, managed to retain their humanity.

However, when it served their purposes, the two

men could revert to the cold and cruel personae that
had characterized them as baronial enforcers.

Rhea went first, Grant falling into step behind her.
Kane gestured for Brigid to precede him out of the cell.
In a reversal of the usual procedure, he brought up the
rear. He walked slowly, knowing that it might be the
last walk he would ever take.

It surely seemed like the longest.

Chapter 21

A circular pit was inset into the stone floor, fifteen feet in diameter and surrounded by an raised metal rim upon which a confusing pattern of glyphs were inscribed. Within the pit, from wall to wall, amber mist seemed to coil, but it was like a dim veil of frozen, semitransparent gold.

Deep within it, the pale naked figure of Shizuka floated suspended, her black hair surrounding her face like a cloud. The livid edges of the raw wound marring her midriff seemed to undulate and ripple.

"She is sedated," Lilitu said. "I promise you she is not in pain."

Grant, Brigid and Kane stared down into the pit without speaking. None of them made contact with each other or with Lilitu, Ishkur and Utu, who stood nearby. Rhea lingered by the door.

At length, Brigid prodded the metal ring surrounding the pit with the toe of her boot and said, "This is Danaan technology. I can tell by the markings."

Utu and Ishkur snorted simultaneously. "What difference does that make?" Ishkur demanded.

"Not much, I suppose," Brigid admitted. "Just

making an observation. I imagine this device served as the foundation for the Celtic legends about the Cauldron of Bran, also known as the Chalice of Rebirth."

"Yes," Utu said. "It has been a boon to my people for many millennia."

Kane glanced at Utu's scarred features and laughed tauntingly. "You could've fooled me."

Utu was not offended. Fingering his face, he replied, "You should have seen me before I entered the chalice. As it was, it was almost too late to save me at all. Time is a factor."

"The same cannot be said for your beloved Shizuka," Lilitu interjected. "She will make a full recovery."

Grant did not remove his gaze from the pit. "Am I supposed to thank you for that?"

"You should," Lilitu countered waspishly. "I did not ask her to come here. She accompanied you of her own accord, hoping to exact a measure of revenge."

"How do you know that?" Kane asked suspiciously.

"Because it's what I would have done." Her eyes glinted in sudden anger. "She killed several of my Nephilim. You should all be grateful that I am trying to save her life instead of ending it."

"How does this thing work?" Grant demanded.

"A blending of scientific disciplines," Ishkur answered autocratically. "You would not understand them."

"Nanotechnology is probably the basis," Brigid remarked.

When none of the overlords responded, Kane figured Brigid's casual assessment was the correct one. In many ways, the Tuatha de Danaan had been technologically superior to the Annunaki.

A thousand years after the Flood, the Tuatha de Danaan arrived on Earth. Humanoid but not human, they were an aristocratic race of scientists, poets and warriors and they made fertile, isolated Ireland their home.

They had met the representatives of the Annunaki during their explorations and struck a pact with them to watch over humanity until the Niburuans returned.

The Danaan took the tribes living in Ireland under their protection and taught them many secrets of art, architecture and mathematics. The essence of Danaan science stemmed from music—the controlled manipulation of sound waves—and this became recorded in legend as the "music of the spheres."

"I'm guessing that the chalice introduces repair nanomachines into the body," Brigid went on, "not too different from the so-called hydra rings we came across a while back. A stasis field—again similar to tech we've encountered before—stabilizes her metabolism while the repairs are being conducted."

Smiling, Kane glanced over at Brigid, then around the antiseptically simple room. Rhea had led them to it through a honeycomb of corridors and chambers. Everywhere there was an ominous sense of intense, hurried activity. They glimpsed people in bodysuits at work in laboratories, bent over mysterious machines.

Nephilim with the ASP emitters and Arabs with subguns marched everywhere

"You seem to be pushing to meet a timetable," Kane said to Lilitu.

She nodded. "We are ready for the final phase."

"Phase of what?" Brigid asked.

A gravelly voice boomed from behind them. "For you to complete your part of our transaction."

Overlord Marduk strode into the chamber, the glow from the chalice pit casting highlights on his armor. Grant raised his gaze from Shizuka and although his face was expressionless, both Kane and Brigid realized he was struggling to tamp down the mad urge to leap at Marduk's throat.

"If not for you," Grant intoned, "we wouldn't be transacting anything."

"Of course," Marduk retorted indifferently. "However, I would much prefer to transact the final piece of business we have between us….with yours and Kane's traitorous hearts within my hands."

To illustrate his point, he extended both fists, working the fingers and knuckles as if he were crushing eggshells.

Kane favored Marduk with a smile of feigned innocence. "There are two kinds of traitors. The first kind lies to and betrays people who trusted him. The second kind of traitor is someone who betrays his own instincts, who violates what his heart and reason tells him is the truth."

He paused meaningfully and his innocent smile

twisted into one of contempt. "As Baron Cobalt you were the first kind and tried to make me and my friends the second. You didn't succeed then, and you won't succeed now."

Marduk glowered at him. "Kane, you are alive only because we have a use for you. I have not forgotten the way you insulted and abused me all those years ago. There will be a suitable punishment—I can promise you that."

Kane sighed as if bored. "Yeah, yeah. Sing a new song, will you?"

He turned toward Lilitu. "Is there anything to drink in this joint?"

Lilitu jerked her head toward Rhea. "If you would be so kind as to fetch refreshments for our guests?"

Rhea hesitated, seeming to be on the verge of arguing, and then she strode swiftly across the medical facility.

"We should not have to remind you that if you do not go to Agartha and return with Ninlil, Shizuka will not be released from our custody," Utu said.

Grant said flatly, "No, I don't need to be reminded. But I'm not going anywhere without her."

Ishkur opened his mouth to voice an objection, but Grant raised his voice. "You can kill me, but I'm not leaving Shizuka. It's not debatable."

Lilitu shrugged. "That is fine with me. Two hostages are always better than one. Kane, Brigid Baptiste and a couple of my own handpicked operatives will undertake the mission. You are more than welcome to remain here, Grant."

Kane and Brigid stared incredulously, first at Grant then at Lilitu. Marduk chuckled, making a sound like iron filings being shaken in a tin can. "Oh, this gets better and better."

Striving for a logical, reasonable tone, Brigid said, "Grant, you know if you stay here, you'll be playing right into the overlords' hands and forcing our own."

"I don't care," he replied, his voice so thick with anger it was an animal's guttural growl. "Shizuka is in there because of *me*. It's my fault. I'm not going to leave her alone with these bastards. Don't waste your time or your breath trying to argue me out of it."

"On the other hand," Kane ventured, "if we just flat-out refuse to go at all—"

"Then all of us are dead," Grant broke in. "It's a rotten choice and I'm sorry you have to make it. But I've already made mine."

In a calmer tone, he added, "Besides, you'll think of something. You always do."

Rhea cleared her throat. When Kane turned toward her, she pressed a large cold goblet into his hands. He inspected the clear liquid suspiciously. "What is it?"

"Taste it and find out," Lilitu said teasingly.

Lifting the cup to his lips, Kane sipped experimentally. It was water, pure cold water. He took three grateful swallows and handed it over to Brigid. "It's just water," he told her.

Brigid sniffed it, then drank deeply and passed it over to Grant, who drained off the rest.

"If all of you have agreed that staying alive is pre-

ferable to being dead," Lilitu said, "you'll be shown to
your guest quarters. You can rest while the final preparations are made."

"'Guest quarters,'" Brigid repeated wryly. "That's
a cute euphemism for a cell."

"Not a cell at all," Lilitu replied, exchanging
knowing smiles with the other overlords. "Not at all."

Kane's stomach churned uneasily, but he said
nothing, not even when Grant folded his arms over his
chest and refused to move from the side of the pit. For
a long, stretched-out tick of time, the two men locked
eyes.

Then Grant touched his right index finger to his
nose and snapped it away in the wry one-percent
salute. It was a private gesture he and Kane had developed during their years as hard-contact Magistrates
and reserved for high-risk undertakings with small
ratios of success. Their half-serious belief was that
ninety-nine percent of things that went awry could be
predicted and compensated for in advance. But there
was always a one-percent margin of error, and playing
against that percentage could have lethal consequences.

Kane returned the salute and turned away.

Two Nephilim escorted Kane and Brigid to an
elevator that whisked them downward. They were
shown to separate rooms at opposite ends of a long
corridor. By the time Kane entered the chamber
assigned to him, drowsiness washed over him in
waves. He sank down on a soft divan covered with silk

and brocade. The effort to swallow a yawn made his ears pop, and his eyes began to water.

Kane suddenly realized what was happening and he snarled, forcing himself to his feet, or at least that was what he thought he made his body do. He was only dimly aware of falling backward, deeply asleep before his head hit the cushioned surface of the divan.

A SMOOTH, SOFT WARMTH like silk slid across his chest, caressing his thighs, lightly touching his groin. He struggled up out of the blackness. His head ached abominably but he forced his eyes open.

Kane felt a firm body press against his, all rustling silk, and he smelled the slightly acrid tang of perfume, the scent of a woman. A voice whispered above him, "Is he not beautiful? For an apeling, that is."

Another feminine voice murmured something indistinct, either a wordless sound of agreement or an endearment. Narrowing his eyes, Kane squinted through the gloom and made out the outline of a woman standing above him. A second woman lay atop him, the gem-hard points of her breasts pressing into his chest. With a distant sense of shock, he realized he was completely naked.

"The beautiful Kane," came the breathy whisper again, and he recognized her voice as that of Lilitu. It held a hard, cold edge of sarcasm. "He became a legend among your kind, little sister…breeding with a hundred of them, planting his seed in their bellies, all for naught. Perhaps this time will be different."

Kane knew what she referred to and his skin prickled with both dread and the memories of humiliation when he had been sentenced by Baron Cobalt to what amounted to stud service.

Although Kane was biologically superior, he knew the main reason he had been chosen to impregnate the female hybrids was simply due to the fact male hybrids were incapable of engaging in conventional acts of procreation, at least physically. Their organs of reproduction were so underdeveloped as to be vestigial.

The familiar odor of the aphrodisiac gel tickled his nostrils, and he felt a surge of nausea. Kane struggled on the divan, but his arms were pulled above his head, and he could only dimly feel his hands at the end of them. When he tried to move them, he realized he was chained to a post at the head of the divan, his ankles cuffed, legs spread apart. Soft flesh moved in a steady rhythm against him.

Kane's thought processes flowed sluggishly, like half-frozen mud. By degrees, he realized Rhea lay atop him, nuzzling his ear and face with her lips. Lilitu stood at the bedside, draped in a filmy silk gown.

"You drugged me," he said hoarsely.

"Yes," Lilitu said. "I apologize for the headache, but it will soon pass."

"Why?"

Suddenly he felt his testicles being cupped, his scrotum tickled by Lilitu's long nails. "You will make love to Rhea."

"Not a chance."

Lilitu chuckled patronizingly. "It's not like you have a choice. You're already aroused. You've been exposed to the same kind of aphrodisiac that was used on you in Area 51. Can't you feel it?"

Kane felt the heat spreading over his groin, but his mind was detached from his body. Lilitu leaned over him, her molten eyes mocking him, amused.

Rhea kissed his lips and then whispered in his ear, "This is not my doing.

"I don't care," he growled, fighting the artificial excitation of the gel.

Rhea sat up, straddling his pelvis. By the dim artificial light, he saw her slim, pale body with its wispy suggestion of silk threads between the juncture of her thighs. Her breasts were small, but very well formed with a great deal of point.

Kane's respiration deepened, his pulse quickening, his blood beginning to burn with a flame that first warmed, then threatened to scorch his nervous system and consume his reason. He knew from bitter experience fighting the effects of the aphrodisiac was futile. In the past, the best he'd ever been able to achieve was a temporary balance between a horrified realization that his body's reactions were out of his conscious control and primordial lust. Always lust won out over horror.

"Do it, little sister," Lilitu urged, breathing rapidly, her eyes narrowed with frustrated passion. "Do it!"

Rhea suddenly climbed off Kane and stood naked beside the divan, staring at Lilitu defiantly. She hugged herself. "No. I will not debase myself for your entertainment."

Lilitu's thin lips worked, as if she intended to spit at Rhea, then she slapped her, the impact of flesh against flesh sounding as loud as a gunshot.

"You half-breed fool!" she spat. "You cannot even manage one arrogant apeling! How can you manage an empire?"

Her words awoke sudden suspicion in Kane's mind, even in its clouded state. Metal jingled and Lilitu brandished a small ring of keys to the locks that chained him to the bed. She tossed the ring contemptuously onto his bare stomach. "Free him, then," she said contemptuously. "Then report back to me. You and Ibrahim leave at dawn."

With a rustle of silk, Lilitu whirled and stalked out of the room. Rhea picked up the keys and opened the lock that held Kane's hands to the post at the head of the bed.

He sat up, snatching the keyring from her fingers and unlocked the shackles around his ankles.

"I'm sorry," she said softly, her big eyes haunted. "I had no choice."

"I hear that a lot from you," he growled, standing up naked in the dark room. He was covered with sweat. "What about Brigid and Grant?"

Rhea averted her gaze from his erection. "Your friends are fine. Sleeping."

He looked around for his clothes and found his backpack. "What the hell was all this about?"

"Lilitu hates you and she hates me." Rhea shook her

head helplessly. "She wanted to rape us...by proxy. But I diluted the aphrodisiac."

Kane shuddered. "I understand why she hates me. I can't figure out what she has against you."

Rhea sighed. "I think I'm a reminder of what she once was."

"Then why doesn't she just kill you?" Kane asked bluntly.

"I don't know." The hybrid woman spoke in such a resigned way, Kane instantly suspected that she did know. Rather than press her further, he asked, "What did she mean about you and Ibrahim leaving at dawn?"

Rhea lifted her bare shoulders in a shrug. "We're going with you to Agartha, to make certain you do as you're told."

"Let me guess," Kane shot back, opening his pack. "You have no choice."

"No," Rhea replied, an edge entering her voice. "And neither do you."

Kane smiled, but it was without warmth or humor. "That remains to be seen, little sister."

Chapter 22

A glowing, phosphorescent lotus blossom sprouted from the base of the interphaser. Skeins of blue-white witch fire streaked along the grooves and convolutions carved into the stone slab at their feet. The light pulsed like the lifeblood in a circulatory system. The entire inscribed surface of the geodetic marker was laced with a webwork of dancing light.

The veil of light expanded from the apex of the interphaser, stretching outward in wavering parabola, giving the illusion of a Chinese hand fan spreading wide, with the pyramidion acting as the centerpiece. Then the aurora of the light disappeared into the interphaser, as if it were liquid and had flowed back into it.

It took a few seconds for their eyes to adjust, and for them to regain their balance. Kane tried not to move until the spasm of vertigo faded. When his vision cleared, he saw the grayish sky above him. It was almost dawn. A cold wind blew dust over him and sighed among the columns of the ancient ruins leaning all about.

Ibrahim el-Amid swallowed hard, shifted his feet and said, "This does not look like Tibet. This looks like—"

"Egypt?" Brigid Baptiste inquired casually.

"Yes." The Arab's one eye narrowed in sudden alarm. He reached for his subgun.

The stiffened edge of Brigid's right hand chopped across the side of the man's throat with a swift, deadly impact. His eye went wide and blank. Ibrahim el-Amid uttered a gurgling noise and toppled sideways, off the stone geodetic marker to the sand heaped at the base of the plinth.

Massaging the side of her hand and wincing, Brigid turned toward the interphaser resting at the center of the carved rock slab. Rhea stepped back from her, her face composed but eyes glinting in sudden fear of the tall, sunset-haired woman.

In a faint voice, full of wonder, she said, "You deceived Lilitu. How?"

"We reset the interphaser coordinates," Kane said. "For Egypt, not Tibet. There's no way she could've known."

Kneeling, Brigid touched the interphaser's inset activation toggles on the miniature keypad. "I'm resetting it again, for Cerberus…just in case we have to phase out of here in a hurry."

Kane nodded approvingly. "Good."

Even after all the phase transits he had made, Kane still wasn't sure how the interphaser did what it did, but the fact it functioned at all never failed to amaze him.

When making transits to and from the Cerberus redoubt, they always used the mat-trans chamber as the origin point because it could be hermetically sealed. The interphaser's targeting computer had been programmed with the precise coordinates of the mat-trans unit as Destination Zero. A touch of a single key on the interphaser's control pad would automatically return the device to the jump chamber, but sometimes the phase harmonics needed to be fine-tuned. The adjustments were normally within Brigid's purview.

Unlike the mat-trans gateway jumps, phasing along a hyperdimensional conduit was more akin to stepping from one room into another—if the rooms were thousands of miles apart.

Kane leaped lightly down from the geodetic marker and checked Ibrahim el-Amid's pulse. The man's swarthy face was locked in a contorted rictus of surprise and pain, his head held at an unnaturally stiff angle.

Brigid, packing away the interphaser, asked, "How is he?"

"He appears to have died suddenly."

Brigid's motions faltered, but only for a second. Someone who didn't know her would not have noticed. She stood up, sliding her arms through the straps of the carrying case. She stepped down on the opposite side of where the Arab's body lay sprawled. Kane took the dead man's weapons, which consisted of a pair of Copperheads with the extended magazines and two autopistols that he identified as Glocks. He guessed they came from the armory at Beausoleil ville.

Rhea jumped down, stumbling slightly in the soft sand. "Isn't Egypt the kingdom of Enlil?"

"It is," Brigid said quietly.

"Where are we in Egypt exactly?" Kane asked, handing her a Copperhead.

She frowned, looking at the subgun. "I'll have to get outside to get a clear sextant reading before I can tell you that."

She glanced around. "As it is, I'd guess we're in the central nave of an ancient temple. Looks like it's been some excavation going on recently."

They stood within ruins spread over a sunken depression. In the early-morning light, the crumbling walls and fallen pillars were like vague dreams rising from the dust of the past. A few stone blocks still showed the chiseled profiles of ancient pharaohs, but the broken columns had long ago been scoured of surface markings. Overhead arched the broken stretches of crenellated walls.

The three people strode toward a flight of shallow steps, guarded on either side by stone sphinxes. The gloomy vastness of the temple extended in all directions, the details dimmed by shadows and drifted sand.

Brigid and Kane wore high-necked, midnight-colored shadow suits that absorbed light the way a sponge absorbed water. Although the material of the formfitting garments resembled black doeskin, and didn't appear as if it would offer protection from flea bites, the shadow suits were impervious to most wavelengths of radiation.

Ever since the Cerberus warriors had found the suits in Redoubt Yankee on Thunder Isle, the garments had proved their worth and their superiority to standard polycarbonate Magistrate armor, if for no other reason than their internal subsystems.

Manufactured with a technique known in predark days as electrospin lacing, the electrically charged polymer particles formed a dense web of formfitting fibers. Composed of a complicated weave of spider silk, Monocrys and Spectra fabrics, the garments were essentially a single-crystal, metallic microfiber with a very dense molecular structure.

The outer Monocrys sheathing went opaque when exposed to radiation, and the Kevlar and Spectra layers provided protection against blunt trauma. The spider silk allowed flexibility, but it traded protection from firearms for freedom of movement. The suits were climate-controlled for environments up to highs of 150 degrees and lows as cold as -10 degrees Fahrenheit. Flat, square ammo pouches were attached to the small of their backs by Velcro tabs.

"Are you hoping to strike a deal with Enlil?" Rhea asked.

Kane shrugged. "We're hoping to find a way out of this that doesn't involve abducting a baby. If that means cutting a deal with the devil, then we cut the deal."

Turning toward Rhea, Brigid asked, "Did Lilitu mention to you about the factionalizing among the Supreme Council?"

Rhea shook her head. "Not really, but I definitely received the impression that overlords Marduk, Zu,

Utu and Ishkur have personal issues with Enlil that have little to do with anything other than old grudges."

Kane took the point as he carefully climbed the steps. "What does Ishkur have against Enlil?"

Brigid frowned. "According to Sumerian myth, Ishkur was believed to be a storm god, much like Enlil, which decreased Ishkur's distinctiveness in Mesopotamia. He sometimes appeared as the assistant to Enlil. In very old texts, he was believed to be the brother of both Utu and Shamash. His consort in early Sumerian and later Assyrian texts was Shala, a goddess of grain, who is also sometimes associated with the god Dagon."

Kane grunted. "Pretty convoluted family history. Is Shala another name for Lilitu?"

"No, I don't think so."

Brigid paused and added, "If Enlil is around, we can always ask him."

"If he is," Kane replied, "he ought to know we're here."

"Let's hope he's more curious than homicidal about us."

The steps were hewed of naked rock. In the dry air, no mold or moss or lichen grew on the edges of the risers to make their footing unsafe. The three people kept close to the inner wall of the stairwell as they climbed.

"Why did Enlil occupy Egypt?" Rhea asked.

"As far as we know," Brigid explained, "he was worshiped here in ancient times as Set."

"Set?" Rhea echoed.

"Yes, a serpent god…or demon. He was very influential during the Third Dynasty reign of Djoser. Apparently Djoser was Enlil's favorite puppet pharaoh. Djoser unified the Upper and Lower kingdoms of Egypt and he also sent several military expeditions to the Sinai Peninsula, during which the local inhabitants were enslaved and forced to mine for valuable minerals like turquoise and copper."

"That sounds like Enlil's MO," Kane observed sourly.

"It does, indeed," Rhea agreed.

"We speculate that originally the Great Sphinx was built in the image of Set," Brigid continued, "but when his cult fell out of favor, the face was resculpted to that of Horus, the sun god. Apparently, Enlil had made the Sphinx his Egyptian vacation home for at least a century, and we know he reoccupied the place over the last couple of years."

Kane glanced over his shoulder at Rhea as they reached the top of the stairs.

"We found the coordinates for the local vortex node over a year ago."

They stepped out of the entryway into a vista of bleak dunes. The only signs of movement came from thin plumes of sand blown hissing by the dawn wind.

"What makes you think we're anywhere close to Enlil's reclaimed territory?" Rhea asked.

Kane stepped out from beneath the overhang, looking in all directions. When he glanced behind him, he did a double take. His gaze remained fixed. "That tells me something," he said quietly.

Rhea and Brigid joined him, looking up and around. A glossy jet-black pillar rose from a heap of rubble. The upper half was sculpted into the likeness of a frowning Annunaki. A dead man hung head down from the statue's elongated neck. A chain bound his crossed feet at the ankles, and he had been suspended there for a very long time.

The desert climate had dried every drop of moisture from his naked body, leaving it in the condition of shrunken, creased leather. There was only a mummified semblance left of his features. The lips were peeled back over his discolored teeth. Part of the scalp was missing, showing bare bone.

"What is this?" Rhea whispered in horror.

In a remarkably steady voice, Brigid said, "I'd say it's a sort of no-trespassing sign."

"Which indicates to me," Kane remarked, turning away, "that we must be in Enlil's territory."

"Why would he want to claim this region?" Rhea asked. "There's nothing here."

"In which case," Brigid replied, "it's not that different from the rest of the planet."

Kane brought a compact pair of ruby-lensed binoculars to his eyes. He swept them over the gently rolling, sandy terrain, then fixed them on a sprawling jumble of debris less than half a mile to the southeast. Even in the uncertain light of dawn, the binoculars brought into sharp relief the broken buildings jutting from the desert floor and shattered colors scattered across the parched ground.

He had no idea if the ruins dated back to ancient times or were of a more modern vintage. It was often hard to differentiate. Two centuries after the nuke-caust, the effects that still lingered were a subtle, underlying texture to a world struggling to heal itself. Ruins were the grim, constant remainders to humanity to never again take the permanence of the earth for granted.

Unpredictable and violent weather patterns were another such reminder, typified by chem storms, showers of acid-tainted rain that could scorch the flesh off any mammal caught in the open. They were linger-ing examples of the freakish weather effects common after the holocaust and the nuclear winter.

Passing the binoculars to Brigid, Kane pointed out the ruins. "Those look to be the best bet."

Brigid squinted through the eyepieces. "Best bet for what?"

"If nothing else, to find another no-trespassing sign."

"I don't think that will be necessary," Rhea said lowly. "I believe we've drawn some attention."

The back of Kane's neck flushed cold at her tone. He and Brigid turned in the direction Rhea stared. He made an instinctive grab for the Copperhead hanging from his combat webbing, but Brigid laid a restrain-ing hand on his forearm.

A dozen gold-armored Nephilim scowled at them

from the shadow cast by a high sand drift. They were as motionless as sculptured monoliths dipped in gold leaf. All of them had their ASP emitters trained on the three people.

"Great," Kane muttered. "A patrol."

"At least we know we're in the right place," Brigid replied softly.

"Great," Kane said again.

A glowering Nephilim took a slow, menacing step forward. "You," he announced in a flat baritone, "will come with us."

"That," Kane retorted just as flatly, "is pretty much the whole idea."

Chapter 23

Lakesh did not even glance at the indicator lights of the huge Mercator relief map when he walked into the command center. His attention was focused on the medical monitor.

The control center was surprisingly well manned, particularly for nearly midnight, but inasmuch as the complex was the brain of the redoubt, it naturally drew personnel from all quarters. Most of the people sitting at the various stations were émigrés from the Manitius Moon base—Mariah Falk, Brewster Philboyd and two men he knew only as Reynolds and Conrad. The only long-term Cerberus staff member he saw was Reba DeFore, the installation's resident medic.

Her presence at the biolink monitoring station surprised Lakesh. A stocky, buxom woman in her midthirties, DeFore always wore her ash-blond hair pulled back from her face, intricately braided at the back of her head. Its color contrasted starkly with the deep bronze of her skin and her dark brown eyes.

"These aren't your usual stomping grounds, Doctor," Lakesh said as he came to her side.

"When I heard that the transponder link with the

away team had been reestablished," she said darkly, "I wanted to check their vitals myself."

DeFore's fingers tapped a sequence into the keyboard, calling up the triangulation tracking program. A topographical map flashed onto the monitor screen, superimposing itself over two icons. The little symbols inched across the computer-generated terrain. The names *Kane* and *Baptiste* glowed beneath the icons.

"Just Kane and Brigid," Lakesh said, trying to tamp down the rising sense of dread.

"The signatures of the entire away team disappeared a few hours ago," DeFore reminded him. "Shortly after they arrived in the Sinai. I'm going to assume that Grant and Shizuka are still alive but their transponder signals are blocked."

"It's happened before," Lakesh commented.

All the Cerberus personnel carried subcutaneous transponders. They were nonharmful radioactive chemicals that fit themselves into the human body and allowed the monitoring of heart rates, brain-wave patterns and blood counts. Based on organic nanotechnology developed by the Totality Concept's Overproject Excalibur, the transponders fed information through the Comsat relay satellite when personnel were out in the field.

The signal was relayed to the redoubt by the Comsat, one of the two satellites to which the installation was uplinked. The computer systems recorded every byte of data sent to the Comsat and directed it down to the redoubt's hidden antenna array. Sophisticated scanning filters combed through the telemetry using special human biological encoding.

The transponders were among the miracles of organic nanotechnology that had virtually disappeared after the nukecaust. Lakesh had managed to resurrect the technique and the technology from the tangled webs of twentieth century experimental medical procedures. Inasmuch as he had been born in 1952, he had an affinity for such things.

"They seem to be in good health," DeFore went on. "Slightly elevated blood pressure on Kane's part. Both of them show a degree of fatigue."

"Their current location?" Lakesh asked.

"Still in Egypt," DeFore stated matter-of-factly. "But now in the vicinity of Luxor. They've traveled several hundred miles since we last picked up their signatures."

Lakesh grunted. "Probably using a parallax point."

Mariah Falk turned in her chair to face them. "The situation can't be that urgent or they would've phased back here."

A former geologist from the Manitius Moon base, Mariah wasn't particularly young or particularly pretty, but she had an infectious smile and a relaxed, easy manner. Her short chestnut-brown hair was threaded with gray at the temples.

"Quite right." Lakesh smiled at her.

"We can't assume anything," DeFore said brusquely. "As far as we know, they're surrounded by an army of Nephilim and Lilitu could be holding them at gunpoint. We're not receiving real-time telemetry. We've got a ten-to-fifteen minute lag."

Philboyd swiveled around in his chair to regard her with a reproachful stare. "What are you getting at, Dr. Glass-Is-Half-Empty?"

DeFore didn't ask him the meaning of the salutation. Instead, she declared, "Anytime we have dealings with the overlords, we're always taking the chance of being outmaneuvered or at the very least, outgunned. Brigid, Grant and Kane are superior, but they're not superhuman."

"I don't recall anyone thinking that about them," Lakesh said stiffly. "No one is that childish."

DeFore frowned up at him. Lakesh matched the woman's frown with one of his own. Their relationship was often awkward, despite the fact she was one of his first recruits. The tension between them had grown more pronounced over the past few years, particularly after the rise of the overlords.

"We may look at them as the three heads of Cerberus," DeFore went on, as if Lakesh had not spoken, "ready to bite the bloody hell out of any hand raised against us, but they're flesh and blood. They're mortal."

Lakesh did not disagree with her, but it had always amazed him that three such contrasting personalities could work so well as a team. The three people were individually gifted. Most of what was important to people born in the late-twenty-second century came easily to Grant and Kane—survival skills, prevailing in the face of adversity and cunning against enemies. But they could also be reckless, prone to taking violent action before exploring other options.

On the other hand, Brigid was compulsively tidy and ordered, with a brilliant analytical mind. However, her clinical nature, the cool scientific detachment upon which she prided herself, sometimes blocked an understanding of the obvious human factor in any given situation.

Regardless of their different styles and attitudes, Kane, Grant and Brigid worked very well as a team, playing on one another's strengths rather than contributing to their individual weaknesses.

"Lilitu came to us," Philboyd argued. "Asking for *our* help, not the other way around."

DeFore stared at him with incredulous eyes, then shook her head in pity. "You didn't actually believe her?"

Philboyd flushed in either anger or shame. "You think I'm that goddamn gullible? Of course I didn't believe her. But I believe she's up to something that could have pretty adverse effects on us."

"I believe the same thing," Lakesh interjected. "And so did friends Kane, Grant and dearest Brigid. Although I disagreed with their choice, I understand that they thought the risk was worth finding out what Lilitu is planning."

"She's an alien," DeFore snapped. "How can anybody understand her thought processes?"

Lakesh shrugged. "She and her brethren are of extraterrestrial ancestry, definitely, but they are not alien, since they were born right here on earth."

DeFore snorted and returned her attention to the icons pulsing on the monitor screen. Although irritated with the medic, Lakesh couldn't really blame her for her skeptical attitude.

Hundreds of years before, when humanity dreamed of roaming the stars, speculation about the extraterrestrial life-forms they might encounter inevitably followed. The issue of interaction and communication with aliens had consumed a number of government think tanks for many decades.

As Lakesh and his colleagues discovered in the waning years of the twentieth century, all of the hypothesizing was nothing but a diversion, a smoke screen to hide the truth. Humankind's interaction with a nonhuman species had begun at the dawn of Earth's history. That relationship and communication had continued unbroken for thousands of years, cloaked by ritual, religion and mystical traditions.

Reba DeFore suddenly sat up straight in her chair. She husked out, "Oh, no…not again."

Lakesh leaned over her shoulder to gaze at the biolink monitor. Although his expression remained composed, he felt cold sweat gather at his hairline as first one and then the other icon vanished from the screen.

Chapter 24

Lakesh took the elevator down to the second level, walked along a short hallway and pushed through a set of swing double doors into the exercise area. He strode past weight machines, stationary bikes, stair-steppers and workout mats.

The small gymnasium had been built to provide the original inhabitants of Cerberus with a means of sweating off the stress of being confined for twenty-four hours a day in an isolated installation. After the nukecaust, just staying alive was as much exercise as they needed, so the equipment had largely lain unused until the formation of the Cerberus away teams the year before.

Following the steady creak-creak of metal cables, he found Domi hauling a weighted pulley system up and down with her arms. Hair damp with sweat, she single-mindedly repeated the motion. Not surprisingly, she was naked. She was always perfectly at ease in her nudity.

Lakesh tried to keep his eyes from dwelling on her compact, perfectly proportioned body. Before arriving at the redoubt, the girl hadn't been accustomed to wearing clothes unless circumstances demanded them, and then only the skimpiest concessions to weather, not modesty.

Born a feral child of the Outlands, she was always relaxed being naked in the company of others and if those others didn't share that comfort zone, she couldn't care less. Despite the scars marring the pearly perfection of her skin, particularly the one shaped like a starburst on her right shoulder, Domi was beautiful in the way a wild mustang was beautiful.

Her body was a liquid, symmetrical flow of curving lines, with small porcelain breasts rising to sharp nipples, and a flat, hard-muscled stomach extending to the flared shape of her hips. With droplets of perspiration sparkling on her arms and legs, her skin looked opaque, its luminosity heightened by an absence of color. Her eyes were closed, the lashes looking like pine needles dusted with snow.

Lakesh was loath to interrupt her, so he stayed quiet and just watched her for a few moments, aware of the foolish smile spreading over his face.

Lakesh had been fond of Domi since the day they first met, more than five years before. In the interim, during shared dangers and joys, that affection had grown to love. She had risked her life to save him when he was imprisoned in Cobaltville and was grievously wounded during the rescue. The starburst-shaped scar on her right shoulder was a lasting memento of the incident, when a Magistrate bullet had shattered her corticoid bone.

Lakesh had not been able to demonstrate his feelings for Domi until a couple of years before when he regained his youth—or least his enhanced middle age. It had been a great source of joy to him when he learned Domi reciprocated his feelings and had no inhibitions about expressing them, regardless of the bitterness she still harbored over her unrequited love for Grant. In any event, he had broken a fifty-year streak of celibacy with her and they repeated the actions of that first delirious night whenever the opportunity arose.

Yet he had felt compelled to keep his relationship with Domi a secret, and he wasn't sure why. At first he tried to convince himself it was concern over raising Grant's ire, but he knew that was simply a feeble excuse. With Grant's heart more or less pledged to Shizuka, the big man was too preoccupied with his attempts to make a new life with her to give the more covert—and intimate—activities among the redoubt personnel more than cursory attention.

At one point, when Domi accused him of being ashamed of their relationship, he had suddenly realized the true reasons he had kept their relationship a secret—he feared she would be swept up in the same karmic backlash that he had long feared would shatter him.

When the punishment had been averted, due he felt to Domi's devotion to him, he had made a rather noisy fanfare of announcing their relationship to one and all. Much to his chagrin, most of the people in the redoubt already knew about it. Or if they hadn't, they could not have cared less—Grant included, or so it seemed.

After watching Domi complete two more reps, he cleared his throat. Instantly, her eyes opened, her entire body instinctively tensing like a bowstring. Then she smiled and released her grips on the weights.

As they thudded down, she stepped away from the machine, flexing her fingers. "A hundred each arm," she said. "Got to keep in better shape now that I've got competition."

Lakesh chuckled shortly, understanding her reference to not only Sela Sinclair but to the ex-Mags who comprised the three away teams. She had worked tirelessly to earn their respect, something that could not be easily won because of her youth, her gender and her background as an outlander.

Handing her a towel, he said, "It's not a contest, darlingest one."

Domi dabbed at her sweat-slick face and her body. "Usually when somebody says that, it's because they just don't notice they're *in* the contest."

He reached for her. "Perceptive as usual."

They embraced and kissed and he felt his body responding to her naked proximity. A little over two years before, he had been an old man who could barely walk a hundred feet without pausing to catch his breath. Ever since that fateful day when his youth and vitality had been restored due to the introduction of cell-repair nanites into his body, he felt he was living in the dream world of all old men.

Holding her out at arm's length, he said, "I know you prefer to exercise while everyone else is off duty, but you're cheating yourself out of sleep."

Disengaging herself from his arms, Domi picked up a red T shirt and pulled it over her head. "Don't need as much as you. Don't have as many worries as you."

"Speaking of worries," Lakesh said gravely, "we lost the away team's transponder signals again. To be precise, we only had Kane's and Brigid's. Shizuka's and Grant's did not register."

In the process of tugging on a pair of khaki shorts, Domi paused to stare at him for a silent few seconds, then she shrugged. "That's exactly what I mean. Prove my point for me."

Lakesh narrowed his eyes. "What point?"

"Brigid, Grant and Kane always go out into the field. You always worry about them, like mother hen, drive everybody crazy with your worrying. And they always come back."

Lakesh experienced a surge of annoyance but he realized the girl spoke the truth. Despite the frequent disagreements and arguments among them, he felt that Kane, Brigid and Grant were his family. In most ways, the exiles of the Cerberus redoubt enjoyed emotional bonds that were stronger than those of blood kin.

Tugging at his nose, Lakesh said quietly, "I suppose I'm afraid if I *don't* worry, they won't come back from their various missions. The day I stop worrying about them will be the day they don't return. And if that happens, I don't know if I'll have the will or the heart to continue with our work."

Domi frowned. "I thought you said Cerberus is the only force standing in the way of humanity regaining its place on Earth or its extinction."

"I've said that, yes," he admitted. "I'm not sure how true it is any longer."

Lakesh had tried many times since his resurrection to arrest the tide of extinction inexorably engulfing the human race. First had been his attempts to manipulate the human genetic samples in storage, preserved in vitro since before the nukecaust to provide the hybridization program with a supply of the best DNA. He had hoped to create an underground resistance movement of superior human beings to oppose the barons and their hidden masters, the Archon Directorate. His only success had been Kane, and even that was arguable.

Still later, he wove the myth of the Preservationist menace, presenting a false trail made by a nonexistent enemy for the barons to pursue and fear. He created the Preservationists to be straw adversaries, allegedly an underground resistance movement pledged to deliver the hidden history of the world to humanity in bondage.

Memories of his abortive plan to turn Cerberus from a sanctuary to a colony still pained him. Several years before, he decided that babies needed to be born, ones with superior genes. Making a unilateral decision, he arranged for a woman named Beth-Li Rouch to be brought into the redoubt from one of the baronies to mate with Kane, to ensure that his superior abilities were passed on to offspring.

Without access to the ectogenesis techniques of fetal development outside the womb that were practiced in the villes, the conventional means of procreation was the only option. And that meant sex and passion and the fury of a woman scorned.

Kane had refused to cooperate for a variety of reasons, primarily because he felt the plan was a continuation of sinister elements that had brought about the nukecaust and the tyranny of the villes. His refusal had tragic consequences. Only a thirst for revenge and a conspiracy to murder had been birthed within the walls of the redoubt, not children.

Beth-Li was long dead, killed by Domi and buried in a simple grave out on the hillside.

Recalling the tragic incident made Lakesh shiver involuntarily.

Domi cocked at her head quizzically. "You cold?"

He forced a laugh. "No, darlingest one. I was just thinking about extinction."

She looked at him with a dubious up-from-under stare, like a child. "That makes you shiver?"

"Wouldn't it you?"

She shook her head. "I try not to think about things that make me shiver. Spoils my appetite. You hungry?"

"I am, come to think of it," he replied. "It's possible we can scrounge up a midnight meal in the galley."

Linking her arm through his, Domi sauntered in

her bare feet out of the gym to the elevator. She chattered gaily about nothing in particular, and Lakesh found himself smiling, despite all of his worries.

Out of all the people who had passed through the gates of Cerberus in the past five years, Domi had undergone the most profound transformation, yet somehow managed to remain the same free-wheeling, outspoken spirit she had been when Lakesh had first laid eyes upon her.

He knew she didn't miss the short and often brutal life in the Outlands. She had quickly adapted to the comforts offered by the Cerberus redoubt—the soft bed, protection from the often toxic elements and food that was always available, without having to scavenge or kill for it.

Domi had enjoyed similar luxuries during her six months as Guana Teague's sex slave. The man-mountain of flab had been the boss of the Cobaltville Pits and he showered her with gifts. He didn't pamper her, though, since she was forced to satisfy his gross lusts. He was obsessed with her, and that had brought about not only his professional downfall, but also his bloody death.

The irony of Teague's demise was most likely completely lost on the girl. Domi was determined to walk her own road, in her bare feet if necessary, yet with a strange contentment born of the confidence that she would always be able to fend for herself.

Lakesh envied Domi's contentment, at the same time fearing she might one day lose it.

Chapter 25

It was the kind of sunrise seen only in the desert. The sky looked like a spreading curtain of blue, smeared with lurid flame-red streaks and molten brass. All around was basically flatland, with not even sproutings of scrub to relieve the monotony of the terrain.

The Nephilim marched single-mindedly across the sand toward the collection of ruins, surrounding Brigid, Kane and Rhea in bulwarks of metal and flesh. Their armor clinked and clanked softly.

"Where are you taking us?" Kane asked, wondering now if he and Brigid should've allowed themselves to be so quickly disarmed.

"Silence," grunted one of the white-eyed men.

By the time the sun was a handsbreadth above the horizon, they reached the crumbling walls. Kane surveyed the ruins, guessing that at one time the broken shell had been a palace or a temple. Now it was only an open-air mausoleum, entombing the dead dreams of the forgotten hands that had built the walls ages ago.

The Nephilim directed them to walk between a pair of massive pillars. The faded inscriptions on the stone were not Egyptian hieroglyphics but cuneiform of a type both Kane and Brigid had seen before.

At the juncture of two of the walls rose a free-standing archway made of dull metal, a little over eight feet tall and four feet wide at its broadest point. It resembled a linteled doorframe in predark cathedrals.

Rhea eyed it apprehensively. "A threshold."

Brigid cast her a suspicious glance. "How do you know that?"

"Lilitu told me about them."

Brigid didn't question her further. Thresholds had been used by the Anunnaki during their first occupation of Earth as both means of instantaneous transportation from geographical point to point and to the orbiting *Tiamat*. Lakesh had opined the devices served as the templates for the mat-trans units of Project Cerberus.

According to him, when he assumed the role of Project Cerberus overseer, he was briefed about the shocking fact that although the integral components of the gateways were of terrestrial origin, they were constructed under the auspices of a nonhuman intelligence—or at least, nonhuman as defined by late-twentieth-century standards. Nearly two centuries would pass before Lakesh learned the entire story.

One of the gold-armored men stepped up to the threshold and passed a small, pulsing gemstone over the surface of the frame, uttering a guttural phrase as he did so.

The gem inscribed a glittering half circle of white

fire that followed the lines of the archway. There was a low, soft thrumming sound like a plucked harp string. Tiny lightnings flickered along its edges.

Within the frame of the threshold, variegated hues of color shifted and wavered. An image strobed, rippled, then coalesced. Rhea drew in her breath in a startled gasp. Beyond the portal lay a vista of dark, distorted shapes. It was like looking through several feet of silt-thick, disturbed water.

The Nephilim gestured toward Kane, then pointed autocratically to the threshold. Although he had traveled through the devices before, Kane wasn't fond of the effects of the transition, so he hesitated long enough for a Nephilim to prod him in the lower back with an ASP.

Taking and holding a deep breath, Kane stepped forward a pace, then two and then three. He moved between the curved frames of the archway and squeezed his eyes shut.

The ruins vanished. Vertigo assailed him, as if he were tied to a giant centrifuge that whirled so fast his mind did not have time to adequately record or measure the sensation. His vision blurred and he felt his belly slipping sideways.

He was conscious of a split second of terrific, senses-spinning speed, of a marrow-numbing chill— then he was on solid footing again.

Kane stood on a paved lane. On either side towered facing rows of black pillars with the top halves fashioned to represent Enlil. The pathway and the columns stretched into the distance, toward two shapes bulking up from the desert.

A vast pyramid blotted out a triangular piece of the blue sky. The early-morning light played along the crumbling facade of the monstrous monolith. He could make out the irregular blocks of stone on the outer edges, looking like broken rows of teeth.

Another huge shape lay before the pyramid, but its details were lost in the shadow cast by the gargantuan structure.

Behind him, the threshold flashed and disgorged Brigid, Rhea and six of the Nephilim. Brigid followed Kane's gaze and nodded in satisfaction.

"Figures," she said.

"What does?" he asked.

"That's the great pyramid of Giza," she replied, tracing its outline with a forefinger. "Also known as Khufu's Pyramid. There's the Sphinx in front of it, and I'm pretty sure that's where we'll find Enlil."

"Why?" Rhea asked.

"We have it on pretty reliable authority he lives underneath it," Kane answered. "Fitting, if you ask me."

Gold-shod fingers pressed painfully against Kane's back. "Walk."

Rhea, Kane and Brigid strode between the towering stone effigies, made acutely uncomfortable by the grim faces sculpted from the slick black stone.

"When Enlil told us a couple of years ago he planned to unearth his old empire, I guess he wasn't just blowing smoke," Kane said.

Brigid smiled thinly. "These monuments to his ego were fabricated recently. Not even Enlil would go to all the expense and labor of digging up every last artifact of his reign as Set."

Rhea gazed up at the foreboding stone visages, and the shadows they cast seemed to darken her eyes. "The Annunaki were a great folk," she said in a voice muted by equal amounts of awe and regret. "With a mastery of unknown forces yet to be rediscovered."

"True, there was much to be admired about them," Brigid said. "But much, much more to be despised."

"That's true of all cultures," Rhea said defensively. "Especially the baronial system that both you and Kane once served so diligently."

Neither Brigid nor Kane could dispute her words, so they opted for silence, both people thinking similar thoughts.

In the century following the atomic megacull, what was left of the world filled with savage beasts and even more savage men. They lived beyond any concept of law or morality, and made pacts to achieve power, regardless of how pointless an exercise it seemed.

Survivors and their descendants tried to build enclaves of civilization around which a new human society could rally, but there were only so many people in the world, and few of these made either good pioneers or settlers.

It was far easier to wander, to lead the lives of nomads and scavengers, digging out Stockpiles, caches of tools, weapons and technology laid down by the predark government as part of the COG, or Continuity of Government, program and building a power base on what was salvaged. The scavengers knew that true wealth did not lie in property or even the accruing of material possessions. Those were only tools, the means to an end. They knew the true end lay in personal power. In order to gain it, the market value of power had to stabilize, to be measured in human blood— those who shed it and those who were more than willing to spill it.

Some of the scavengers used what they had found in the Stockpiles and elsewhere to carve out fiefdoms, tiny islands of law and order amid a sea of anarchy and chaos. These people formed ruling hierarchies, and they spread out across the ruined face of America. They profited from the near annihilation of the human race, enjoying benefits and personal power that otherwise would have been denied them if the nukecaust had not happened.

The hierarchies spread out and divided the country into little territories, much like old Europe, which had been ruled over by princes and barons. The different hierarchies conquered territories, and claimed them as baronies. Although these territories offered a certain amount of sanctuary from the crazed anarchy of outlying regions, most of them offered as little freedom.

At first, people retreated into baronies for protection, then as the decades went by, they remained because they had no choice. Generations of Americans were born into serfdom, slavery in everything but name, particularly after the institution of the Program of Unification and the rule of the nine barons.

Although all of the fortress-cities with their individual, allegedly immortal god-kings were supposed to be interdependent, the baronies still operated on insular principles. Cooperation among them was grudging despite their shared goal of a unified world. They perceived humanity in general as either servants or as living storage vessels for transplanted organs and fresh genetic material.

As the group drew closer to the Sphinx, Kane and Brigid realized alterations had been made to it. Although the giant statue was still that of a human-headed lion in repose, with both forelegs outstretched, the features had been resculpted.

The head rising from the beast's body was narrow and long, with a sharply pointed jaw, high, ridged cheekbones, nose as thin as a knife blade and a strangely small, prim, almost triangular mouth. A series of serrated spines curved up from the center of the brow to the crown of the head. The eyes were the most unsettling feature of the face—almond shaped, they were wide open and stared out into the barren desert with a fathomless stare. A fear that was almost a blind xenophobic terror knotted into a cold fist in the pit of Kane's stomach.

"Halt," a Nephilim ordered.

The three people obeyed, still staring at the gigantic face of Enlil looming over them. Brigid said in an incredulous, angry whisper, "He restored the Sphinx to its original form."

"You seem surprised," Kane murmured.

"It seems like an incredible waste of time and resources."

"It's his time and his resources to do with as he wants," Rhea said.

Kane opened his mouth to voice a rejoinder, but an armored man intoned, "Kneel. You will all kneel."

No one obeyed. A Nephilim pressed the triple viper heads of his ASP emitter hard against the back of Kane's head. "Kneel," he repeated.

Reluctantly, slowly, Brigid and Kane lowered themselves to one knee. Rhea dropped to both knees, her head bowed, while her companions glared defiantly up at the Nephilim.

A low grating sound, as of metal scraping against metal, commanded their attention. A section of sand directly between the outstretched forepaws of the Sphinx trembled. The scraping noise turned into a rumbling timpani, almost like a fanfare.

The ground collapsed in upon itself, and a round portal irised open with a hissing squeak of hydraulics. Dim light spilled upward in a wavering shaft. A figure rose into view, apparently pushed from below.

For a confused instant, Kane thought he gazed at a life-sized statue of Enlil made entirely of gold, inlaid on the shoulders, pectorals and forearms with glittering jewels. The morning sun glinted from the gilded body armor and accentuated the inhuman leanness of his frame.

The corded tendons of Enlil's long neck resembled ropes braided beneath the reddish-and-bronze flesh. It gradually lightened to a shade of gold on the skin drawn tautly over the strong, high-arching bones of his face. His eyes gleamed like molten brass, bisected by black, vertical-slitted pupils. They seemed ageless, yet at the same time old beyond memory.

Scales glistened with a metallic luster on the flesh of his throat and around his jawline, as if his skin were dusted with silver. Kane knew the outer layer of his epidermis was like finely wrought mesh, an organic equivalent of chain-mail armor. A back-curved crest of glittering spines sprouted from his hairless skull, gleaming like wires made of burnished steel.

Enlil was a creature of alien, inhuman beauty, his flesh and eyes and mind a melding of dragon, myth and machine.

He moved with a serpentine grace toward them, his austere face suddenly creased in a raptorial grin. In a voice like the chiming of a bronze bell, he spoke a single word. "Kane."

Kane had no chance to rise before a gold-coated hand closed around his throat and yanked him to his feet, then swung him completely clear of the ground. Enlil's hand mercilessly compressed tendons, muscles and ligaments. Kane clutched desperately at his wrist in order to keep his vertebrae from being dislocated.

"A long time coming, this," Enlil rasped. "The reckoning. A long time."

Enlil's fingers continued to squeeze Kane's throat.

Blood thundered in his ears. Kane was a strong man, but he dangled like a kitten in the hand of a sadist, toes barely touching the sand.

He managed to choke out one half-gagged sentence. "Not here…to fight…"

"I agree," Enlil said, dropping his voice to a gloating croon. "You're here to *die*."

Chapter 26

Brigid made a motion to lunge to her feet, but a hand fell heavily onto the back of her neck. Fingers dug into clumps of nerve ganglia, and she bit back a cry of agony. She shouted, "Enlil! Stop!"

Enlil did not even glance her way. His eyes seethed with cruelty and the hot, banked fires of ruthless triumph. "Why would I do that?"

He spoke in a strange voice, velvet soft and rasping at the same time. "You apekin from Cerberus have violated the spirit of our pact many times. Only the fact that you stayed out of my direct sphere of influence saved you. Now that you are within the reach of my hand, why should I not crush you?"

Kane kicked at Enlil, struggling as his body began to convulse involuntarily due to lack of oxygen. Rhea flowed to her feet with such surprising speed she easily evaded the clutch of a Nephilim.

"My great and imperial lord," she said quickly, unctuously. "We are are here only to help you and to warn you of treachery."

Enlil's eyes flicked toward the hybrid woman. Uncertainty and surprise registered on his face. "You are a Quad-Vee."

Rhea ducked her head, bending at the right knee, spreading her arms wide in supplication. "And as such, I am your hereditary servant."

Enlil regarded her with bemusement, then amusement. A faint smile ghosted over his thin lips. "Indeed."

"Please, my all-powerful lord," she went on. "I beg you to hear us out."

Enlil returned his molten gaze to Kane's face, and then he flung him aside as if he were a dummy stuffed with straw. Landing heavily on his left side, Kane lay in the sand, trying to cough, trying to breathe, trying to move. Assaulted by waves of pain and nausea, Kane dragged himself to his elbows, pulling mouthfuls of air into his straining lungs.

Enlil speared Brigid with his piercing gaze. "Where is Grant?"

Stubbornly, Brigid shot back, "Tell this gilded zombie of yours to take his hands off me and then we can talk."

Enlil's smile widened. He spoke a few words of guttural Nibiruan. The Nephilim shifted his grip to the high collar of her shadow suit and he jerked Brigid to her feet. She did not give them the satisfaction of voicing a cry of pain.

Enlil stepped very close to her, bending his head. His breath gusted hot on her cheek, but she refused to flinch. In a gravelly whisper, he said, "So lovely."

He pressed a metallic finger against her lips. "So fearless."

The finger traced a line over her chin, down her throat and continued between her breasts, outlining her right, then her left.

Brigid looked unblinkingly into his eyes. She said tonelessly, "You can lay off the supervillain posturing, Enlil. I'm not afraid of you."

"No?"

"No. If you don't listen to what we have to tell you, then your little dug-out empire will be overrun and destroyed in pretty short order."

"By Cerberus?" Enlil inquired mockingly.

Kane staggered to his feet. "Not by us," he said hoarsely. "But by members of your own family…Utu, Zu, Ishkur, Marduk and Lilitu."

Enlil did not react with either denial or outrage. Still, he turned away from Brigid and swept his gaze broodily over Kane, then Rhea. He said, "Come with me."

BRIGID, RHEA AND KANE joined Enlil on a disk of a translucent, plasticlike substance about four feet in diameter. From beneath it emanated the faintest susurrus of electronic hums.

The disk dropped straight down a vertical shaft. Brigid had seen identical lifts in the Annunaki catacombs beneath the Moon. She guessed it operated on the same anti-grav principles.

Their descent eased to a gentle stop. They stepped off the disk into a dimly lit room. A tall statue loomed menacingly twelve feet over their heads. Hewed from the same slick black stone they had seen earlier, it was a full-figure representation of Enlil, but in his former incarnation as Set. The statue wore the traditional headdress and yoke collar of a pharaoh. The long, lean arms lay folded across its chest, grasping the symbols of Egyptian divine rule—the many-tailed flail and the shepherd's crook.

Enlil nodded toward the statue. "This is the original, stored safely down here for many millennia. It looks much the same as it did the day it was completed."

Brigid glanced around, her eyes narrowed. "So this is the much-debated chamber hidden beneath the Sphinx."

"One of many chambers," Enlil said, heeling around and stalking down a passageway. "Follow me."

The three people fell into step behind him, walking along a corridor made of huge square-cut stone blocks. A Nephilim bearing all of their weapons brought up the rear.

The gentle curve of the ceiling arched twenty feet above them and revealed fantastic sculptures, most vaguely man-shaped and standing out sharply in cameo. A multitude of greenish-yellow elongated rods hung from the ceiling like glowing stalactites.

Kane and Brigid had seen a similar design years before in lunar caverns. The walls on either side were covered with vividly colored friezes portraying dark-skinned women wearing filmy robes, their bodies fondled by bipedal reptiles wearing fantastic head-dresses.

Kane repressed a shudder, then sidemouthed to Brigid, "Thanks for the assist, Baptiste."

"Thank Rhea instead."

"I'd rather thank you."

Brigid only raised a sardonic eyebrow and Kane responded in kind. Neither person said anything, but Kane repressed a smile. Even after five years together, he couldn't help but reflect that Brigid Baptiste was quite possibly the toughest woman—and one of the toughest people, for that matter—he had ever met.

He found her intelligence, her iron resolve, her wellspring of compassion and the way she had always refused to be intimidated by him not just stimulating but inspiring. She was a complete person, her heart, mind and spirit balanced and demanding of respect.

For a woman who had been trained to be an academic, an archivist, and had never strayed more than ten miles from the sheltering walls of Cobaltville, Brigid's resiliency and resourcefulness never failed to impress him. Over the past few years, she had left her tracks in the most distant and alien of climes and breasted very deep, very dangerous waters.

Kane found the thought of losing that person too horrifying to contemplate, not just because of the vacuum she would leave in the Cerberus personnel, but because of the void her absence would leave in his soul.

Light glowed ahead, far down the passageway. They passed statuary, stone sphinxes, priceless porcelains and wall hangings. The cruel hand of time had not softened the features of relics that dated back to the beginning of human culture.

Enlil swept into a hexagonal-walled chamber, about twenty feet in diameter. Rhea, Kane and Brigid stepped into it, their eyes drawn to a thronelike chair with huge oval plaques rising from the back, inscribed with cuneiform symbols. The sweeping armrests glittered with a pattern of jewels.

They looked across the chamber—and rocked to sudden halts when the scale-pebbled faces of overlords Dumuzi, Shamash, Nergal and Ishkur turned toward them.

"Do you know how amused I am by this moment?" Enlil asked.

Ishkur bent at the waist in a mocking bow, and his laugh was like the hissing of a snake. "You did exactly what I thought you would do."

Fear coiled in Kane's belly. "You're a spy, working for Enlil against Lilitu?"

Ishkur nodded. "I told him about the mission Lilitu set for you. I believed you would try to outwit her and come to him directly."

"And I did not think you would be so foolish," Enlil said. "I stand corrected."

Ishkur nodded graciously.

"We weren't going to use a baby as a pawn," Brigid stated. "You should have known that about us from the start, Enlil."

Struggling to regain his mental and emotional equilibrium, Kane fixed his gaze on Nergal. "Not too long ago you tried to pull off the same thing Lilitu is attempting—take control of *Tiamat*."

"My reasons were not the same as Lilitu's," he retorted stiffly. "Nor were my methods."

Brigid snorted. "You could've fooled me."

"That would not be difficult. " It was Rhea who spoke, and her voice held a hard edge that sent a shiver of dread up Kane's spine. "But you did not fool Lilitu."

She thrust out her right hand at Ishkur. There was a flash of light, as of a mirror reflecting an errant beam of sunshine. Then, as though razor-keen steel sliced through scaled flesh, tendon and bone, blood gouted from Ishkur's neck and his head leaped from his shoulders.

It fell, rolled and bounced with astonished dead eyes toward Enlil.

Chapter 27

Enlil's eyes became incredulous circles of pale bronze as they followed the rolling, bumping head of Ishkur. They turned to molten pools of rage, and he took a long, lunging step toward the hybrid woman.

Rhea held up her right hand, palm outward. From the center of her hand stabbed an intensely bright white needle of light. It slashed across Enlil's left cheek. Crying out, he staggered back, clapping a hand over the wound. The odor of burned flesh filled the big chamber. There was very little blood, since the energy of the beam cauterized the edges of the gash.

The Nephilim who had accompanied them into the chamber stepped before Enlil, raising his ASP emitters.

"Stay where you are," Rhea commanded imperiously. "All of you stay where you are or you will meet the same fate as that traitor."

"Rhea—" Brigid began.

"*All* of you!" Rhea repeated stridently. "You and Kane get over there with the others."

Seeing no other option, Kane and Brigid obeyed, stepping over the headless body of Ishkur to stand with the overlords. Although numbed by shock, Kane realized a tiny energy weapon had been implanted in the palm of Rhea's hand.

Enlil snarled out a stream of invective in liquid Nibiruan.

Rhea shook her head. "I don't understand that language…at least not yet."

"You have called down the wrath of *Tiamat* and have doomed your mistress," Enlil spit.

"Lilitu is not my mistress," Rhea said dismissively.

"It matters not!" Nergal thundered. "Lilitu may delude herself that she will not be held responsible for the murder of Ishkur, but Tiamat will not make the distinction between you and her!"

A mocking smile slowly spread over Rhea's face. "Tell you what. Why don't we go and ask her?"

An expression of confusion replaced the fury contorting Enlil's face. He blinked. "What?"

Rhea jerked her head in an upward nod. "You heard me. Let's go ask big bad mama *Tiamat*."

"You blaspheme," Dumuzi said querulously.

Rhea chuckled contemptuously. Brigid and Kane knew *Tiamat* was revered as the mother goddess of the Annunaki, so her attitude bordered on sacrilege.

The overlords gaped at her in dumbfounded astonishment for a long, tense moment. Then they began shouting demands, both in English and Nibiruan. After listening impatiently to the cacophony, Rhea cried out, "Enough!"

A beam of light lanced from her palm and inscribed a black scorch mark on the wall. When the overlords fell silent, Rhea said, "Enlil, you will take us to *Tiamat* and you will take us now."

A crafty gleam shone in Enlil's eyes. "I will have to reprogram the threshold—"

"Don't insult my intelligence," Rhea broke in coldly. With her left hand she gestured around her. "This is your personal shuttlecraft. Don't waste your time or mine by denying it."

Brigid and Kane exchanged bewildered glances but kept their own questions to themselves.

Enlil regarded the hybrid woman stonily for a silent few seconds, as if he contemplated denying either her request or her assertion they stood within a space vehicle. At length he asked, "And if I refuse you?"

Rhea flexed the fingers of her outstretched right hand. "Then you die, here and now. All of you."

"And the doom *Tiamat* will visit upon you and Lilitu will be beyond calculation," Shamash snapped.

"It very well might be beyond calculation, but you will also be beyond caring." Rhea showed her teeth in a cold half grin. "Enlil, you may hold the title of lord of the earth and air, but Lilitu is the queen of darkness, not only of this world, but of the next, as well."

Enlil continued staring at Rhea, and despite his lack of expression, Kane could sense his inner turmoil and confusion. "What of the apelings?"

"They will go with us."

"Why?" Nergal demanded.

"We have our reasons."

"'We,'" Dumuzi echoed.

Rhea did not deign to look his way. "Prep us for launch."

Lips working as if he were bottling up the desire to spit or scream, Enlil turned and stamped over to the high-backed chair. He depressed an inset gem. "First, I would like to dispose of Ishkur's remains."

Rhea nodded. "Proceed."

Enlil spoke in Nibiruan to his Nephilim and with no expression on his craggy face, the gold-armored man slid his gauntleted hands under Ishkur's armpits. He swung the dead overlord over the wide yoke of his shoulders, picked up his head as if it were a misplaced melon, then carried the two parts of the corpse out into the passageway.

Enlil sat down in the chair and his fingers depressed several of the inlaid gems encrusting the arms. The brass plaques exuded a shimmering radiance.

With a series of electronic hums and a sequence of mechanical clanks, the hexagonal chamber began changing. The wall Enlil faced shifted as a long section of the wall dropped down on invisible pivots like a shelf. From within it flashed the multicolored lights from glass-encased readout screens.

Staring intently at Enlil, Brigid said softly to Kane, "The operation of the ship must be keyed to the pattern of his mind energy."

A steady, throbbing drone grew louder. Round portals in the floor irised open, and padded shock couches rose. A heavy panel of metal slid over the doorway with a rumble, sealing with a thud.

Rhea turned toward Brigid and Kane. "Strap yourselves in."

Brigid eyed her challengingly. "Why are you treating us like enemies?"

"At this point," Rhea said, "you're pawns and you've been useful. But you're too dangerous to leave behind."

"Then kill them now," Nergal growled. "I didn't when I had the chance, I've regretted it every second of every day since."

Rhea glanced toward him, amused. "That is what you wish of me?"

Nergal's eyes glinted raptorially. "Yes."

"Then I shall not do it," Rhea countered, her eyes flicking back toward Brigid. "Unless you convince me it's necessary."

Venting sighs, Brigid and Kane sat in the chairs and secured the shoulder harnesses. Hesitantly, the other overlords followed suit, strapping themselves in.

The control console emitted a hum like a hive of bees. An array of screens all around the hexagonal walls flashed, blurred with pixels, then resolved into sharp focus, showing different views of the desert outside.

Rhea stood behind Enlil's control chair, eyes on his fingers and what gems he manipulated. The floor vibrated beneath their feet, in tandem with a whine that climbed steadily in pitch. Dimly came metallic clickings and clanking.

"The anchors are detached," Enlil declared. "All launch systems engaged."

"Pray proceed," Rhea said curtly.

"I suggest you strap yourself in," Enlil said.

Rhea cast him a defiant scowl, but edged toward a shock couch and sat down, adjusting the straps so they crisscrossed over her breasts. She kept her right hand extended toward Enlil.

He pressed a pair of jewels on the armrests and green indicator lights lit up. A flicker of movement on a screen caught Kane's eye. A giant metal-collared iris opened slowly. The sky beyond showed bright with the midmorning sun.

With a strange, lifting sensation, the ship rose, lifting away from its subterranean hangar. One of the screens showed an exterior view of the launch, apparently transmitted from a scanner set up near the Sphinx.

The ship was one of the nondescript Annunaki skimmers, a featureless disk of dull gray alloy. Neither Kane nor Brigid was surprised.

They watched as the Great Pyramid and the Sphinx swiftly receded on the screens, becoming mere ripples and smears of contrasting texture and color.

Kane felt the pressure of acceleration, then a brief shudder that jolted him from the inside out. He looked questioningly at Brigid.

"The artificial gravity has kicked in," she surmised quietly.

Then g-force slammed Brigid and Kane into their couches and kept them there all through the bumpy, teeth-rattling ride through the atmospheric layers. Before the pressure became painful, it ebbed away.

"The inertial dampers have been engaged, too," Kane put in.

The screens showed only cloud cover, misty, billowing froth sweeping over the hull. Scraps of vapor slid past, then suddenly only sepia and starlight showed on the monitors. The skimmer broke through the exosphere and whirled free of Earth's gravity well.

Kane glanced around at the vast wilderness of stars displayed on the screen—remote, diamond-bright and beautiful.

"On course," Enlil announced calmly. "But you will remain seated until I say otherwise."

"Do you have any idea in hell of what's going on here?" Kane whispered to Brigid.

Lips compressed, she shook her head. "Only the humiliating sense that we've been majorly duped."

"By Rhea or Lilitu?"

Brigid hesitated a second before replying cryptically, "I'm wondering if there's actually any difference."

Rhea glared at them from her shock couch. "Silence."

Kane met her glare with an inoffensive stare. She continued glaring at him and he continued with a stare of wide-eyed innocence. Finally, she looked away and Kane repressed a smile. Still, he felt as confused as he ever had.

As a Quad-Vee, Rhea had been bred as a highest-ranking class, one step beneath the barons, but still servants. Balam claimed that the Quad-Vees possessed a higher percentage of human DNA than the baronial breed of hybrid, but they were still superior to humanity.

What made the Quad-Vees so superior had nothing to do with their physical endowments. Their brains could absorb and process information with exceptional speed, and their cognitive abilities were little short of supernatural.

Almost from the moment they emerged from the incubation chambers, they possessed IQs so far beyond the range of standard tests as to render them meaningless. All of Nature's design flaws in the human brain were corrected, modified and improved, specifically in the hypothalamus, which regulated the complex biochemical systems of the body.

They could control all autonomous functions of their brains and bodies, even to the manufacture and release of chemicals and hormones. They possessed complete control over the portion of the brain known as the limbic system, and by tapping into it they developed degrees of telepathic and extrasensory ability.

But since they were bred for brilliance, the Quad-Vees had emotional limitations placed upon their enormous intellects. They were captives of their shared hive-mind heritage, which derived from the Annunaki.

Locked into a remorseless, almost sterile intellectualism, the hybrids did not allow visceral emotions to play a large part in their psychologies. Even their bursts of passion were of the most rudimentary kind. They only experienced emotions during moments of extreme stress and then so intensely they were almost consumed by them.

Kane estimated less than thirty minutes passed before Enlil said, "You may get up now if you wish. But let me extend a word of caution. If anyone interferes with the operation of this ship, you will die."

Unbuckling her harness, Rhea sneered. "An empty threat."

Enlil turned his head toward her, a savage grin creasing his face. "No threat, simply a statement of fact. This vessel is attuned to my neural pattern. An attempt to displace my control will engage a self-destruct program. Even *Tiamat* has a similar program."

Brigid and Kane rose from the couches, as did Dumuzi, Shamash and Nergal. The three overlords fixed their raging eyes on Rhea, who affected not to notice.

"Who are you, woman?" Shamash demanded.

Rhea tossed her long hair back. "You will find out in short order, my lord."

Enlil suddenly stiffened in his chair. Musical notes wafted from the control console, a series of chimes that sounded somewhat like the opening bars of a song.

In a voice tight with tension, Enlil said, "We're being hailed."

Nergal stepped up beside the chair. "By *Tiamat?*"

Shaking his head, Enlil hitched around so he could stare directly at Rhea. "No," he said, his voice made hoarse by incredulity. "By Lilitu."

Chapter 28

Eyes blazing fiercely, Nergal whirled on Rhea. "How is this possible? Explain this trick!"

Voice purring with amused contempt, Rhea answered, "It is no trick. If you care to, you may open a channel and speak with Lilitu directly aboard *Tiamat*."

The outraged eyes of the assembled overlords fixed on Enlil. Shamash spoke in Nibiruan, and although Brigid and Kane couldn't understand the words, the accusatory tone was unmistakable.

Enlil did not respond. His body trembled with the effort of bottling up his anger. Kane half expected him to explode with a frenzy of volcanic fury, lashing out at anyone within arm's reach.

But with a full-throated snarl, he punched a jewel on the arm of the chair. A monitor screen flickered, fluttered and coalesced into the head and shoulders of a smirking Lilitu. She drawled one soft, mocking word. "Lover."

Enlil half rose from the command chair. "You are mad! I will see to it that *Tiamat* takes everything from you and strips you of your royal rank!"

Lilitu laughed, cruelly, tauntingly. "You have no more influence over *Tiamat* than I... Less at this point, I think. What little you do retain will vanish in short order."

Nergal, Dumuzi and Shamash stiffened, their faces registering surprise and fright.

"This undertaking will be your death," Enlil said flatly.

"The death of many things is close at hand," Lilitu retorted silkily. "Certainly your dominance over the council, and the illusion that you control *Tiamat*. Your masquerade has been exposed."

Enlil did not respond, but his broad shoulders sagged in resignation.

Pushing past Rhea, Kane stepped toward the view screen. "Lilitu—what have you done with Grant and Shizuka?"

Lilitu's eyes glinted, first with annoyance then with malice. "You will learn that when you arrive. *Tiamat* is even now guiding you to her bosom."

Her image winked out, replaced by a dark, massive shape that caused fear to surge in a cold tide within Kane.

Sleek, deadly and dark with pinnacled towers silvered by starlight, the vast body of *Tiamat* sailed majestically over Earth. From her hull rose spires and minarets tipped with glittering points, reminiscent of the dorsal fins of a mind-staggeringly enormous dragon.

Tiamat's bow resembled a gargantuan horned head

crafted from alloy and the back-swept pylons supporting twin engine nacelles were outspread like the wings
of a raptorial bird. Weapons emplacements bristled
from the stylized foreclaws. The main body tapered
amidships, narrowing down to the stern like a tail. The
ship's running lights cast strange shadows across its
hull, lending it a pronounced supernatural air.

As before, Kane struggled to view *Tiamat* as a
vehicle, a warship, but the cruiser bespoke a self-
assured, almost arrogant awareness of the power at
her command. Under the armor that plated the
enormous sweep of its metal hull, the ship was a living,
thinking entity.

Although he could not grasp the ship's scale, since
there was nothing around by which to measure it, he
knew *Tiamat* measured out to be a mile long, almost
as broad at her widest point, with an overall mass of
two million metric tons.

Suddenly a stream of gibbous light flowed from
Tiamat's undercarriage and washed the screen with a
pale luminescence. The people within the skimmer
felt a jar that jolted the deck beneath their feet.

"Tractor beam," Brigid said unnecessarily.

The skimmer drifted alongside *Tiamat*'s starboard
side, toward a huge hexagon inset deeply into the hull.
The steel-rimmed well was about sixty yards in
diameter, large enough to easily admit Enlil's disk
ship. It was sealed by a black, reflective material that
at first glance was glass, but was completely opaque.

"Mother *Tiamat* pulls us to her, " Rhea said.

Brigid angled an eyebrow in her direction. "Rhea, what did Lilitu mean about Enlil's control over *Tiamat* being an illusion?"

Rhea did not answer for long moment, her smooth brow furrowing in sudden confusion. "I—I'm not certain..."

Her words trailed off and she looked dazedly at Brigid. "I'm not sure of anything any longer...even of what I'm doing."

Brigid's eyes narrowed. "Who are you? You're not really Lilitu's sister, are you?"

Rhea's face was suddenly shadowed by doubt. "I am...but I am not."

Her lips stirred as she tried to say more, but she did not seem able to voice the words.

On the monitor screen, two lights flashed green at the outer rim of the hexagon. The black glass portal split down the center and the two halves slid smoothly into a pair of recessed slots.

"She's opening the door for us," Kane commented, hoping the dread rising up within him wasn't evident in his voice or expression.

Enlil turned toward Brigid and Kane, gesturing toward the pile of their equipment dropped by the Nephilim. "There are your weapons," he grated. "You might as well take them. When men venture into the unknown, they are fools if they go unarmed."

They cast a watchful glance toward Rhea, who shrugged diffidently. "Do as you wish. Take them or not, it will make little difference."

As the Cerberus warriors retrieved their guns, Kane said quietly, "I sure as hell hope you have an idea of what we've gotten ourselves mixed up in, Baptiste."

She shook her head. "Only speculation, mainly about motives."

"I don't understand."

"Deception and betrayal," Brigid stated grimly. "And the final reckoning that includes us, for some reason."

THEY DISEMBARKED from the skimmer into the cavernous hangar deck. On the ceiling at least fifty feet above them, crescent-shape light fixtures flickered, then shed a wavery, watery illumination.

In a staggered sequence, lights flashed on along the length of the hangar's ceiling. The dim illumination produced by the crescents wasn't bright enough to dazzle them, but they saw a long expanse of featureless bulkhead and deck made of smooth, dull gray alloy. The ceiling lights led to a set of double doors at least one hundred yards away.

On their initial visit to the gargantuan ship, Kane and Brigid found that many of the subsystems had yet to be restored to full functionality. Fortunately, the lift to the command deck was online, sparing them all a very long and very tiring walk up many flights of stairs.

The elevator shaft stretched upward, disappearing into a gray blur far above. The car was like a glass cylinder, the walls, floor and ceiling all transparent. As it rose, Kane and Brigid glimpsed masses of piled and jumbled and incomprehensible objects.

Kane knew that anything of Annunaki cultural influence had been hidden away in the belly of *Tiamat*. The history, the science, the art of a long vanished civilization survived in the vaults of the vessel.

Whether they were relics, weapons or perhaps only rubbish, they were of the Annunaki and of a past empire that Kane fervently believed should remain dead.

The lift hissed to a stop and the door slid open on the vast command deck. The overlords marched out first, led by Enlil with Rhea striding behind them. Brigid and Kane brought up the rear, feeling small and almost insignificant.

The chamber was enormous, holding bank after bank, chassis after chassis of computer stations, view screens and instrument panels. Massive wedge-shape ribs of metal supported the roof and the curving walls of the bridge.

The huge overarching girders bore cuneiform markings and hieroglyphs, arranged in neat, compact vertical rows. Both Kane and Brigid had seen identical symbols before, as well as a very similar layout, but on a smaller scale.

Years before they had explored a crashed spaceship, buried deep beneath the ancient city of Kharo-Khoto in Mongolia. At the time they assumed the vessel had been built by the Archons because of the mummified corpse of one found lying within a dysfunctional stasis unit. Later they realized the ship had been of Annunaki design and manufacture, a scout ship dispatched by *Tiamat* herself and appropriated by Balam's people.

Like the interior of the ship beneath the Black Gobi, the lines of the vast bridge were deceptively simple, but when they tried to follow the curves and angles, they found their heads swimming and their eyes stinging. There was a quality to the architecture that eluded the human mind, as though it had been designed on geometric principles just slightly beyond the brain's capacity to absorb.

Flames danced in anachronistic tripod-supported braziers, filling the air with the cloying odor of incense and illuminating bas-relief carvings on the bulkheads. They depicted sharp cameos of reptilian figures engaged in mysterious activities.

Covering the far bulkheads were a pair of side-by-side rectangular crystal-fronted screens, stretching from the deck halfway to the ceiling. Twin views of Earth were displayed upon them.

In the center of the bridge, looming tier by tier, rose a massive metal edifice that glistened brightly under the glare of banks of ceiling lights. They blazed like miniature but incandescent suns. It resembled a Sumerian ziggurat, but one wrought in plates made of some gleaming alloy. A forest of black support pylons soared all around the base of it, and from within each one came a gurgling, liquid sound as of running water.

Both Kane and Brigid remembered Balam's description of the ziggurat: "This is the control nexus of *Tiamat*—or her cerebral cortex."

They heard a rhythmic, familiar drone. Following the sound with their eyes, they saw a fusion generator, enclosed between slabs of armaglass exactly of the same type and size as the one in the Sinai.

A horseshoe-curved console faced the pair of screens. From the center of the inside curve rose a high-backed chair. Ornately sculpted and glittering with all variety of precious gems, both knew it was more of a throne than a command chair

Directly above it hung a solid gold disk six feet in diameter, embossed on one side with the bas-relief image of a ferocious winged dragon, and the obverse bore the likeness of a beautiful, majestic woman, who exuded a matronly air. The images were stylized representations of the two aspects of Tiamat, the destroyer and the mother goddess.

Lilitu occupied the chair. Her lean body was encased in silver-blue armor, her elbows propped on the armrests, fingers steepled beneath her chin. Sitting in chairs on either side of her were Marduk, Utu and Zu.

Catching sight of her, Enlil bellowed in wordless fury and lunged forward. He rocked to a sudden, clumsy halt when the eyes of the dragon image of Tiamat on the golden disk flashed, glowing progressively brighter. The entire disk exuded a borealis-like shimmer around its rim.

A stuttering sound, like the dots and dashes of Morse code amplified a hundredfold, suddenly thundered throughout the vast bridge. They were so loud

Kane and Brigid winced, feeling corresponding vibrations in their bones.

"*Tiamat* rebukes you," Lilitu said with a peculiar gentleness. "You are no longer our mother's favorite."

Chapter 29

With muted metallic clank and a stamping rush, Nephilim wearing the colors of Utu, Zu, Marduk and Lilitu formed a protective half circle around the control console. Kane counted twenty of them.

"They're here just in case you lose all sense of restraint," Lilitu said, extending a hand toward Rhea. "Come to me, sister."

Rhea hesitated, her brow furrowing. She appeared to be on the verge of refusing, then she took a tentative step forward. With uncanny swiftness, Kane moved. He crooked an arm around Rhea's neck, forcing her head up while his other hand closed tightly around her slender right wrist. He jerked her arm up, the lens of the implanted beam weapon trained in a direct line with the gold disk bearing the dragon image of *Tiamat*.

Rhea cried out sharply in pain and Lilitu echoed that cry with an angry one of her own. She rose from the throne, shouting orders in Nibiruan. The Nephilim extended their ASP emitters, but the gesture was futile.

Enlil turned toward Kane, baring his teeth in a fierce, approving grin. "Well done, Kane."

"Shut up," he said coldly. Raising his voice, he said, "What have you done with Grant and Shizuka?"

Brigid leaned close, whispering, "I don't think this is a good idea, Kane."

Although he didn't shift his gaze from Lilitu, he shot back, "If you have a better one—"

The stuttering electronic notes reverberated throughout the bridge. The sound crashed in metallic echoes from the bulkheads. The dragon eyes of the disk glowed with a threatening malignancy.

The overlords swiftly moved away from Kane, Brigid and Rhea. Brigid whispered, "Okay, here's a better idea. Let Rhea go."

"Why?"

"Because *Tiamat* is ordering you to."

Kane gave her a quick, incredulous glance, then looked up at the disk. "What are you talking about, Baptiste?"

Brigid nodded toward the brazen image. "I'm fairly certain that's a direct interface with *Tiamat*'s main neural core. She probably remembers us from the last time we were here."

Kane repressed the urge to respond with a profanity. Instead, he mentally replayed what he recollected of Brigid's speculation about the nature of *Tiamat*'s bio-technology and the kind of artificial intelligence perfected by the Annunaki. Although the wiring of the human brain and a computer shared many similarities, the crucial difference lay in the ability to learn new behaviors. According to Brigid, *Tiamat* remembered everything in her long experience and more than likely that extended to individuals, particularly if they had posed a danger either to her existence or to those she was charged with safeguarding.

"*Tiamat* wants to know what you're trying to do, Kane," Lilitu announced. "What do you suggest I tell her?"

"I want to know about my friends," Kane said, addressing the disk. "And I want to know what the hell is going on here."

In a strained voice, Rhea said, "She can destroy you in one second if she wishes."

"Maybe," Kane conceded. "But you'd die, too. And I'm betting you're the entire reason we're here in the first place."

The hybrid woman's body tensed within Kane's arms. She twisted, trying to get a look at his face. "What do you mean?"

Groping for a response, Kane shook his head in frustration. "I'm not sure. But I've got the distinct feeling that both Lilitu and *Tiamat* need you."

Rhea shivered. "I fear you're right. Let me go, then. I'll stay with you and Brigid, and do what I can to protect you."

Kane exchanged a quick, questioning glance with Brigid, who gave him a terse nod. He released Rhea. Although she rubbed her wrist and regarded him reproachfully, she stayed between him and Brigid.

Impatiently, Lilitu called, "Come here, sister!"

"Where are the people he has asked about?" Rhea said stubbornly.

"What difference does it make?" Lilitu snapped. "You are in no position to—"

The dots-and-dashes signal blasted through the bridge again. Lilitu flinched, as though the impact of the sound was painful.

"Very well," she intoned, glaring up at the dragon face. She spoke in Nibiruan to Quarlo, who stood upon her right. He marched swiftly across the command deck.

"What do you hope to accomplish by this, Kane?" Enlil growled.

Before Kane could respond, Brigid shot back, "That's not a question you should be asking us, Enlil, it's one you should be directing toward Lilitu. What does *she* hope to gain from this latest factionalizing of the Supreme Council?"

"Power, what else?" he muttered.

"That's very glib," Brigid replied. "But power over whom and to do what? This isn't the first time the royal family has fought among yourselves. You and your half brother Enki were at each other's throats for centuries."

Enlil did not dispute her declaration. Enki had been the last living full-blooded Annunaki, living in isolation on the Moon. He had told Brigid how his people had factionalized violently over the issue of humankind's fate. The decision was reached to go along with Enlil's plan to drown humanity, return to

Nibiru and then return to Earth after an appropriate period of time.

Although Enki took covert steps to ensure there would be human survivors of the catastrophe, he had no choice but to leave Earth with the rest of his brethren. Enki and a small group of supporters had become attached to Earth and its inhabitants and were overwhelmed with guilt and remorse. They could not return to Nibiru or any of their outposts on the other planets in the solar system. They could not conceive of living in peace with Enlil and the others of the Supreme Council who had approved and engineered the near genocide of humankind.

Over the course of the centuries on Earth, the perceptions of these few Annunaki about life had changed. They acquired a new need, a new passion that sent groups of them across the widest gulfs of space. They had stopped seeking power and even knowledge, and found themselves driven by a motivation grander than the simple survival of their race—a motivation to aid the development and fulfillment of all sentient life.

Because Enki and his faction could not undo what had been done to humanity, they sought to share Annunaki achievements with other races. They thought of life-forms springing into existence all over the universe, evolving races that needed their knowledge. Having acquired all the skills and technology that they were capable of acquiring, they spread across the galaxy, driven by a need to rectify their crime against humanity.

Although the main force of the Annunaki returned to Nibiru, Enki and many others did not. They became explorers, not exploiters. They learned that all life was growing. There was no limit to what life could be. Individuals and races had their limits, of course, but the process of life itself was unlimited. They came to understand that every living, sentient creature could contribute to its growth. Individuals and even races might perish, might be forgotten, but what they had accomplished could never be extinguished. It would echo for eternity because it had become part of the evolution of all life.

In infinity of possibilities, there seemed to be only one restriction—no race could know the potential of another race, and therefore, could not pass judgment on its inherent worth. As hard as it was to realize, the older races had to allow the younger races to develop on their own, make their mistakes without interference. This epiphany was what Enlil could not accept.

Balam claimed that when the biological functions of the royal Annunaki pantheon ceased, their mind's energy was converted to digital information and stored within *Tiamat*'s database.

Brigid and Brewster Philboyd had witnessed Enki's physical form turning into energy and joining with *Tiamat*, becoming bytes and bits of disembodied, digitized information, either awaiting access or rebirth into a new body.

Quarlo returned, escorting two slow-moving figures. After the first flush of relief at the sight of

Grant and Shizuka, Kane and Brigid felt the surge of anger.

Grant's face bore raw abrasions and his right eye was swollen nearly shut. He walked with a pronounced limp. His hands were bound before him by a pair of stainless-steel cuffs.

Shizuka, although showing no injuries, looked distinctly unwell, her complexion sallow, eyes dull and lusterless.

Lilitu spoke to the Nephilim who pulled the two people to a halt beside the console. She said, "Here are your friends. Rhea, come to me."

"How are you two doing?" Kane asked.

"I feel worse than I look," Grant replied flatly. "I think I've got a couple of cracked ribs and maybe even a sprained ankle."

He nodded toward Shizuka. "She's very weak."

Shizuka forced a feeble smile. "Unlike Grant, I probably don't feel as bad as I look, if that's any consolation."

Kane swung toward Lilitu, barely able to restrain himself from firing a burst from his Copperhead. "What did you do to them?"

Marduk took it upon himself to answer. "Grant objected to his woman being removed from the healing chalice. He forced me to persuade him that she was well enough to be brought forth."

"It looks like you persuaded him very enthusiastically," Brigid stated coldly.

Marduk lifted an armored shoulder in a shrug, a

feigned smile of shame crossing his face. "I admit things got out of hand a bit. But no permanent harm was done."

With a forefinger, Lilitu beckoned Rhea. "Get over here."

Rhea took a step forward, but Kane put a restraining hand on her shoulder. "What do you need her for, Lilitu? More importantly, what does *Tiamat* need her for?"

Lilitu hissed like an outraged cat, her eyes flashing. "How dare you! This is none of your affair!"

Enlil snorted, his voice harsh, his tone peremptory. "You have made this the affair of us all. Whatever lies you have told *Tiamat* about me, she will not harm me. I demand to know the truth, here and now."

He turned his face to the suspended golden disk and spoke in earnest Nibiruan. Slowly the circle of metal revolved, showing the embossed image of the beautiful woman. A sequence of eerie musical notes floated through the bridge.

Enlil cast Lilitu a triumphant grin. "Our mother demands that you explain yourself to me. I have told her how your servant murdered Ishkur."

Lilitu's lips peeled back from her teeth. She cursed in the language of Nibiru, and her eyes were ugly.

The strange music crooned low and ached with sad notes. Rhea gazed at the disk with wonder and the beginnings of awe. Touching her temples with the tips of her fingers, she whispered, "I understand her. Mother *Tiamat* is greatly grieved by this discord and hatred among her children."

The vague music flowed into a loud, jangling discord, causing everyone to wince. Light flashed dazzlingly from the rim of the disk, and one musical note, magnified a million times, slammed against them like crashing thunder.

Rhea's lithe body stiffened as if she had received an electric shock, back arching, her eyes wide and wild. Her skin suddenly seemed to glow, emitting a ghostly golden pall. For an instant, a strange radiance shone deep from within her eyes. She opened her mouth and spoke. "I am the mother of gods—I fashion all things! War monsters ride in blood at my heels and nine banners go before me when I fly to battle! Behold me in my power, children of Nibiru and man, and fear me!

"The timeless Anu watches over my path and this world is my domain and you are my children! You are all family! Why, then, do you threaten? Why do you injure one another?

"I am *Tiamat*, mother of all things, sharp of claw and unsparing of fang! There is no other and you must speak the truth to me!"

A great, fearful sigh went up among the overlords and as one they faced Rhea and bowed all in a line, as a row of wheat bows beneath the passing of the wind.

Only Lilitu did not bow. She remained standing, her head tilted at a defiant angle. "I *will* speak the truth, Mother *Tiamat*, but not that written by the holy men, the scribes, not that found in scrolls or on clay tablets, or the truth as interpreted by scholars. After thousands of years, after thousands of lies, you will hear *my* truth."

Chapter 30

Lilitu spoke of two lifetimes, as a goddess and a baroness, as a child of Nibiru and an heiress to a vast kingdom on Earth.

Lilitu was born upon a very old world already in its death throes. In planetary terms, Nibiru was drawing its final breath. Its wild orbit caused it to be unusually variable in heat and cold and caused drastic weather changes, geological upheavals and gravity disruptions.

But in biological terms, Nibiru's final breath was long enough for the Annunaki to evolve from a race of saurian bipeds into a prosperous, even magnificent civilization. If life on any planet in any solar system was a rigorous, merciless test of survival of the fittest, it was on Nibiru, and the Annunaki passed.

They did not allow nature to stand in their way. As on Earth, adaptability was the primary key to survival. They conquered their wild environment, but they were not conquerors by nature. They were organizers first and foremost and they tamed Nibiru by organizing themselves, learning to subsist on the resources of a nearly depleted world.

When the Annunaki mastered space flight and then

the secret of hyperdimensional travel, they turned to the other worlds in the solar system to supply the deficits of their own.

A small, green planet Lord Anu called Ki best fit their needs. The world was everything Nibiru was not and exactly what the Annunaki had desired and hoped for—a planet incredibly rich in natural resources, thickly forested, oceans brimming with edible flora and fauna, populated by life forms no more advanced than hominids. More importantly, Ki was large enough for the exercise of individual power, to slake the thirst of even the most ambitious of the lords of Nibiru.

Their ambitions expressed themselves in competitions of how best to exploit the abundant resources of Ki and over centuries of colonization, the competition led to strife and eventually to war, the first of many between the overlords.

It was into this atmosphere of strife and conspiracy that Lilitu was born to a branch of the royal family of Anu and Ea. Her childhood was one of quiet, sheltered luxury that only the nobility could command. She was raised to be a queen, one of the Supreme Council. Her cousins, Enlil and Enki, were matriculated to be kings, and so it was assumed she would wed one of them.

However, due to one of the many internecine conflicts among the overlords, Lilitu's branch of the family was snapped off and they were expelled from the royal court.

Over the next few years, Lilitu became a shrewd and ruthless manipulator, multiplying her family's holdings into a sprawling empire near the Red Sea.

When Enlil became a member of the Supreme Council of the Nine, he cast a covetous stare on the kingdom Lilitu had built and decided that in order to add it to his own holdings, he had to claim her as his bride.

Despite vociferous objections from other members of the Supreme Council, Enlil and Lilitu were wed. Shortly thereafter, she gave birth to a son, Ninurta. Now that the blood of Lilitu's disgraced house was in the succession to the throne, a conspiracy of betrayal and usurpation began.

Plots and counterplots were engineered against Lilitu and Prince Ninurta. Bowing to the pressure of Anu and his own greed, Enlil convinced Lilitu to flee to safety in the Indus Valley, but in reality he exiled her.

Barely surviving an assassination attempt, she lay near death, guarded by a handful of loyal Nephilim. Enlil claimed Lilitu had deserted him for another and left their son to be the sole heir to the throne.

For centuries afterward, Lilitu schemed to regain her position on the Supreme Council and reclaim her son. Her actions were condemned as evil and her confederates were called the Lillu, the demon children of Lilitu.

Although not immortal, she embarked upon a millennia-long war against the Annunaki Supreme Council. It was a game played among all the overlords, using humanity as pawns, then as knights.

Like her brethren, Lilitu exploited humankind for her own purposes and thousands of them died, trapped by snares set to capture overlords. Her influence spread throughout the ancient world. In Egypt and Syria she was known as Anat, a war goddess and in Greece as Hecate, the personification of eternal night.

As Shamahat, she used the mighty Sumerian king Gilgamesh to further her agenda, then deposed him when he grew arrogant and independent.

As the mysterious Queen of Sheba, she seduced King Solomon.

Lilitu financed and backed the revolt of Zu and Marduk, in their attempt to occupy the Nippur spaceport with their own forces. But when Enlil appointed Ninurta the commander-in-chief of the opposing forces, Lilitu withdrew her support and committed suicide rather than raise a hand against her own son.

But as a wife of Enlil and a former member of the Supreme Council, Lilitu's soul, her mind energy was permitted to join with *Tiamat*, and her legend lived on as Lilith, the Queen of the Night, as the mother of evil spirits, the woman who wooed evil like a lover and never lost her beauty.

Lilitu's body was mortal, but her spirit was reborn in a new vessel, incarnated within the frame of Baroness Beausoleil. Unlike the other overlords, she knew who she was, she retained her memories and her humiliations from her previous life—and she bided her time, waiting for the reckoning.

"'ADAM AND EVE MAY ENTER herein, but not Lilith the Queen,'" Lilitu announced, eyes burning with contempt. "So ran the ancient prayer. Pah! As if any of the proud daughters who bore my name cared anything for humans. Fear of me, of my name, has spanned the ages."

She threw her head back and spread her arms wide. "Lilith, Lilitu, the woman whose beauty never fades, whose fire is unquenchable, who knows the wisdom of the black ages! The stars may burn out, the heavens crash asunder, but there will always be a Lilitu to bestride the earth!"

Lilitu pointed a finger at the golden disk. "I am your dark daughter and you are the mighty mother! You know the grave wrongs, the unspeakable crimes that have been inflicted upon me, and I demand redress!"

Lifting both hands, she curved the fingers into talons. Lips curled back over her teeth, she screeched words in the Nibiruan tongue, and the blazing fury of her eyes swept over Kane, Grant, Shizuka, Brigid and Rhea, then fixed with an unblinking intensity upon Enlil, who flinched. "I demand a balancing! I demand justice!"

Rhea shuddered violently, her face sheened with perspiration. "And you shall have it, daughter. You shall have it within my womb."

Rhea turned toward the metal-sheathed ziggurat. Slowly, deliberately, she strode toward it.

"What the hell is going on here?" Grant rasped. He glanced toward Kane with surprised eyes. "You've got guns?"

He nodded. "I don't think they'll do us much good. How did Lilitu get you here?"

"Through a threshhold. We arrived about an hour before you did."

In a voice tight with tension and pain, Shizuka said, "This is madness. I don't understand any of it."

Keeping her eyes on Rhea, Brigid said quietly, "I think I do. We were never anything other than Lilitu's backup plan, a way to divert Enlil's attention from her real intentions."

"Which are what again?" Kane asked.

Brigid didn't respond for so long, Kane almost repeated the question. At length, she whispered, "Like she said, a reckoning."

She glanced over at Enlil, who affected not to notice.

Rhea reached the base of the ziggurat, but her steady, almost somnambulant gait did not falter. The smooth alloy skin swirled, shifted and opened. Jeweled fire spilled out. Rhea stepped through and vanished from sight. Everyone stared in silence, gaping at the unearthly beauty of the rainbow radiance.

Lilitu spoke from behind them, gloating and awe-struck at the same time. "The womb of *Tiamat*."

Chapter 31

At a sharp command from Lilitu, Quarlo and three of the Nephilim herded Brigid, Kane, Grant, Shizuka and Enlil toward the ziggurat. Enlil resisted, digging his heels into the deck.

"No! You cannot do this!" Enlil struck out at them, struggling. "I will not permit it!"

Lilitu snarled out a laugh. "Oh, no, my little Overlord. You have no choice."

Enlil snarled, reaching for her throat. She evaded his grasp and snatched Brigid's pistol from her holster. With a speed that blurred the eye, she raked the barrel of the TP-9 across Enlil's forehead.

Crying out, he staggered and would have fallen, if not for the Nephilim at his back. They set him down on unsteady legs. Lilitu watched him. Her lips smiled, but her eyes were hateful. Blood ran down the sides of Enlil's nose.

The throbbing glow blazing from the portal held every hue and tint in the spectrum, from brilliant rays of yellow to auras of deep purple and shimmering bands of variegated pink and red.

"Why do you want us in there?" Kane demanded,

trying to keep the fear within him from building to mindless terror.

Lilitu's smile became a fierce vulpine grin. "*I* do not want you in there. It is the wish and will of *Tiamat*. This is the night of the gods which was preordained."

As they were force-marched to the base of the ziggurat, Kane saw what he took to be a pulsing black membrane stretched over the opening. Brigid touched it with careful fingers. "It's some sort of force field, not cloth or anything organic."

Kane was not comforted by her description, especially when she stepped through the field and disappeared completely from view. Taking a deep breath, he followed her. A blast-furnace gust of air scorched his face, but in spite of the heat, he felt cold.

Then he was lost in total darkness, unable to feel or sense anything but darkness. He tried to speak, but his vocal cords seemed paralyzed and although he extended his arms, he touched nothing.

Slowly, sensation and sight returned to him as his eyes adjusted to the darkness. Kane stood with his companions in a dim vestibule. There was the silence of death in the cold air, and the dry, faint odor of eternity. Despite the gloom, he saw that the Nephilim had not been admitted.

"What the hell is this place?" Grant muttered, his voice sounding curiously small.

"We are within the essence of *Tiamat*," Lilitu stated. "All of her ancient wisdom and ancient science are stored here. We are but dreams within her and like all other dreams, we will fade, but she will remain."

"Nice and mythologically correct," Brigid muttered dryly, sounding not the least impressed. "More than likely we're in the equivalent of an access port to the ship's main CPU. A maintenance tunnel."

A faint, chiming melody rang through the darkness, a ghost of crystal bells, the echo of haunting music.

Lilitu moved forward. "This way."

They walked down a narrow, low-ceilinged hall, Enlil's gait was slow and reluctant. A pallid light shimmered down the length of the passageway, guiding them. It ended against a blank wall. A solitary seat, molded of metal, faced them. Upon it sat Rhea, very still, her hands folded over her breasts. A capsule of pale golden light surrounded her. She reminded Kane of an insect trapped in amber.

Her eyes glinted like two pieces of yellow diamond in her pale, angular face and although they were not Rhea's eyes, they were full of a deep sorrow. For a moment, Kane's fear was tempered by pity for the intelligence behind those eyes, entombed for thousands and thousands of years, following a single path, a program without deviation.

Brigid was the first to find her voice. "Rhea—can you hear me?"

Again came the faint music as of wind-touched crystal chimes. Rhea spoke softly, "I hear you, child of Earth. But the spirit of Rhea is blended with all of my other children. That is ever the blessing and curse of *Tiamat*."

Lilitu chuckled, a sound like the buzz of a rattlesnake's tail. "That is what Rhea was bred for—to serve as your voice, your limbs, your eyes and ears."

Rhea's head slowly turned toward her. Although her face did not register any particular expression, she said, "Explain."

"You have lived long, Mother, but your existence has been restricted to these artificial catacombs. I know you want to leave them, to experience a new life, walking through green fields, breathing fresh air, knowing the touch of the sun on your face. This is my gift to you, Mother."

A sickness rose in Kane as he began to understand.

"Explain," Rhea said again.

"The organic body your spirit inhabits was created at the same time mine was, so like all of the overlords, it possesses a compatible genetic imprint. We will rule together, you and I. As mother and daughter, we will impose a new order on Earth, that is neither human nor Annunaki. But before that can be done—" Lilitu swung around toward Enlil "—we must depose the Supreme Council."

"You dare not, witch!" Enlil snapped.

Lilitu regarded him with mock surprise. "Do I not?"

"No," he grated. "To depose me, you will have to kill me."

"And your infant mate, Ninlil," Lilitu said sibilantly. "Do not forget her. She must die, too. I will not tolerate pretenders to the Annunaki throne."

The sickness in Kane became a violent revulsion for

the ancient, evil ways of the Annunaki. He fingered his Copperhead, loath to open fire in such a small space, but not seeing very many other options to keep Lilitu's scheme from succeeding.

Rhea's voice echoed hollowly. "Those of the Supreme Council who would visit violence upon others of the council will perish by it. That is the law, ever and always."

"We will make new laws!" Lilitu shrilled, malignant fires burning in her eyes. "We are now free, not bound by the strictures of the past."

"And that was why you kept Rhea with you?" Brigid demanded. "You figured that if *Tiamat* took possession of her, you would have control over her and so be exempt from the old system of Nibiruan justice."

Lilitu pointed Brigid's TP-9 at Enlil. "I don't need *Tiamat* to exact my own justice!"

"I am the leveler of justice among the Annunaki," Rhea said matter-of-factly.

"Then level it!" Lilitu cried, finger tightening on the trigger.

"And betimes," Rhea went on in a detached tone, "my justice was harsh and swift."

Her heavy-lidded eyes closed and the strange crystalline melody suddenly increased in volume.

The autopistol in Lilitu's hand exploded with a brutal concussion and a blinding flash of flame. Lilitu shrieked, staggering on wide-braced legs, staring at fingers seared to the bone by smart metal turned molten. The stench of seared human flesh cut sharply into everyone's nostrils.

Clutching her smoldering, mutilated hand by the wrist, Lilitu fell to her knees, keening in agony and disbelief.

Enlil voiced a deep roar of joyous fury and pounced on the kneeling figure of the woman, fitting his hands around her neck. He uttered a bellow of triumphant Nibiruan.

The bellow turned into a gargling cry of shock when his body froze, locked in position. Enlil turned toward Rhea, eyes wide and accusatory, opening his mouth to voice a demand. Instead, he cried out in frustrated fury as he arms were jerked backward, as if responding to powerful tugs of invisible puppet strings.

Then, his body armor came apart, flying away from his limbs and torso in a litter of fragments. The fragments dissolved into handfuls of glittering dust. Flesh and blood came away with the armor. Throwing his head back, Enlil screamed, tongue protruding from between his jaws.

Face wet with tears, Lilitu gasped to Rhea, "How can you do this to me? This was all for you!"

Rhea opened her eyes and when she spoke the timbre and tone were more like her own. "I share my mind with *Tiamat*, so she has the same memories of your cruelty as I do, sister. If the old laws are not to be obeyed, if the ancient ways are to be spat upon as barriers to individual ambition, then there is no longer any reason for *Tiamat* to exist as she has existed."

She closed her eyes again and *Tiamat*'s voice

intoned, "Nor is there a reason for any of her children to continue to subjugate and enslave one another. As long as *Tiamat* exists, she will be used to further these ambitions. Before this night has ended, the rule of the old gods and their old ways will come to an end."

Enlil fell limply to the floor, blood dripping from dozens of wounds about his lean frame. The cocoon of amber light enclosing Rhea began to constrict. At the same time, the cold, crystalline music pealed, sounding note after note, increasing steadily in volume.

"That sounds suspiciously like a countdown to me," Brigid murmured tensely.

Shielding his eyes from the lambent glow, Grant said curtly, "I think this is probably as good a time to get the hell out of here as any."

"I agree," Kane said vehemently. "Let's do it."

As he stepped toward the passageway, he glimpsed a blur of movement out of the corner of his eye. He turned back around just as Brigid plunged through the shimmering haze surrounding Rhea and secured a double-grip on her wrists.

With one swift, practiced movement, she pulled her up from the chair and draped her limp body over a shoulder.

She locked eyes with Kane for an instant and said flatly, "She didn't ask for this."

Before Kane could reply, the sweet tinkling of music chimed wildly through the chamber.

"I don't think *Tiamat* approves," Grant observed.

Brigid stepped past him. "She ought to be used to disappointments, particularly with the psycho crew she called her children."

Chapter 32

The floor shivered violently beneath their running feet. As Kane put out a hand to steady himself, the vibrations running through the wall stung his fingers. He hazarded a quick over-the-shoulder glance. Coruscating light like a miniature sun going nova flared at the far end of the passageway.

Brigid stumbled, burdened by Rhea's deadweight. Reaching out, Kane slid the unconscious woman from Brigid shoulder to his own, making the exchange as they ran.

She gave him a grateful smile. "What's the plan?"

"The hangar bay is our best bet," Kane answered. "We don't have the keys to activate the threshhold."

When the opening through the ziggurat came into view, Shizuka blurted, "It's shrinking!"

"It's closing!" Grant barked. "Don't stop!"

Putting her head down, Shizuka increased her speed, legs pumping. She leaped through the opening in a headlong dive. Grant followed her half a heartbeat later, tucking his head against his shoulder.

Brigid jumped next, and Kane hurled Rhea through the aperture before springing up, arms extended before him, legs held straight and close together. A gust of heat seared his senses, followed by a deep bass hum in his ears. He felt double, glancing impacts against his heels as the portal silently sealed.

Even as he hit the floor, he realized he had avoided having his feet amputated by a fractional margin. Raising his head, he squinted through the smoke-filled bridge. The disk bearing the likenesses of *Tiamat* revolved in a blur of gold, shedding an iridescent radiance. A screeching rumble pressed against his eardrums.

Fragments of metal pattered down all around. The bulkheads showed cracks, and the vast deck creaked, heaved and shuddered all around them.

Overlords and Nephilim alike, half blinded by smoke, were running like panicked deer. Grant, Brigid and Shizuka were close by, looking around in confusion. Rhea stirred on the deck, eyelids fluttering.

Kane lifted his Copperhead and slowly raised himself to his knees. He was almost instantly knocked back down by a green-armored Nephilim lumbering past. The white-eyed soldier turned toward him, leading with his ASP emitter. Kane put two bullets into his forehead before he could launch a plasma bolt.

The bridge was screaming pandemonium, with overlords shouting contradictory orders and Nephilim darting about madly. Through a part in the roiling vapors, Kane saw half a dozen blue-armored men hustling Marduk toward the lift doors.

The air suddenly filled with the sizzling phosphorescent buds of ASP bolts. The plasma rounds smashed into the group of Marduk's Nephilim from the rear, punching holes in their body armor and knocking them down. The fusillade sent them scrambling to take cover behind the control consoles.

The overlords and their Nephilim were turning on one another, like trapped animals, savagely attacking anything that strayed within their range of vision and weapons.

A cluster of Lilitu's Nephilim hove out of the smoke, their emitters flaming. Kane and Brigid directed a barrage of gunfire in their direction. The bullets clanged against their armor, sparks flaring up at the impact points and the kinetic energy sending them staggering.

Another group of Nephilim opened fire, shooting indiscriminately. Kane flattened himself on the deck, covering Rhea.

Brigid blasted off a long staccato burst from her Copperhead, pounding dents in their breastplates. "Grant!" Kane yelled.

When the big man turned in his direction, Kane tossed him the Copperhead. Smoothly, Grant snatched the subgun out of the air and placed the stock against his shoulder, opening up with a full-auto barrage at the armored figures, regardless of their color. He ignored the plasma bolts blazing through the air around him.

The Copperhead's line of steel-jacketed rounds tore into a purple-armored Nephilim's head, ripping bloody chunks out of his face. Brigid's own stream of subsonic rounds caught Overlord Shamash in his armored chest with a sound like a sledge banging repeatedly against an anvil and knocked him behind the throne.

Zu gaped up at the ziggurat and shouted in panicky Nibiruan. Kane followed his stare and felt his skin prickle with a supernatural chill. A pulsing golden flame surrounded the metal structure, and in the heart of it throbbed a ruby-red star.

"I don't like the looks of that," he said loudly.

Grant gave the ziggurat a glance, and retorted, "Neither does anybody else."

The overlords stared up at the ziggurat with terrified eyes, then began a surging run across the bridge. They were hampered by their body armor and the Nephilim bunched around them in a protective bulwark. A console exploded with a bone-jarring bang and a flare of dazzling white light. Hoarse screams interwove with the echoes of the detonation.

Rhea's upper body suddenly jackknifed up from the floor, her eyes wide and wild. "What is happening?"

Before anyone could formulate a response, her head turned to the left and to the right, absorbing and assessing everything going on around her. Pushing herself to her feet, she said crisply, "Come with me."

"Come with you where?" Shizuka demanded.

"Come with me to stay alive," she snapped. "The old order dies this night. Stay here if you wish to perish with them."

After exchanging very brief glances with one

another, the Cerberus warriors followed Rhea across the bridge through the haze of eye-stinging, throat-closing smoke. Brigid stroked a short burst from her Copperhead and saw a magenta-armored Nephilim jerk, lurch and fall.

Blossoms of light mushroomed up from the bases of the black pylons surrounding the ziggurat, spewing vapor and liquid. Splinters of metal swirled in the air. Great groaning shudders racked the bulkheads, the deck plates jouncing beneath their sprinting feet.

Running beside Rhea, Kane said impatiently, "I wish you'd tell us exactly what's going on here."

"I wish I could, too," Rhea countered, her voice strained with exertion. "But all I have is a broad impression of *Tiamat*'s intentions, of her emotional state. She cannot understand how her beautiful children can be so evil. She is filled with despair and she wishes her existence to end. If you do not wish your existence to end, as well, then you must run instead of question."

A profane retort leaped to Kane's tongue, then he felt the heavy jolt of an explosion and a sear of heat, even through his shadow suit. He needed no further urging to run.

He, Brigid, Shizuka and Grant put their heads down and sprinted, following the surprisingly fleet-footed Rhea on a circuitous route through the smoke-occluded bridge. The astringent vapor made everyone's throats feel raw and abraded. Frightened voices shouted in Nibiruan all around. Fountains of fiery sparks erupted.

Glowing sparks of silver showered down. The smell of hot metal filled their nostrils.

Ahead of them loomed an open lift car, much smaller than the one that had whisked them up from the hangar. They leaped into it and Rhea pressed a tab on the wall, sealing the transparent door. Panting, blinking sweat from his eyes, Kane was too breathless to speak. Shizuka coughed rackingly into her fist. Her dark eyes reflected pain.

The descent stopped and the door slid into its groove, opening to reveal a short stretch of polished floor leading to an open archway. They raced for it, trying to maintain their balance and footing on the convulsing floor.

On the other side of the archway lay the docking bay and Enlil's skimmer. Although they entered the cavernous hangar by maintenance hatch and had less distance to run, dashing across the open space made Kane feel completely exposed and naked. The slow, heavy tolling of the crystalline notes continued to echo through the vast chamber.

To Kane's deep surprise and relief, he and his four companions reached the disk ship without mishap. They stumbled to wheezing halts around it, leaning against the smooth, slick exterior.

Breasts heaving, Brigid asked, "Now what? How do we get in—"

Rhea laid her hands against it. A section of the hull split wide in a triangular shape, as if it were cloth slit open by an invisible blade. A ramp extended outward, the smart metal of the ship forming a long walkway.

"Oh," Brigid said contritely, fingering hair out of her face. "It must be keyed to Annunaki genetic material. Right?"

Rhea gave her an enigmatic glance. "Something like that. Now we must tarry no longer."

Grant all but carried the exhausted Shizuka up the ramp and into the vessel. Kane brought up the rear, not liking the way the overhead lights strobed. He didn't voice the fear that the giant ship would fall apart before they could escape the hangar.

A new, sudden fear sprang full-blown into his mind, when after Brigid entered the ship, the hull sealed, leaving him standing outside on the ramp. "Hey!" he shouted, running up the walkway. "I'm still out here!"

A hand tangled in the thick hair at the back of his head and jerked him backward with neck-wrenching force. Kane relaxed his body, allowing it to go in the direction it was pulled. He used his legs as catapults, his head as a battering ram.

Moving with serpentine reflexes, Lilitu evaded his attempt to body-smash her. She released her grip on Kane's hair and sidestepped. He hit the hangar floor with his left shoulder and skidded several yards.

He turned onto his back just as the toe of Lilitu's boot slammed solidly into the pit of his stomach. Cramping knives of pain stabbed through him, and a second kick rolled him completely over. He forced himself up by his elbows.

Between clenched teeth, tasting blood and bile, Kane demanded, "How'd you get here?"

Lilitu laughed tauntingly. "I never take the chance of being trapped. I always have an exit in mind, unlike you, apekin."

Kane tried to sweep Lilitu's legs out from her under her, but she was much quicker. She brought her foot down hard on the base of his neck and ground her heel into his throat. The expression on her blood-streaked, smoke-stained face was one of venomous, malevolent delight.

"No," she said in a hoarse whisper. "You will not escape. I sealed your friends and my traitorous slut of a sister in the ship. Only I can free them and I will not. All of them will die, trapped like vermin. And you, Kane, you will die as all humanity will eventually die—beneath the heel of the Annunaki!"

Her right hand was a welter of blood, flayed tissue and bone chips, but she did not seem to feel the pain—or she had been driven mad by it. Lilitu increased the pressure of her foot on his neck as he fought for air, the edges of his consciousness turning black.

Desperately, Kane flung up his right leg, pounding the knee into the back of Lilitu's thigh, directly into a clump of nerve ganglia. She cried out, her leg buckled and she fell, but directly on top of Kane.

Lilitu began a vicious attack at once. Her teeth gleamed in a snarl, and her left hand battered Kane about the head and face. She was immensely strong, and Kane tasted the salt of his own blood filling his mouth. She dragged her nails over his face, trying to blind him, but he managed to jerk his head aside. Flesh tore in four vertical scarlet lines from temple to jaw. They thrashed over the deck in a limb-flailing whirl.

Her uninjured hand went to his throat, tightening around it. The woman's face tilted crazily above him, swimming off into a blurry fog. Distantly, with a rather detached sense of horror, he heard the strange, dry sound of cracking vertebrae.

Kane stiffened his right wrist, locking the fingers in a half-curled position against the palm and drove a killing leopard's-paw strike toward Lilitu's face, hoping to crush her nose and propel bone splinters through her sinus cavities and into her brain.

Swiftly, she lowered her head and Kane's hand impacted against the crown of her skull. Needles of pain lanced up his forearm, through his elbow joint and into his shoulder socket. If not for his shadow suit, Lilitu's cranial spines would have lacerated his hand.

Her fingers loosened around his throat. Not much, but enough for Kane to drag in a raspy half-lungful of oxygen. His vision cleared a little and he brought his left fist up in a hammer blow against the side of Lilitu's head. She went sprawling, landing on her maimed hand. She shrieked in maddened agony.

Setting his teeth on a groan, Kane climbed to his feet, letting his battle instincts take over. He backed away from Lilitu, putting a good dozen feet between the two of them. As he moved, he never took his eyes from the woman's face as she struggled to her feet.

With a howl of malicious triumph, Lilitu rushed forward. Kane stood his ground and met the charge head-on. She swiftly ducked a right hook and evaded a body blow. Throwing her arms around his torso, Lilitu bodily lifted him off the floor and carried him straight against the skimmer, pile-driving Kane into the hull.

Agony blazed through Kane's body as the air was forced out of his lungs. He felt his rib cage cracking beneath the inhumanly powerful pressure that Lilitu exerted. White spirals of light burst behind his eyes. In desperation, Kane brought up both his hands, cupped them and slapped them as hard as he could over both of the woman's ears.

The twin concussions forced Lilitu to loosen her back-breaking grip slightly, but she cinched down again, forcing a grunt of pain from Kane's lips. Red-hot needles shot up and down his spine. Lilitu jammed the crown of her head against Kane's chin, the spines cutting the flesh, forcing his upper body to bend over the encircling, pinioning arms. He knew Lilitu's homicidal fury could break his back.

Cupping his hands once more, Kane slapped them over the woman's ears again, using every iota of his strength. Lilitu shrieked as her eardrums imploded under the concussive pressure from the blows. Her grip loosened and Kane fought his way out of the murderous embrace.

Lilitu recovered far more quickly than he anticipated and bounded atop him. He fell backward with her to the hard hangar floor. Her clawlike fingers sought his eyes again. Kane arched his back and rolled, bucking the woman off him. Lilitu levered herself to her full height and voiced a strangulated wail of frustrated fury.

"You are a fool!" she screeched. "This is the night you dance to oblivion, screaming for the mercy of *Tiamat!*"

"Scream for it yourself," stated Rhea's flat voice.

Twisting, Kane saw Rhea standing at the foot of the ramp, with Brigid at her side, aiming the Copperhead at Lilitu.

"How were you able to open the seal?" Lilitu demanded.

When Rhea did not answer, Lilitu smiled and spread her arms. "Come to me, sister."

Rhea regarded her blankly, then whispered, "How can anything so beautiful be so evil?"

She thrust out her right arm as if intending to push Lilitu backward. Light flickered from the palm of her hand. A little curl of smoke puffed up from between Lilitu's breasts.

Lilitu's jaws gaped open, but she did not go down. Her reptilian eyes glared unblinkingly and Kane thought of the serpent in the Garden of Eden that first brought evil to humankind. For a nightmarish instant, he believed Lilitu was the same monstrous creature and could never die.

Then, with blood bubbling over her lips and dead eyes rolled up in her head, Lilitu toppled backward, arms and legs spread wide. Scarlet seeped slowly from beneath her.

"I made sure there was enough energy left in the beamer for one last shot," Rhea said softly. "I thought I would have to use it on myself. Perhaps, in a way I did."

Kane drew in a deep breath and winced as his rib cage twinged. He touched the lacerations on his face and mopped blood from his neck. He felt drained of all emotion and strength, and he did not object when Brigid helped him up and led him into the ship.

Grant and Shizuka were already strapped in. Kane took the seat between Grant and Brigid, directly behind the control chair occupied by Rhea. With a barely perceptible hum, the disk rose and floated toward the giant bay doors of black glass. They opened smoothly, and the ship shot out into space as if launched from a catapult.

"Accelerating," Rhea announced. "Maximum thrust in five seconds. Brace yourselves."

Lateral thrust pushed everyone deep into the shock couches. Inertia dampers whined in protest and awakened nausea in their stomachs. The skimmer shuddered. When Kane thought his body couldn't tolerate another second of punishment, the pressure ceased.

Sounding unaffected, Rhea said, "Max velocity achieved. We are 248 kilometers from *Tiamat*."

On the monitor screens that displayed a rear view, they saw a bloom of fire unfolding fluttering petals. Only vaguely could they discern the dragon-shape silhouette of *Tiamat* within the flower of flame. Strobing flickers ran across the blaze.

The shimmer around the outline of the great ship pulsed and throbbed as it advanced. Pale ectoplasmic waves shimmered out from the curving contours of the vessel. The pallid borealis fanned out slowly in a fitful mile-wide aura.

Kane, Brigid, Grant and Shizuka watched the death of *Tiamat*, each lost in his or her own thoughts and saying nothing. The concept that they had witnessed the end of an entity who was the mother-goddess of so many ancient cultures sapped the mind of anything to which they could compare the sight.

Slowly, Rhea swiveled the control chair to face all of them. "You may get up now if you wish. *Tiamat* is no longer a danger to us."

Brigid arched an eyebrow. "*Tiamat* has self-destructed?"

Rhea's face remained immobile, her eyes and expression inscrutable. "I didn't say that. Only that she no longer poses a danger."

"What about the other overlords?" Grant demanded. "They're dead?"

Rhea slowly turned the chair around, back toward the screens. "Nor did I say that."

Unbuckling the safety harness of his shock couch, Kane stood up, silently ignoring the ache in his arms and legs and the throbbing soreness of his bruised ribs. "Just what *are* you saying?" he challenged.

The chair continued rotating, presenting its back to Kane. Rhea said quietly, "Only that *Tiamat* no longer poses a danger…for the time being."

Kane gazed at the images on the screens, noting how the shimmering sphere of light surrounding *Tiamat* appeared to burn in space, shot through with incandescent particles, like a fireworks display as seen from a vast distance. Then, rolling multicolored clouds overlapped, engulfing *Tiamat* until she could no longer be seen, only a fiercely radiant hairline of luminescence stretching across space, like an inestimably long cloud.

Still, Kane fancied he heard the tolling of the crystalline chimes, pealing again and again. He knew they tolled for him, for all of his friends, heralding a time of victory or death that was still to come.

But not yet, he told himself fiercely.

Kane's hands moved to rest lightly on the shoulders of Brigid Baptiste and Grant.

No, not yet.

* * * * *

ROOM 59

*Welcome to Room 59, a top secret,
international intelligence agency sanctioned
to terminate global threats that governments can't
touch.
Its high-level spymasters operate in a virtual
environment
and are seasoned in the dangerous game
of espionage and counterterrorism.*

*A Room 59 mission puts everything on the line;
emotions run high, and so does the body count.*

*Take a sneak preview of
THE POWERS THAT BE
by Cliff Ryder.*

*Available January 8,
wherever books are sold.*

"Shot fired aft! Shot fired aft!" Jonas broadcast to all positions. "P-Six, report! P-Five, cover aft deck. Everyone else, remain at your positions."

Pistol in hand, he left the saloon and ran to the sundeck rail. Although the back of the yacht had been designed in a cutaway style, with every higher level set farther ahead than the one below it, the staggered tops effectively cut his vision. But if he couldn't see them, they couldn't see him, either. He scooted down the ladder to the second level, leading with his gun the entire way. Pausing by the right spiral stairway, he tapped his receiver. Just as he was about to speak, he heard the distinctive *chuff* of a silenced weapon, followed by breaking glass. Immediately the loud, twin barks of a Glock answered.

"This is P-Five. Have encountered at least three hostiles on the aft deck, right side. Can't raise P-Six—" Two more shots sounded. "Hostiles may attempt to gain access through starboard side of ship. Repeat, hostiles may attempt access through starboard side of ship—" The transmission was cut off again by the sustained burst of a silenced submachine gun stitching holes in the ship wall. "Request backup immediately," P-Five said.

Jonas was impressed by the calm tone of the speaker—it had to be the former Las Vegas cop, Martinson. He was about to see if he could move to assist when he spotted the muzzle of another subgun, perhaps an HK MP-5K, poke up through the open stairwell. It was immediately followed by the hands holding it, then the upper body of a black-clad infiltrator. Jonas ducked behind the solid stairway railing, biding his time. For a moment there was only silence, broken by the soft lap of the waves on the hull, and a faint whiff of gunpowder on the breeze.

Although Jonas hadn't been in a firefight in years, his combat reflexes took over, manipulating time so that every second seemed to slow, allowing him to see and react faster than normal. He heard the impact of the intruder's neoprene boot on the deck, and pushed himself out, falling on his back as he came around the curved railing. His target had been leading with the MP-5K held high, and before he could bring it down, Jonas lined up his low-light sights on the man's abdomen and squeezed the trigger twice. The 9 mm bullets punched in under the bottom edge of his vest, mangling his stomach and intestines, and dropping him with a strangled grunt to the deck. As soon as he hit, Jonas capped the man with a third shot to his face.

"This is Lead One. I have secured the second aft deck. P-Two and P-Three—"

He was cut off again as more shots sounded, this

time from the front of the yacht. Jonas looked back. *A second team?*

And then he realized what the plan was, and how they had been suckered. "All positions, all positions, they mean to take the ship! Repeat, hostiles intend to take the ship! Lead Two, secure the bridge. P-Three, remain where you are, and target any hostiles crossing your area. Will clear from this end and meet you in the middle."

A chorus of affirmatives answered him, but Jonas was already moving. He stripped the dead man of his MP-5K and slipped three thirty-round magazines into his pockets. As he stood, a small tube came spinning up the stairway, leaving a small trail of smoke as it bounced onto the deck.

Dropping the submachine gun, Jonas hurled himself around the other side of the stairway railing, clapping his hands over his ears, squeezing his eyes shut and opening his mouth as he landed painfully on his right elbow. The flash-bang grenade went off with a deafening sound and a white burst of light that Jonas sensed even through his closed eyelids. He heard more pistol shots below, followed by the canvas-ripping sounds of the silenced MP-5Ks firing back. *That kid is going to get his ass shot off if I don't get down there,* he thought.

Jonas shook his head and pushed himself up, grabbing the submachine gun and checking its load. He knew the stairs had to be covered, so that way would be suicide. But there was a narrow space, perhaps a yard wide, between the back of the stairwell and the railing of the ship's main level. If he could get down there that way, he could possibly take them by surprise, and he'd also have the stairway as cover. It might be crazy, but it was the last thing they'd be expecting.

He crawled around the stairway again and grabbed the dead body, now smoking from the grenade. The man had two XM-84 flash-bangs on him.

Jonas grabbed one and set it for the shortest fuse time—one second. It should go off right as it hits the deck, he thought. He still heard the silenced guns firing below him, so somehow the two trainees had kept the second team from advancing. He crawled to the edge of the platform, checked that his drop zone was clear, then pulled the pin and let the grenade go, pulling back and assuming the *fire in the hole* position again.

The flash-bang detonated, letting loose its 120-decibel explosion and one-million-candlepower flash. As soon as the shock died away, Jonas rolled to the side of the boat just as a stream of bullets ripped through the floor where he had been. He jumped over the stairway, using one hand to keep in touch with his cover so he didn't jump too far out and miss the boat entirely. The moment he sailed into the air, he saw a huge problem—one of the assault team had had the same idea of using the stairway for cover, and had moved right under him.

Unable to stop, Jonas stuck his feet straight down and tried to aim for the man's head. The hijacker glanced up, so surprised by what he saw that for a moment he forgot he had a gun in his hand. He had just started to bring it up when Jonas's deck shoes crunched into his face. The force on the man's head pushed him to the deck as Jonas drove his entire body down on him. The mercenary collapsed to the floor, unmoving. Jonas didn't check him, but stepped on his gun hand, snapping his wrist as he steadied his own MP-5K, tracking anything moving on the aft deck.

The second team member rolled on the deck, clutching his bleeding ears, his tearing eyes screwed tightly shut. Jonas cleared the rest of the area, then came out and slapped the frame of his subgun against the man's skull, knocking him unconscious. He then cleared the rest of the area, stepping over Hartung's corpse as he did so. Only when he was sure there were no hostiles lying in wait did he activate his transceiver.

"P-Five, this is Lead. Lock word is *tango*. Have secured the aft deck. Report."

"This is P-Five, key word is *salsa*. I took a couple in the vest, maybe cracked a rib, but I'm all right. What should we do?"

"Take P-Six's area and defend it. Hole up in the rear saloon, and keep watch as best as you can. As soon as we've secured the ship, someone will come and relieve you."

"Got it. I'll be going forward by the left side, so please don't shoot me."

"If you're not wearing black, you'll be okay."

Jonas heard steps coming and raised the subgun, just in case a hostile was using the ex-cop as a hostage to get to him. When he saw the stocky Native American come around the corner, Glock first, Jonas held up his hand before the other man could draw a bead on him.

Martinson nodded, and Jonas pointed to the motion-less man in front of him and the other guy bleeding in the corner of the deck. "Search these two and secure them, then hole up. I'm heading forward. Anyone comes back that doesn't give you the key word, kill them."

"Right. And sir—be careful."

"Always." Jonas left the soon-to-be-full operative to clear the deck and headed topside, figuring he'd take the high ground advantage. Scattered shots came from the bow, and he planned to get the drop on the other team—hell, it had worked once already. "P-One through P-Four, Lock word is *tango*. Report."

"P-One here, we've got two hostiles pinned at the bow, behind the watercraft. Attempts to dislodge have met with heavy resistance, including flash-bangs. P-Two is down with superficial injuries. We're under cover on the starboard side, trying to keep them in place."

"Affirmative. P-Three?"

"I'm moving up on the port side to cut off their escape route."

"P-Four? Come in, P-Four?" There was no answer. "P-Four, if you can't speak, key your phone." Nothing. *Shit*. "All right. P-One, hold tight, P-Three, advance to the corner and keep them busy. I'll be there in a second. Lead Two, if you are in position, key twice."

There was a pause, then Jonas heard two beeps. *Good*. Jonas climbed onto the roof of the yacht, crept past the radar and radio antennas, then crossed the roof of the bridge, walking lightly. As he came upon the forward observation room, he saw a black shadow crawling up onto the roof below him. Jonas hit the deck and drew a bead on the man. Before he could fire, however, three shots sounded from below him, slamming into the man's side. He jerked as the bullets hit him, then rolled off the observation roof.

That gave Jonas an idea. "P-Two and Three, fire in the hole." He set the timer on his last XM-84 and skittered it across the roof of the observation deck, the flash-bang disappearing from sight and exploding, lighting the night in a brilliant flash.

"Advance now!" Jonas jumped down to the observation roof and ran forward, training his pistol on the two prostrate, moaning men as the two trainees also came from both corners and covered them, kicking their weapons away. Jonas walked to the edge of the roof and let himself down, then checked the prone body lying underneath the shattered windows. He glanced up to see the two men, their wrists and ankles neatly zip-tied, back-to-back in the middle of the bow area.

"Lead Two, this is Lead. Bow is secure. Tally is six hostiles, two dead, four captured. Our side has one KIA, two WIA, one MIA."

"Acknowledged. Bridge is secure."

Jonas got the two trainees' attention. "P-One, make

sure P-Two is stable, then head back and reinforce P-Five, and make sure you give him the key word. P-Three, you're with me."

Leading the way, Jonas and the trainee swept and cleared the entire ship, room by room. Along the way, they found the body of the young woman who had been at position four, taken out with a clean head shot. Jonas checked her vitals anyway, even though he knew it was a lost cause, then covered her face with a towel and kept moving. Only when he was satisfied that no one else was aboard did he contact everyone. "The ship is clear, repeat, the ship is clear. Karen, let's head in, we've got wounded to take care of."

"What happens afterward?" she asked on a separate channel.

"I'm going to visit Mr. Castilo and ask him a few questions."

"Do you want to interrogate any of the captives?"

Jonas considered that for only a moment. "Negative. All of them are either deaf from the flash-bangs or concussed or both, and besides, I doubt they know anything about what's really going down today anyway. No, I need to go to the source."

"I'll contact Primary and update—"

"I'm the agent in charge, I'll do it," Jonas said. He sent a call to headquarters on a second line. "No doubt Judy will flip over this. Do you still have a fix on that Stinger crate?"

"Yes, it's heading south-southwest, probably to Paradise," Karen replied.

"Naturally. See if you can get this behemoth to go any faster, will you? I just got a really bad feeling that this thing is going down faster than we thought." He gripped the handrail and waited for the connection, willing the yacht to speed them to their destination more quickly, all the while trying to reconcile the fact that his son was involved in a plot that could very well tear a country apart.

* * * * *

Look for THE POWERS THAT BE
by Cliff Ryder in January 2008
from Room 59™.
Available wherever books are sold.

ROOM 59

CRISIS: A massive armed insurgency—
ninety miles off America's coast.

MISSION: CUBA

A Cuban revolution threatens to force the U.S.
into a dangerous game of global brinksmanship,
thrusting spymaster Jonas Schrader into an
emotional war zone—exacting the highest price
for a mission completed.

Look for

THE powers THAT be

by cliff RYDER

CAPITAL OFFENSIVE

Sabotaged U.S. satellites set civilization
on a death spin....

A secret terrorist organization has hacked its way into
defense satellites, leaving American global security
severely compromised. Stony Man gets a lead on
a rogue Argentinean general and his twisted vision
of a scorched, reborn planet Earth—but tracking the
technology and the villain is a race where seconds
count...and the losers will be humanity itself.

STONY®
MAN

*Available in December
wherever books are sold.*

TAKE 'EM FREE

2 action-packed novels plus a mystery bonus

NO RISK

NO OBLIGATION TO BUY

Look for

AleX Archer
SERPENT'S KISS

While working on a dig on the southern coast of India, Annja finds several artifacts that may have originated from a mythical lost city. Then Annja is kidnapped by a modern-day pirate seeking the lost city. But she quickly sides with him and his thieves to ward off an even greater evil—the people deep in the Nilgiris Mountains, who aren't quite human...and they don't like strangers.

Available January wherever you buy books.